"GIRL, YOU HAVE NO IDEA WHAT YOU'RE GETTING INTO," TUCK CHALLENGED.

"Perhaps not, but I intend to find out. This is *my* inn. I intend to live here and operate it as a proper hostelry for wayfarers."

That brought sharp laughter and catcalls, which seemed to bolster Tuck Loudon. He joined in the laughter wholeheartedly. "I'll give you a week, Gretchen. At the end of that time you'll be begging me to send you back to Boston. I'll wager on it."

The resulting laughter both reddened her face and stiffened her resolve. "Not on your life, Mr. Loudon. You're wasting your money." She turned away, heading for the stairs.

"I was thinking of the same payment as the last time."

The words stopped Gretchen in her tracks. Sensation swept over her body at the memory of his kisses. Slowly, she turned to face him. "You will freeze in hell before that happens again, Mr. Loudon."

"Now that, I really will bet on."

Other **Thirteen Colonies** books
by Carolyn Chase

RENEGADE HEARTS
SCOUNDREL'S CARESS

The SMUGGLER'S EMBRACE

CAROLYN CHASE

A DELL BOOK

Published by
Dell Publishing
a division of Bantam Doubleday Dell
Publishing Group, Inc.
666 Fifth Avenue
New York, New York 10103

Produced by Cloverdale Press, Inc.
96 Morton Street
New York, NY 10014

ISBN: 0-440-20361-9

Printed in the United States of America
Published simultaneously in Canada

April 1990

10 9 8 7 6 5 4 3 2 1

RAD

The SMUGGLER'S EMBRACE

Chapter One

Western Massachusetts
1765

A CHILLY, PERSISTENT drizzle had mercifully ended, giving way to a patchy, hesitant sun that did little to warm the sharp breeze drilling in from the northeast. Despite her heavy woolen traveling suit and beaver wrap, Gretchen North felt she would never stop shivering.

Would this horrid journey never end? She was on her second day from Boston—it seemed an eternity—and every mile, every inch had been uncomfortable. She couldn't decide which was worse, the cold or the incessant lurching of the coach that tossed her about until she felt her body was one mass of bruises and aching muscles. Then there was the constant noise of the coach squeaking and scraping as it traveled over rutted roads made nearly impassable by spring rains.

No, Gretchen decided, the worst had been her insufferable traveling companions, Parson and Mrs. McMurdden. The woman's high-pitched voice, strained to its limits to be heard over the sounds of the coach, had grated on Gretchen's nerves. And her prying questions had been intolerable: Why was Gretchen traveling alone? Where was she going? Why wasn't she married? None of her business, any of it. Thank heaven the McMurddens had alighted at Worcester, leaving Gretchen to "enjoy" the last leg of her journey alone.

She looked out the window, clutching her fur to her throat. Rain still dripped from sopping trees, and puddles, some the size of small ponds, filled many of the fields. It was a very wet spring in Massachusetts in 1765. Doubtlessly she should have waited until May or even June to make this journey, but there had been no time to waste. It was either now or never. Aloud she muttered, "Two days ago you were very brave, full of eagerness for this trip. Where is your courage now, Gretchen North?"

She closed her eyes and tried to relax, to sway with the movement of the coach rather than fight it. It required some effort, but gradually the noise, the motion, and even the cold began to recede, and her mind retreated to the comforts of Boston— and her reasons for leaving it.

Perhaps, she thought with a tinge of guilt, she had treated Uncle John and Aunt Sarah North unjustly. After all, they had raised her from childhood, given her every advantage, lavished money on her. Whatever might be said of them, they could not be accused of lacking generosity. Her full trunk atop the coach was proof of that. But they were not warmhearted people. Although they had no children of their own, they never accepted Gretchen as a daughter. She was always the intruder, the child of John's wayward brother, their ward, for whom they were doing their duty as family.

Gretchen sighed. She could not blame Uncle John and Aunt Sarah for wanting to be rid of her. They were only right to want her married and out of their home. And at age eighteen she knew she should be married. Most of her friends were already mothers; some had even lost a tooth or two. Gretchen had thought it only an old wives' tale that a woman lost a tooth with every child. Now she knew it was only too true.

Gretchen still had her teeth—fine white teeth— and her maidenhood. But she had had a proposal. At sixteen, she had fancied herself in love with Tom Henessey, he of the curly dark hair and dancing Irish eyes. That innocent affair had resulted in a flurry of "chance" meetings and a few chaste kisses. But with all the ardor of puppy love, Gretchen had been willing to marry him.

Then Uncle John had learned of the romance and had driven Tom away. The son of a coppersmith was hardly a suitable match for the niece of one of the wealthiest merchant families in the Bay Colony. In retrospect, Gretchen had to admit that Uncle John had probably been right. Marriage to Tom Henessey would have been folly. She had been young, naive, delighted at the prospect of a clandestine romance—but she had not truly loved him. She suspected, in fact, that part of the attraction had been the desire to challenge Uncle John.

But following this episode, the pressure to marry became intense. There was certainly no shortage of suitors. The generous dowry Uncle John had provided had seen to that. Gretchen's lush golden hair and vivid blue eyes had not hurt her chances, either. Many declared her one of the prettiest girls in Boston. And she knew she was ready for marriage, ripe to fulfill the needs of a man, as her friends described it. The stick of a girl she had been as a child was gone at last. It seemed to happen overnight that she was suddenly a woman. Her equilibrium changed as she walked or ran. Uncle John had invested in a whole new wardrobe—an elegant one, suited to a girl of her position.

There were incessant teas and balls and soirées. She was hardly ever without the companionship of some suitor or other. One particularly persistent gentleman had been in his sixties! Gretchen had honestly tried to choose, but none had appealed to her. And as Uncle John had reiterated the financial and social virtues of one or the other, she had begun to feel like cattle at auction.

Then Uncle John had imposed an ultimatum: Choose or the choice would be made for her.

Desperation rose in her, along with a terrible restlessness. Try as she would, she simply did not want the life—or the men—being offered her. But what did she want?

The origins of her discontent were well known to her. It was the blood of her father coursing through her veins. Winthrop North was the second son, five years younger than his brother John. He, too, had worked in the family business, married, and settled into a life of ease. Then Priscilla North, Gretchen's mother, had died giving birth to her. Gretchen had no memory of her mother, of course, but her portrait showed a very beautiful, dark-haired woman, with an air of delicate sweetness to her features.

Gretchen's memory of her father was not much more pronounced. In his grief over the death of his beloved Priscilla, Winthrop North had abandoned home, position, and family and gone westward to the frontier. He had returned occasionally, hugging Gretchen, holding her on his knee, regaling her with stories of life in the west, of Indians, Frenchmen, and trappers and of battles to win to hold on to a new land. In Gretchen's mind, her father became the most romantic of men. He was huge in size, bursting with health, and the handsomest man she had ever seen. He left no doubt where her own golden hair came from, and with his flourishing moustache, tanned complexion, and hearty laugh, he exuded masculinity. No wonder her suitors seemed pale and dull in comparison.

She had wept and clung to him each time he

left, but he insisted the frontier was no place for a young girl. She was better off with her Uncle John and Aunt Sarah, he had explained. When she was grown, a woman, he would send for her. But he never did, though his rare letters promised and promised. Gretchen wrote to him often, pouring her frustrations onto multiple pages in her neat hand, for she had learned to read and write. Then came the reply she almost couldn't bear. Winthrop North was dead. She had wept for days, inconsolably. Another letter followed. It stated that Gretchen had inherited from her father a property called the North Inn in Springfield, Massachusetts.

John North had urged her to sell it and add the proceeds to her dowry. But Gretchen had hesitated. This North Inn was all she had left of her father. Then Uncle John had announced that he had found Gretchen a husband. Ephraim Waring was an associate in the family business, a widower in his forties with two young children, a man as dry and forbidding as John North himself. She had pleaded with her uncle, wept openly, but to no avail. He insisted he knew what was best for her. Ephraim Waring was a good man who would take care of her.

Alone in her room, Gretchen had clutched the deed to the North Inn as her salvation. She would not marry Ephraim Waring. Never! She would go west as her father had, claim her inheritance, and start a new life. She had hidden her packing and sneaked out at night. This endless carriage ride was the result.

Gretchen opened her eyes, looking out at the

suddenly leaden skies. What was she getting into? She simply didn't know what lay ahead. But it just had to be better than a marriage she did not want. A new, nearly untouched land lay before her, and adventure beckoned as it must have to her father. Taking comfort in this thought, she began to observe with greater interest the passing countryside. She was her father's child, wasn't she?

After a time, she heard the shouts of the driver and coachman, although she couldn't make out the words. Then suddenly she heard the savage crack of the whip and felt the vehicle take on greater speed. Looking out the window, she saw a river ahead, wide and deep, almost overflowing from the heavy rains. To her eyes it was a raging torrent, the current bearing logs and branches downstream. They weren't going to try to cross that! It wasn't possible.

Her answer came as the coach plunged downhill into the water. She held on with both hands as the current buffeted the carriage. For a moment she feared being swept downriver, but the forward movement continued. Apparently the horses were strong, and the river not as deep as she feared.

Suddenly she was thrown to the floor, landing quite unceremoniously on her back, legs in the air, skirt and petticoats flying most disgracefully. Quickly she covered herself and scampered back into her seat. Cautiously, she peered through the window of the coach. They were stopped in what appeared to be midstream. She heard the driver cursing and cracking his whip, but the coach wouldn't move. They were stuck. Gretchen opened the door for a better view and immediately squealed as muddy water sloshed inside, soaking her feet. Slamming the door to stay dry, she stuck her head out the window and called, "What's wrong, driver?"

"I believe ya' might say we's stuck in midstream, ma'am."

Gretchen couldn't hide her annoyance. "You never should have tried to cross, driver. Couldn't you see how swollen the river is?"

He muttered under his breath, indicating his irritation with her. "I saw it, ma'am, but I figgered we'd make it."

"Well, you figured wrong! What are you doing to do, driver? We can't stay here."

After swearing an oath, the driver turned to confer with the coachman. "We's gonna hafta lightened the load, ma'am. Take all the luggage off and give the horses a chance to pull us outta here."

"Then I suggest you get at it, driver. I'd like to get to Springfield before dark."

The driver cleared his throat. "Yer gonna hafta get out, too, ma'am."

"Me?" she asked in a mixture of shock and disbelief.

"'Fraid so, ma'am. The horses'll need ev'ry pound we kin give 'em."

She looked at the water in dismay, fear starting to rise in the pit of her stomach. "But . . . but I . . . can't swim."

"No need to, ma'am. The water's not deep. Or'narily it's just a little stream. Ya' kin walk out."

Gretchen looked down at the raging current

doubtfully. "That seems most unlikely to me, sir."

"Nuthin' to it, ma'am. I'll help ya."

But as he started to climb down from his seat, Gretchen was distracted by a shout from the far bank. Looking over, she spied three men on horseback. The driver hollered back that he was stuck and could use a little help. The horsemen immediately plunged their mounts into the water, heading for the coach. Two rode toward the lead horses of the carriage. The third broke off and came toward her.

Even from the far bank, Tuck Loudon had seen the golden hair that no bonnet could hide. Closer vision provided no disappointment. Fair hair, eyes a brighter blue than he had ever seen, delicate skin, so very fair, lips so turned out and smooth they seemed to have no other purpose than for a man to kiss. His appraisal also took in the sharp rise of her bosom beneath the dark gray suit.

"Seems you're contemplating a swim, ma'am."

She had noticed how beautifully he rode, his steed, a handsome bay, carrying him through the water effortlessly. He wore what appeared to be a leather suit, with fringes that bounced as he rode. Beneath his wide-brimmed hat was the handsomest face she had ever seen—squarish with a singular cleft in the chin, a full lower lip and a firm upper. His brown eyes were bright. His face was both bold and sensitive, itself a remarkable contrast.

"I'd rather not, if the choice is mine, sir," she replied.

He grinned, revealing a full set of strong white

teeth. "I understand the water is quite refreshing this time of year, ma'am."

"I am not a 'ma'am', but a 'miss'—and I'd rather not test the waters if I can possible avoid it."

Tuck regarded her with surprise. Her appearance, her clothes, her voice all spoke Boston—and more, a most wealthy and privileged Boston. What on earth was she doing here? A proper Boston maiden traveling alone in the west? Unbelievable! She might as well be a creature from another world. "What do you propose I should do, ma'am—I mean, miss?"

Gretchen looked down at the water, then back at him. "If you would give me a ride to the far shore, sir, I would . . . happily pay you. I have funds."

"Pay me? I am not in the business of rescuing damsels in distress," he scoffed. "Or even those stuck in a coach in midriver."

There was a mocking note in his voice that set Gretchen's nerves on edge. But determined to make the best of the situation, she quipped, "I believe there is a first time for everything, sir."

"Some beginnings are better not made—or so I've heard."

"I will not harm you, sir—I assure you," she teased.

In an instant, he spurred his horse toward her, taking her by surprise. His arm swept around her waist and for a terrifying moment she was floating over the raging water. Then just as quickly, she found herself safely nestled sideways on the saddle in front of him. The horse began to move rapidly, sending sprays of water with each stride. Gretchen felt giddy with excitement. Then she became uncomfortably aware that his arm still held her. Indeed, it had slid up her waist and now cradled her breasts. She squirmed, then realized that movement might send her toppling into the stream. Her only choice was to sit up straight and pretend not to notice it.

In a moment, they reached the far shore. The man spurred his horse up the embankment and came to a stop. But he did not release her. Gretchen turned her head sideways to look at him. Still he did not loosen his grip, and his eyes were dancing with mischief. She coughed expectantly. Surely a gentleman would allow her to dismount. But he only grinned at her in that taunting way of his. Gretchen was all too conscious of his arm still cradling her breasts. She sat erect, and as her embarrassment gave away to anger, she again turned her face to speak to him. He was not smiling now, and his eyes were filled with a strange intensity.

Her mouth was slightly open as his lips came to hers. Perhaps that accounted for the softness, the sweetness, the fullness against her lips. Sensation swept her whole body and she trembled. She had never been kissed like this. She gasped her astonishment into his mouth, unable to halt her feverish clutching as her hands moved over his broad shoulders, his neck, his head, knocking his wide-brimmed hat to the ground.

The kiss seemed to last an eternity, lips moving, searching out exquisite sensations, savoring them, until a sharp ache in Gretchen's neck—for her head was turned at an awkward angle—brought her back to her senses. She broke away and leaned her head back, gasping as her fingertips came to her lips.

His smile was slightly mocking, tinged with both delight and triumph. "You did offer payment for the ride. I can't remember when I was so well paid."

Without warning, his lips joined hers anew and she was powerless to stop it. She twisted in the saddle to ease the pain in her neck, and leaned against him, immersed in the sensation, sopping it up, feeling it permeate her body until she was tingling all over. Then she felt wetness at the corners of her mouth as his lips seemed to claw at hers, ravenous, and she felt like she was melting as his tongue teased hers, then plunged inside. Only belatedly did she again come to her senses, realizing she was sucking his tongue, pulling him inward, while his hand cupped her breast. Shocked, she pushed him away, panting breathlessly, "Sir, this is . . . *uncalled* for."

Tuck Loudon stared back at her, a lazy grin on his face. "I thought it rather nice myself," he drawled.

"Well, I didn't!" She tried to squirm away from his grasp, but he was too strong for her. "I thank you for rescuing me, sir. If you will release me, I will dismount now."

"Do you have to?" he asked with a wicked glint in his eyes.

She knew he wanted to kiss her again. She also

knew she must not let him. "I do indeed." She felt
his arm relax, and heard him let out his breath in a
deep, exaggerated sigh. She slid to the ground and
smoothed her skirt. Her cheeks flushed hot with
embarrassment. The nerve of the man, toying with
her this way.

"What on earth brings a woman like you out
here?"

Unable to look at him, she busied herself by
tugging at her skirt. "I am on my way to
Springfield—to claim my inheritance."

"Springfield will never have seen the likes of
you," he said with a hearty laugh. "I'm not at all
sure Springfield is ready for you."

Seeing his hat on the ground, she bent, picked
it up, and thrust it at him angrily. "I'm sure I'll get
along just fine, thank you."

"This is rough country out here—hardly a tea
party in Boston. Are you really traveling alone?"

"I am," she declared with a toss of her golden
head.

"Is someone going to meet you, take care of
you?"

She bristled under his relentless questioning.
Who did he think he was, acting so superior? "I am
quite capable of looking after myself, sir. I don't
need your help—nor anyone else's."

He laughed again. "I must say you do have
spirit, but I suspect Springfield will afford you a
few surprises."

"I'm sure I'm quite capable of handling them."
His laughter flooded over her, and she felt herself
blushing. To hide her embarrassment she turned

away, striding to her trunk, which had been off-loaded. She stood with her back to the man as she watched the two other horsemen begin to lead the coach out of the water. It took effort. There was much shouting and cracking of the whip, but finally the carriage broke free of the mud and dashed pell-mell through the water and up the bank, stopping near her. In a minute her trunk was aboard, and she opened the door to reenter.

A hand clasped her arm and helped her inside. Seated now, she turned and saw that the man had gotten down from his horse. She noticed that he was quite tall, with a thin waist and slim hips. She knew she was blushing as she murmured. "Thank you for your assistance, sir."

"It was nothing." He grinned broadly. "Your payment was overly generous, I must confess." Now he laughed. "Have a pleasant journey, Miss . . ."

"North, Gretchen North."

"A most fetching name. Perhaps I'll see you in Springfield."

The coach lurched away before she could reply, and Gretchen settled into her seat, thankful the episode was over.

Almost at once it began to rain again. It was a hard shower, much more of a downpour than the earlier drizzle. Yet Gretchen was almost unaware of it. Certainly she felt no chill as before, for she was hot with both shame and indignation. But try as she might, she could not dispel the memory of his kisses. Her fingertips returned to her lips, sealing in secret knowledge. Tom Henessey's fumbling embraces had been nothing like this. Memory of sensation spread over her body, and she formed a visual image of the man who had done this to her. Thick, brown, curly hair, so soft between her fingers. She shook her head impatiently. She had to forget it, and she vowed not to lose her head like that again. She must have been mad!

Suddenly she frowned. Who was he? She didn't even know his name. Well, she reasoned, perhaps that was for the best. Then she let out a small cry as his words came back to her—he had said he would see her in Springfield!

Chapter Two

MUCH TO GRETCHEN'S disappointment, the North Inn was not in Springfield, but some miles north of town, leaving her to wonder if the establishment was named for her father or for its location. She spent the night in Springfield at an inn, eating in her room to avoid the rowdies drinking downstairs. As she lay abed, listening fearfully to the raucous laughter and bawdy songs from below, she worried that the North Inn might be such a place as this.

Her mind returned again to the man on horseback. She could only pray that he would not mention the incident to anyone—but it was a faint hope, for his behavior had proved he was no gentleman. Perhaps she should be relieved that the North Inn was out of town.

The rain ended overnight, and Gretchen awoke to a brilliant, sunny spring day which elevated her spirits. Using the commode in her room, she sponge-bathed, donned her chemise, then hesitated about what to wear. Though she still had some distance to travel, she was sick to death of her traveling suit, and she wanted to look her best when she arrived at the North Inn. Thus she made her decision—a favorite gown of bright blue, the skirt draped back to reveal a splendid petticoat fringed with Belgian lace. The problem was, the gown required a corset. She made a face at that, but if she did not cinch it too tightly, perhaps it would not be too uncomfortable during the ride. She wanted to make her most favorable impression upon arrival.

After a quick breakfast of boiled eggs, sausage, and barley bread—white bread was apparently unheard of out here—she hired a small two-wheeled cart and driver to carry her and her trunk northward to her inheritance.

As she rode, Gretchen clutched her heavy woolen cloak around herself, for the morning breeze was chilly. She hoped for a time of reflection, contemplating the rolling countryside, for it was beautiful. The wide, deep Connecticut River lay off to her left, surrounded by pristine woods—mostly maples just beginning to leaf out—and wildflowers bursting into bloom after the spring rains. How lovely! She was so right to have come. She also wanted to imagine the North Inn, what it would be like, how she would act as proprietress of an establishment for travelers and wayfarers.

Her attempts at reverie came to naught, for her driver, a Welshman named Bill Llewellyn, was nothing if not garrulous. Young and obviously none too quick of wit, he insisted on refighting the French and Indian War, much to her boredom, rambling on about colonial victories at Lake George and Lake Champlain, and the capture of Fort Ticonderoga, where he had apparently fought. He even recounted the entire strategy, in endless detail, by which General Wolfe defeated General Montcalm at Quebec and captured the city for the British. Gretchen mused that if she'd ever had the slightest interest in wars and warring, Bill Llewellyn had squelched it forever.

"Yessir, missy, seventeen sixty-five is goin' to be the best year God e'er struck. The French's gone, the Algonquins on the run. This whole country"—he gestured across the river toward the west—"will open up. Wimmin and chillun, whole families, can live safe now. No more mauraudin' savages. This here country's goin' to become so full o' folks, a body'll hafta go, hell, west o' the Hudson River, just to find apiece o' land. I hear they's maybe a million folks in the colonies, and damn near all o' 'em is wantin' to come out here. And I guess they's room. There ain't no end to land out west—least nobody's found it yet."

"Really?"

"Yes, indeedy, missy. We's got land, all the land in the world. An' it's rich land, where a man can stick a plow in the ground and just watch the crops grow. King George, he don't know what he did when he 'feated them French and Indians. He ain't even begun to find out yet. But he will. Smart man. I figger George the Third is just 'bout the greatest king they e'er was."

"He does seem remarkable. He surely is popular in Boston." She sought to distract him. "How much further to the North Inn, Mr. Llewellyn?"

"Not fer, missy. Ya'll be in Holyoke 'fore ya knows it."

"Holyoke?"

"Thass whar the North Inn is. An' the folks there say it *Whole Yolk*, not *Holy Oak*. Better get that straight on yer tongue if ya's gonna live here, missy."

She mentally corrected her pronunciation. "Thank you, Mr. Llewellyn. I'll remember."

"What brings ya out here, missy?"

"My father was Winthrop North. Perhaps you have heard of him."

He glanced at her sharply. "Oh yeah, I heerd o' him, all right."

"My father left me the North Inn as my inheritance. I've come to claim it." She saw his eyes widen as he gaped at her, slowly shaking his head. "Is there something wrong with that, Mr. Llewellyn?"

Abruptly he turned back to the horse, cracking his whip over the animal's head, but he continued to shake his head, as though he'd just heard something too amazing to be believed. "Nuttin a'tall, missy." Thereafter he became silent for the rest of the journey, for which Gretchen was thankful.

Holyoke was indeed only a settlement, perhaps

a dozen or fifteen homes clustered around a town square. The houses looked tidy enough, with spring flowers in bloom and well-tended gardens already being planted. She saw children at play and a couple of woman hanging out laundry. The domestic scene was cheerful. On the east side of the square, next to the small church, was Follen's General Store, a busy place with several wagons pulled up in front. She saw a couple of women emerge carrying sacks of foodstuffs.

There was no mistaking the North Inn. It stood at the north end of the square, well back from the roadway, with a curved drive in front. It was easily the largest structure in town. It stood two stories high and perhaps fifty feet long and was sturdily built of split logs. The half dozen windows in front were of real glass, set in lead panes. It really was a handsome-looking place. Gretchen felt a surge of pride that she owned such an establishment.

To the right of the inn, as she faced it, was a small livery stable, which she apparently owned as well. Alighting from the cart, she noticed the North Inn sat atop a high bluff overlooking the river. Boats and barges were moored to the wharf, and she saw men carrying parcels and barrels up a flight of steep stairs toward the back of the inn. When she turned back to the cart, Bill Llewellyn had already hoisted her truck atop one shoulder.

"Ya want this inside, missy?"

"By all means, Mr. Llewellyn. This is my new home."

Gretchen marched forthrightly ahead of him, unlatched the front door, and stood aside for him

to enter. She was rewarded with a loud thunk as
he dropped the trunk just inside the door. When
he emerged she had the requisite coins in hand,
plus a small gratuity for his services.

As Bill Llewellyn mounted the cart and began
his return journey, Gretchen had a sense of being
utterly alone. She shivered despite the midday
sun, then scolded herself. What was there to be
afraid of? Squaring her shoulders, she marched
into the North Inn.

The interior was dark, and it took a few mo-
ments for her eyes to adjust from the brilliant
sunlight. Slowly she realized that it was one large,
cavernous room, filled with roughhewn wooden
tables and benches. There were candles and lanterns on the tables, but much of the light came
from a roaring fireplace at one end of the room.
Odors assaulted her senses—burning wood and
smoke, of course, but also tobacco and a sour,
rancid smell she decided must be the spirits consumed in this place. Her eyes fully adjusted now,
she saw the inn was anything but clean, with
sawdust and litter covering the floor, and mugs,
pewter tankards, and wooden bowls called trenchers on the tables. She watched in disgust as a
burly, bearded man spit a huge blob of tobacco
juice on the floor.

"Well, what haf we here? Dearie, ya step right
o'er here, and let ol' Buck buy ya' a pint."

As he lurched to his feet, she heard laughter
from the others, felt them leering at her. Before he
could move toward her, however, she turned and
walked deeper into the room to stand before a

counter. There were numerous barrels and casks behind it. Mugs and larger tankards hung from the ceiling. Obviously this was the taproom, the place where the spirits were dispensed. Behind the counter was one of the most loathsome-looking men she had ever seen. He had a huge, round head with dark hair pasted against his scalp with pomade. An ugly scar ran from his left ear to his chin, twisting his mouth into a droop. He was short in height, but powerfully built, with heavy shoulders, a thick waist, and arms the size of young trees.

She felt intimidated, but she squared her shoulders and spoke in a firm voice. "Are you in charge of this establishment, sir?"

He stared at her, and she realized there was a gray, almost vacant look in his eyes. What a repulsive individual.

"And if I yam?"

The question unnerved her. Again she summoned her courage. "I am Gretchen North. My father—my late father—was Winthrop North. He bequeathed this property to me. I have come from Boston to take charge of it."

Still he stared at her. It was as though he had never seen a woman before. "You did what?"

"I believe you heard me, sir." Nervously, she undid the bow at her throat and slid the hood of her cloak back, shaking out her hair. "I have come to claim—"

"Wouldja look at them goldilocks!" The voice came from behind her. She recognized it as belonging to the man who called himself Buck.

Another voice chimed in. "Ne'er did see such hair."

Turning nervously, she saw several men getting to their feet and coming toward her. As they clustered around her, one man reached out and touched the back of her head. She stepped away. "Oh, please . . . don't."

"Such purty hair. Ne'er seen the like o' it."

"Stop it, I say!" At once she pulled the hood back over her head and turned to address the man with the scarred face. "I asked if you operate this establishment."

He gaped at her a moment longer. "In a manner o' speakin'. I's the barkeep."

"Very good. That's some progress." She felt someone behind her pull down her hood and snake his hand through her hair. "Stop it, do you hear?" She wheeled to face the man. He was older and bewhiskered, slight of build, with a silly, toothless grin on his face.

"Ne'er seen hair like that."

His hand came toward her again, but she halted it with a vigorous stomp of her foot. "I will not have it! Stop touching me!" She turned back to the barkeep. "What is your name?" she demanded.

"Timothy, Timothy Wolf."

"Very well, Mr. Wolf. Henceforth you take orders from me as the new owner. My orders are for you to get this disgusting, filthy place cleaned up and aired out." She knew her voice had become strident, but it was her only defense against fear.

"Didja say owner?"

Fear gave way to impatience.

"Are you deaf as well as insolent?"

"New owner? Ain't poss'ble, ma'am."

"It certainly is. I have the deed to prove it."

"Tuck Loudon owns this here place."

She bristled and stood taller. "I assure you this Tuck person does not. I have the necessary papers to prove my ownership."

"That may be so, but yer gonna haf to take it up with Tuck Loudon himself."

"Where can I find this person?"

Wolf rendered an elaborate shrug. "Dunno. Ain't seen him fer a cupla days." He looked past her toward the men gathered behind. "Any o' you blokes seen Tuck lately?"

"Yeah, rode in last night," someone answered.

Gretchen turned to the voice. "I demand you bring him here immediately. I want this settled at once."

The wizened old man hesitated, obeying only when the barkeep ordered, "Miles, go tell Tuck he's gotta vis'ter."

That brought laughter from the others. The man called Buck said, "Some vis'ter. But Tuck'll know what to do with her."

Another said, "An' if he don't, I sure do." More raucous laughter followed this comment.

Gretchen sat primly, quite stiff backed, on her trunk and waited, doing her best to ignore the crude comments about her appearance and questions about where she came from and how she got to Holyoke. It was insufferable to her, and she had a sense of acute disappointment that her beloved father had run such a place. It was not at all as she had imagined. In her mind's eye she had envisioned a clean, airy place with curtains and elegant furnishings, a comfortable hostelry for ladies and gentlemen who were traveling. Why, this place was nothing more than a tavern, and a most disgusting one at that. Her father could never have operated such an establishment.

She could not possible have been more surprised when the door was flung open. Standing before her was the man on horseback, the one who had rescued her from the river. There was no mistaking the handsome face, the shock of thick brown hair. He was dressed much as he had been the day before. Again she was taken aback by his overpowering physical presence, and she felt a wave of heat suffusing her skin.

Her surprise was naught compared to his. He had hardly forgotten the girl at the riverbank. How could he? The memory of her soft lips and willing response still stirred his loins. But he had not linked her name with the North Inn and Winthrop North. Even when Miles Burnett said North's daughter had arrived to take over the inn, he still had not thought of her. "Well, what have we here?"

She sensed he was as surprised to see her as she was to see him. Her eyes widened as a broad, mischievous smile slowly spread across his face. His presence seemed to fill the whole room. "You're M-Mr. . . . Tucker?" she stammered.

He laughed generously. "Hardly. Tucker is my first name. Tucker Loudon. My friends call me Tuck."

His laugh was too strong. Indeed everything about him was too forceful. Oh, how could she have been so foolish? "Of course. My mistake." She knew she was blushing and struggled for her poise. "It seems, Mr. Loudon, you've come to my rescue again." But she was anything but grateful, she thought to herself.

"I trust I will be as well rewarded as the last time."

Now she was angry. The heat of his words seemed to spread over her body, most uncomfortably so. And that triumphant look on his face made her blood boil. She could not let him make her seem a fool. Coolly, she replied. "I doubt if such a reward will be called for again."

Once more his laughter taunted her. "That would be a most regrettable loss."

Everything about him was a challenge, even the way he stood—legs apart, hands on hips, the wide grin on his face, the insulting laughter. She knew she had to stand up to him, or else all was lost for her. "I'm sure you'll survive, Mr. Loudon." She gave him a piercing look. "There seems to be some confusion about the ownership of this—" she made an expansive gesture to encompass her surroundings—"this establishment. I would appreciate your explaining to this gentleman"—she gestured anew—"this barkeep that I am indeed the legal owner."

Tuck turned down the corners of his mouth in an expression of extreme doubt. "Miles Burnett says you claim to be the daughter of Winthrop North."

"I am, indeed. I am Gretchen North."

"So you said yesterday. I remember." He shook his head. "I never put two and two together. I just never figured you in a place like this. Still can't," he added pointedly.

"But I assure you I most definitely *am* here, Mr. Loudon."

He seemed to hesitate, frowning, pressing his lips into a hard line. Then he strode to one of the tables, shoved the plates aside, and hopped up to sit at the end of it. "Do you have proof of who you say you are?"

The question took her by surprise. "Proof? You want proof?" How dare he?

"That's what I said."

She couldn't believe him. Surely there could be no doubt. Why else would she ride two days to this godforsaken place? "Are you contesting my ownership, Mr. Loudon?"

"I am. What makes you think you or anyone else can walk in here and lay claim to this place?"

She studied his face, searching for some clue to his motives. He seemed so angry, but why? "I can't imagine what business it is of yours, Mr. Loudon, but very well." She delved into her purse, extracting a packet of papers. "I have a deed, giving me ownership of the North Inn. This is the North Inn, isn't it?"

"So it is called," he admitted.

She handed him the deed. "I believe everything is in order, Mr. Loudon." She watched him read the document, searching his face for some reaction. Annoyance was there, even dismay. It gave her a sense of triumph, and renewed confidence.

But his next words struck her like a blow. "Miss North, papers like this are a dime a dozen out here. They don't have much value, I'm afraid." He refolded the document, then turned and waved the deed toward the patrons arrayed behind him. "We've all seen papers like this, men. Don't mean a thing, do they? Out here, possession is nine-tenths of the law."

She heard the muttered agreement and sensed an undercurrent of menace in it. Obviously, Tuck Loudon was the leader of these men. Her worst suspicions were confirmed. He was no better than the lewd, filthy men who surrounded him. Steeling her resolve, she asked, "Are you claiming ownership of the North Inn, Mr. Loudon?"

"I don't see why not. This is no place for you."

Now she saw open hostility in his eyes and it triggered her own. "I assure you I am the legal owner, Mr. Loudon. The North Inn is all I own in the world. It is mine, and no one is going to take it from me. I'm sure there is some sort of government, even here. And I'm sure the Crown will agree with me and preserve my rights."

Tuck swore under his breath. "I hardly think we need to get the Crown involved in this, Miss North." Having the authorities butt in was the last thing he needed.

For the first time that day, Gretchen dared to smile. She had discovered his weak point. Naturally, he had been claiming the North Inn as his own. The authorities would reveal his deception—

perhaps even send him to jail. She knew she had won.

"Then I gather you are not prepared to dispute this matter?"

He hesitated, looking down at his boots, as though studying them. Now he sighed deeply, hopped off the table, and looked down at her with an expression of limitless disgust. When he spoke, his voice was devoid of the teasing charm he'd used before.

"All right, Miss North, I'll agree you may be the owner of the North Inn. But Holyoke, and especially this tavern, is no place for a woman like you."

She looked at him imperiously. "I'd like to know why not."

He shook his head in disbelief. "Lord, woman, just look around you. This place is inhabited by—" He bit off his words. "Let's just say, you are unacquainted with the sort of people who come to the North Inn. Have you ever been in a tavern before, Miss North?"

She hesitated. The very question was an affront. "Of course I have." Another pause. "I'll admit . . . not very often, but—"

His malicious laughter flooded over her. "Like never, I'm sure. Miss Gretchen North, daughter of Winthrop North, you don't belong here. You belong in Boston. Your appearance, your attire, everything about you bespeaks Boston. Go back there. Attend your tea parties, your soirées, your poetry readings, whatever proper Boston maidens do to amuse themselves. This is the last place on earth for you to be, believe me." He looked out over the patrons. "Am I right, men?"

A hearty chorus of agreement came, and Gretchen felt the derision in it. And despite her victory, she was beginning to feel a little afraid—these men would be formidable adversaries. "I don't believe there's any call to speak to me this way," she said bravely.

"I think I need to." There was a challenge in his tone. "This is no place for you. You have no more idea how to run the North Inn than"—he shrugged—"than I do about giving a sermon in church. Go back where you belong."

"I can't . . . I won't!"

"I'll tell you what, Gretchen." His tone softened a little. "I'll run this place for you. It makes a little money from time to time. I'll send the profits to you. I promise I will."

Any doubts Gretchen had had were quickly swallowed up in anger. Now he was treating her like a child! Her voice took on an edge as she defiantly said, "You will do no such thing, Mr. Loudon. I am quite capable of running this establishment and that is exactly what I propose to do—whether you like it or not."

"Lord God Almighty!" Again he shook his head. "Girl, you have no idea what you're getting into."

"Perhaps not, but I intend to find out." Her back straightened and she wheeled to face the barkeep. "Mr. Wolf, I insist you clean up this pace at once. It is disgusting. And please have my trunk carried upstairs to the largest room."

"God, girl!" Tuck's voice rose. "You can't live up there. It's no place for you. The Widow Sparrow lives across the green. I'll speak to her about taking you in."

"You needn't trouble yourself, Mr. Loudon. This is *my* inn. I intend to live here and operate it as a proper hostelry for wayfarers."

That brought sharp laughter and catcalls, which seemed to bolster Tuck Loudon. He joined in the laughter wholeheartedly. "I'll give you a week, Gretchen. At the end of that time you'll be begging me to send you back to Boston. I'll wager on it."

The resulting laughter both reddened her face and stiffened her resolve. "Not on your life, Mr. Loudon. You're wasting your money." She turned away, heading for the stairs.

"I was thinking of the same payment as the last time."

The words stopped Gretchen in her tracks. Slowly she turned to face him. "You will freeze in hell before that happens again, Mr. Loudon."

"Now that, I really will bet on."

Chapter Three

PICKING UP HER skirt, a particular necessity because of the dirt and litter on the staircase, Gretchen followed Timothy Wolf and the little man called Miles as they carried her trunk upstairs. The second floor was bisected by a narrow hallway. There appeared to be numerous rooms off both sides. The two men turned to the left.

The corridor and rooms she passed were all uniformly filthy. Had no one ever swept or mopped? But what affronted her the most were the odors, which only worsened as she approached what was to be her room. There was smoke and burned tallow to be sure, also stale cooking smells, but what assaulted her senses, almost making her gag, were the vile stenches she could only associate with unclean bodies and chamber pots. What a filthy place.

She waited as the men carried her trunk through a narrow doorway, then she stood aside as the two men emerged. Wolf grunted as he passed her. "Is this the largest room, Mr. Wolf?" she asked him.

He glanced at her malevolently. "They's all 'bout the same size. This is the one yer ol' man slept in. I figger it's good 'nuff fer you."

Was everyone here always so rude? Before she could enter, Miles Burnett had to stop, render his toothless grin, and exclaim over her "purty" hair. She pushed past him to keep him from touching her.

The room was square, perhaps twelve feet long on each side, and sparsely furnished. To her left on the outside wall was a small fireplace filled with cold ashes. In the far corner to her right was what passed for a bed—actually a lumpy straw pallet on the floor, its covers dishelved and filthy. There was a bench against the wall which matched those in the tavern below. The only other piece of furniture was across the room to her left; a small roughhewn table bearing a washbasin full of dirty water, and a pewter pitcher. The stench in the room was abominable. Good heavens! Her father had lived here? Never!

Her trunk had been carelessly dropped in the middle of the floor. Passing around it, she went to the single window, opened it, and threw out the shutters to let in fresh air and sunlight. Below her she glimpsed a lovely view of the Connecticut

River and the rolling land beyond. But in her melancholy state she had no appreciation for it, and she turned back an in the better light saw just how terrible this room was. Behind the door she saw a small closet. Opening it, she saw it contained some filthy, smelly clothes. She started to touch them, but pulled back her hand in disgust.

Her eyes smarted, then were quickly washed with tears. Everything was so horrid! Not at all what she expected. All her life she'd lived in a fine Georgian home with lovely furnishings, everything neat and spotless. She had not even realized such filth existed. And people actually slept in this place! The full force of her predicament stuck her, and she visibly slumped, gripping the closet door to keep from falling. Slowly she lowered her head against her extended arm. Her shoulders shook with silent sobs.

Downstairs in the tavern Tuck Loudon kicked a bench so hard he hurt his toe—which did little to help his mood. Of all the rotten, bloody luck! Why in God's name did she have to come here—*now,* of all times? She could ruin all his plans, everything he'd worked for. Damn it all to hell!

A slurred voice interrupted his thoughts.

"Thass some lookin' wench. We's gonna haf some fun roun' here."

Tuck regarded Buck Shaw in utter disbelief. "You fool! That girl is pure poison."

The big man laughed, showing yellow teeth. "Looks like good poison to me."

"You haven't a brain in your head, Buck. Do you realize what will happen if she finds out what's going on around here? She'll blab, maybe even go to the authorities. Our deal is off and our goose is cooked."

Shaw blinked. "Ne'er thought o' it that way."

"You damn well better start thinking of it."

Timothy Wolf emerged from the stairwell and approached Tuck. "Ya better git rid o' her."

Damn it, why did she have to come here now?"

The barkeep shrugged. "No point in wondrin'. She just gotta go, thass all."

"I know." Tuck shook his head in frustration. "Why does she have to be so bloody stubborn?"

"Ya better think o' some way to git rid o' her," Wolf repeated.

"I know, and I will." Tuck started for the stairs. "Got to be some way to handle her."

At the top of the stairs Tuck hesitated. Ridicule simply hadn't worked. Apparently she had more spunk than he figured. Maybe he could reason with her. He passed down the hallway. Yes, sweet reason. Females always went for that. Pausing outside her door, he heard the sounds of weeping. So, she wasn't as tough as she pretended, was she? Tuck wasn't surprised. And in this state, likely she'd be more willing to listen to reason.

"Not very commodious, it is, Miss North?" he called out cheerfully as he entered the room without knocking.

Gretchen recognized the voice, but did not raise her head to look at him. She didn't want him, of all people, to see her crying. She struggled for a moment to gain control of her voice, only partially succeeding. "My father . . . lived here?"

"Now will you let me take you to the Widow Sparrow? This is no place for you."

There was a softness to his voice, a concern and caring, that affected her, causing the unwanted tears to fall anew. In a moment she felt his comforting arm around her shoulders. And did she ever need to be comforted! Still not looking at him, she said, "I asked you. Did my father live here?"

But Tuck didn't answer her question. Instead he said, "I don't recall Winthrop North mentioning he had a daughter. Did you know him very well?"

Feeling the gentle pressure of his arm against her shoulders, Gretchen felt unnerved. "I-I . . . suppose not. H-he came west when I was very little . . . after my mother died. I was raised by my aunt and uncle." She sighed. "I only saw him a few times. I suppose—I guess I didn't really know him." Now she raised her head to look at him, unmindful of her tear-stained cheeks. "But he was . . . my father. I loved him."

He felt he understood her—a young child, practically an orphan, raised by relatives, coming out here to claim what was left of her father, hoping to know him. It was a good thing she never would. But he said, his voice soft, "Of course you loved him. And he was worthy of your love."

His words thrilled her. "Was he really?"

"Truly." It was a lie. Winthrop North had succumbed to the very spirits he dispensed to the patrons of the inn. He had become a shell of his former self. He turned her to face him, putting his

other arm around her shoulders. She was unspeakably lovely, all liquid eyes and maddening
mouth. "I might add that he has a lovely
daughter—and a most courageous one to come out
here. Pity he didn't know her better."

He did not intend to kiss her, just to comfort
her, but he couldn't help himself. Of their own
will, his lips were drawn to hers, which were salty
now from her tears, but oh, so sweet. And how
soft!

As before, she shivered under the exquisite
sensation. Instinctively she clutched at him, deepening the kiss—but only for a moment. When she
stepped back, her eyes flashed with anger. "You're
taking advantage of me," she accused.

"I don't mean to," Tuck countered. "Such lips as
yours were meant only to be kissed."

She resisted as he bent to her again. "You
wagered that you'd kiss me again, didn't you? You
caught me in a weak moment when I needed
someone to comfort me. So you've won. Congratulations!"

"I was not serious about the wager, nor is that
why I kissed you." He stepped toward her. "I
simply couldn't resist."

She stepped back again, breaking free of his
arms. "Then may I suggest you try harder to
control yourself in the future. I am not the type of
woman who—"

"I know you're not, and I will try harder to resist
you—although I fear I may fail in that," he added
wickedly.

The man was insufferable. Gretchen knew she

must be on her guard with him. She could trust no
one out here. "If you find me so hard to resist,
then why are you trying to get me to go back to
Boston?"

He fixed her with a penetrating stare. "Because
it is the wisest thing to do. The North Inn is no
place for a lady. Go home. I'll visit you there and
show you that I do know how to be a gentleman."

"That would be a novelty."

Gretchen untied her cloak and removed it from
her shoulders, placing it on top of her trunk. She
meant it as a gesture showing her determination to
stay, but at once she realized her mistake. Her
gown was of the latest fashion, which meant the
heavy corset both cinched her waist and pushed
up her bosom, creating a deep valley in the wide,
square neckline. The brightness in his eyes left no
doubt of his appreciation. She had worn such
gowns many times, but now she was blushing, or
about to. Why did this man have such an effect
upon her? "It is the fashion, Mr. Loudon," she
explained, trying to be nonchalant.

The rounded tops of her breasts were a most
unsettling invitation, but Tuck knew better than to
stare. He raised his gaze to her eyes. "And a most
becoming one, Gretchen—which is an even better
reason for you to return to Boston. I fear you will
have scant opportunity to wear such a garment out
here."

"Then I will obtain a proper wardrobe. I am my
father's child, Mr. Loudon. And I am staying
here." She looked around the filthy, unkempt

room again, slowly shaking her head in disbelief.
"I cannot believe my father lived here."

Tuck hesitated. "I do believe this was his room,
yes."

Gretchen shook her head obstinately. "He
couldn't have. Not my father."

Part of him wanted to tell her what Winthrop
North had really been like, but then he realized he
hadn't know him that long. And North had been
making an effort to shape up the last weeks of his
life, perhaps in anticipation of this girl's coming.
"He had the room fixed up better then."

"What do you mean?" Her blue eyes widened
and her brows raised questioningly.

He pointed toward the straw mattress. "North
had a rather nice four-poster, as I remember. Over
there was a fine writing desk and a comfortable
chair." Again he turned. "On this wall was a
handsome chest of drawers."

"Where are all his things?"

His shrug was elaborate. "That's hard to say
anymore."

Awareness came to her. She turned, moved
away from his arm, and gaped at him. "You mean
someone . . . *stole* them?"

"Various 'someones,' I'm sure. I told you, possession is nine-tenths of the law out here. After
your father died, people just helped themselves."

"And you let them do it," she snapped.

"I couldn't have stopped them, if that's what
you mean."

"Where are my father's things? I want them
back."

He intended his smile to be sympathetic, but she didn't react to it that way. "I'm afraid they're long gone, Gretchen."

"What do you mean, *gone*?" she demanded.

"Just as it sounds—gone, scattered. Some was probably taken downriver and sold. You'll never find them now."

She stared at him, breathing heavily under her anger. "And I suppose you helped yourself, too?"

He clenched his teeth into a grimace and rubbed his chin. "He did have a painting, a seascape, I admired. I'll see that it is returned to you."

"How very generous of you, Mr. Loudon!" Gretchen's voice ladled contempt.

"I told you what it's like out here, Gretchen. I repeat, this is no place for you."

How the man irked her! "That again! Go back to Boston and my tea parties—I believe that's the way you put it, is it not? Well, I'm not going to, Mr. Loudon. You may be certain of that! Now, where is my father's painting?"

"At my home. I do not live at the North Inn."

"But you say you operate it," she pointed out.

"Only in a manner of speaking."

"Some manner! The filth and stench in this place is unspeakable."

He looked around, as though seeing it for the first time. Then he shrugged his shoulders. "Things have been let to slide a bit since his death, I suppose."

"You suppose!"

"Things were better when your father was

alive," he admitted. "It's inevitable when an owner dies, a place falls—"

"Just answer me one question, Mr. Tucker Loudon. Who could possibly bear to live in such conditions?"

"Your customers, Gretchen." He grinned. "I guess you'll want to know who your clientele is. All right, let's see. A good many are boat people. They ply the river in rafts and boats. I assure you the accommodations here are far better than they are used to. Then there are woodsmen, trappers and such coming in from the west. They cross the river on the ferry down below. They trade their wares, then seek a little"—he coughed—"diversion of various varieties."

"You mean get drunk."

"Oh yes, most definitely that, Gretchen. It's how your father made his money, and I assume you will, too—if you remain." He laughed. "No harm in getting drunk and having a little fun. Your father offered a public service with the North Inn. You will do the same—if you have the stomach for it, that is."

"Oh, I definitely have the stomach for it, Mr. Loudon—but it will change, believe me, starting right now."

She wheeled toward the doorway, but he grabbed her wrist to stop her, turning her back to face him. "Gretchen, listen to me—"

"I will not. And you're hurting my wrist. . . ."

"That's because you're pulling at it. Just hold still and listen."

"I will not," she repeated.

In one quick movement he pulled her hard against himself and smothered her lips with his. It was a savage, ferocious kiss. But she twisted away. "So, you're both a brute and a rogue!"

"Anything to silence you." Again he pressed his mouth to hers, holding tight against her struggles, and he knew again her startling response, the luscious softness of her moving lips, even as she struggled against him.

At last he released her and stepped back, witnessing the heaving of her breasts as she panted. "Let me take you to the Widow Sparrow's. You can stay a few days if you like." Seeing the red lips part in protest, he implored her, "Please, Gretchen, listen to me. You have no idea what you're getting into. At the very least, think about it awhile before you make up your mind."

She looked at him wild-eyed and still gasping for breath. She had never felt this way before. Her righteous anger—he had forced himself on her again, and in a most brutal fashion—vied with the strange sensations overwhelming her body. She felt tingly all over, full of anticipation and a crazed, unfulfilled wanting. How dare he confuse her this way! When he reached for her again, she backed away and raised her hand in warning. "No more."

"Gretchen, I only want—"

"I know what you want!" she cried.

He sighed deeply. "I want only what is best for you, Gretchen," he said at last. "Obviously I care about you, or I wouldn't be acting so ungentlemanly"—he gave a wan smile—"and making such a damnable fool of myself. I have forced myself on you and I apologize. But you are so beautiful, so desirable, I—" He shook his head sadly. "I mean it when I say I can't resist you."

She started to speak, but it seemed Tuck Loudon, was not yet finished.

"Yes, you are beautiful and desirable, but you are also young and innocent, a gentlewoman, sheltered from the rude and unseemly your whole life. This is a rough place, Gretchen, highly dangerous for someone like you. I can't permit you to remain. Your father would never have approved of my letting you stay."

His words, especially the reference to her father, affected her, causing her anger to lessen. "There is truth to what you say," she admitted. "My father did not want me to come here."

"Then obey him, even from the grave. I will personally see you back to Boston safely."

She studied him a long moment, searching his handsome, masculine face for any hint of deception. She saw none, but that didn't mean there was none. After all, she hardly knew him, and he had done nothing to earn her good opinion. "I don't trust you, Tucker Loudon. As far as I know you are just like the others downstairs—albeit perhaps a bit more clever. You want me back in Boston, away from here, and you are prepared to use any means to achieve it. So be it. But I warn you it won't work. I'm here. I'm staying. I look upon you as an adversary—and I don't plan to lose."

"Gretchen, it's a terrible mistake."

She met his gaze. "To you, perhaps, but not to

me." She hesitated. Then almost to herself, she said, "I can't go back to Boston."

"Of course you can," he protested.

"No, never. My uncle is forcing me to marry a man I abhor. There can be nothing here at the North Inn worse than what awaits me if I return to Boston."

Chapter Four

GRETCHEN MADE IT only a few steps down the corridor before the turmoil within her threatened to dissolve into tears. She vowed not to cry—especially not in front of Tuck Loudon. She ducked into one of the rooms and closed the door in an effort to collect herself in peace.

This room was filthy, too. Everything was so horrid. He was right. This was no place for her. The enormity of her task weighed heavily on her. All she wanted to do was fly away from this place and escape the filth, the lewd remarks, and the sullen stares she faced at every step. So strong was the impulse that she actually reached for the doorknob. Then she heard Tuck Loudon's heavy tread in the corridor. She held her breath as he clumped noisily down the stairs. When he was gone she breathed a sigh of relief.

The pause brought her back to her senses. She wouldn't leave; she couldn't give up so soon. If she returned to Boston now, it would be in shame and embarrassment. No, she must try to succeed. She opened the door and stood in the hallway, shaking her head at what she saw. She didn't even know how to start to begin to do anything about it. It was impossible.

Utterly discouraged, she slowly strode back into her room. She gazed dully at her trunk, filled with fine clothes, her cloak tossed atop it. Was this really all she had in the world—a trunk and the North Inn? Then she remembered Ephraim Waring and aloud repeated her own words, "There can be nothing here at the North Inn worse than what awaits me if I return to Boston." It was true. The North Inn was her inheritance, and she had better start making the best of it. Filled with new resolve, she turned toward the stairs.

As soon as she descended she saw the man called Buck and several others at a table, tankards before them, leering at her. "Ain'tcha the fancy one!"

"Just c'mere and give us a good lookatcha."

She glanced down at herself. Her dress. She should have donned her cloak, or at least covered her bosom with a scarf.

Holding her head up, she walked past them. Miles Burnett was sweeping the floor in a highly lackadaisical fashion. In truth, he was doing little more than moving the dirt around, but at least he was making an effort. Then she spotted Timothy Wolf carrying a tray of mugs and wooden trenchers through a rear door. She followed and entered a large kitchen, which was warmed by a pair of huge fireplaces. Over each fire, carcasses of animals were revolving on spits. One appeared to be a deer, the other a small boar or pig. A smaller spit contained several fowl; pheasant or quail, she supposed. Numerous pots hung over the hot coals. The odors were tempting, and Gretchen realized how hungry she was.

Wolf carried his heavy tray to a corner by a rear door, where a scullery maid was washing bowls over a pair of wooden tubs. Gretchen was at first startled by the sight of her, for she was quite deformed, with one wall eye and a pronounced droop to her lower lip. Her spine was curved and she moved with great difficulty. Gretchen's natural sympathy surfaced. What a poor, unfortunate creature.

Now Gretchen's attention focused on a woman wielding a large knife. She was standing over a butcher's block, cutting meat for stew.

"Venison?" Gretchen asked.

"Umm," the woman grunted without looking up.

"Is that for tonight's supper?"

The woman nodded sullenly.

Was there no one in this establishment who could be friendly? "I'm Gretchen North, daughter of Winthrop North."

"Heerd ya was here."

Finally the woman raised her head to look at

Gretchen. She had a square, almost mannish face, with flat cheekbones, a nearly lipless mouth, and humorless brown eyes. Her graying hair was tied back in a severe bun. Beneath a formless dress and stained apron, she had a heavy body almost entirely lacking in femininity. Gretchen could only think of her as burly or brawny, words usually attached to men. "Are you the cook?"

"Thass what I is." The woman seemed to appraise Gretchen for a moment, taking in her face and hair, her attire. Then she shook her head, clearly disapproving, and returned to her work. "Ya ain't gonna be much help."

"I hope to be," Gretchen said sincerely. "What is your name?"

"Name's Molly, Molly Dugan."

"Well, Mrs. Dugan—"

"I ain't no missus. Never married, never wanted ta, never let a man touch me."

There was hostility in Molly's voice. "Why don't I just call you Molly, then?" Gretchen suggested. The older woman's reply was at best a grunt. For a moment Gretchen watched the heavy arms slice at the bright red meat. "Your cooking smells delicious, Molly, but all this"—she motioned toward the fireplaces—"must be a great deal of work."

"'Tis that, right 'nuff."

"Do you have someone helping you?"

"Nope." She raised her head to look at Gretchen. "Does it all m'self."

"Surely not!" Gretchen glanced toward the scullery maid.

"Mary's a looney, not fit fer cookin'." She returned to her meat cutting.

Gretchen glanced at Wolf, who was standing nearby, obviously listening to this conversation. "Are there no other employees, Mr. Wolf?"

His gray eyes were full of hostility as he said, "Meg Gwynne'll be in affer a while. She's the servin' wench."

Gretchen recoiled at the term, but knew it was used. "That's all the employees of North Inn?"

"Miles Burnett helps out with the stables," he said defensively. "He's sweepin' right now."

Before Gretchen could speak Molly blurted out, "That drunken pipsqueak's no help!" She looked at her new employer. "Used to be more folk workin' here, but al o' 'em left."

"Left? But why?"

Molly Dugan shook her head rather violently and struck savagely with her knife. "'Cause this ain't no fit place fer no decent person."

The finality of her voice struck at Gretchen, and she looked to Wolf for confirmation. He frowned, shrugged his heavy shoulders, and walked out of the kitchen. Gretchen watched Molly work a moment before she spoke again. "The upstairs rooms are filthy. No one can live there."

"Folks do."

"Well, I won't! Where can I hire some people to clean the rooms and do some laundry?" Molly Dugan simply looked at her for a long moment, then slowly shook her head, as though she were dealing with an utter fool. "I asked a perfectly civil question, Molly."

"Dunno. Ain't my problem."

Gretchen stood there a moment longer, trying to tamp down her annoyance, then abruptly marched out of the kitchen. To her chagrin, she saw Tuck Loudon sitting with Buck and the others, talking and laughing. When they looked in her direction, she sensed the laughter was aimed at her.

"Gentlemen, Miss North is wearing the latest fashion from Paris, France," Tuck announced.

"A Frenchie dress. That ain't right. We just fought a war with 'em frogs," Buck sneered.

"Too true, Buck my man, but isn't she just lovely? Pretty soon all the ladies will be dressed like that. We won't mind a bit, will we?"

"Not my woman!" The voice belonged to a third man. "She ain't gonna show herself off like that."

Gretchen could feel the heat rising in her cheeks. She saw the amusement in Tuck's eyes and knew he was taunting her in front of these ruffians.

"I think she's purty," Buck announced. "C'mere, lass, an' let ol' Buck haf a good look-atcha."

"I'll do no such thing." She turned to Tuck. "I hope you're having fun at my expense."

"Oh, I am that, all right," he assured her.

Gretchen strode to the foot of the stairs, then turned back to him. "Since you used to operate this establishment, Mr. Loudon, perhaps you can tell me where I might hire some people to help clean up the mess you left me."

"Mess?" He made a parody of looking around. "I don't see any mess."

"Well, I do. Where can I hire people to clean and—"

"I haven't the slightest idea, my dear Miss North. But I will tell you one thing. Hiring people to clean up the North Inn is the least of your problems."

"It'll just git dirty agin." Buck's guffaw suggested just how amusing he thought he was.

"Miss North, if you want the place clean, I suspect you're going to have to do it yourself."

"That's the best idea you've had yet, Mr. Loudon." She wheeled away from him and started up the stairs, still smarting from the encounter.

Upstairs she delved into her trunk. To her dismay she realized the pretty gowns of silk and satin would be useless here. Delving deeper, she found a simpler dress of brown broadcloth. She held it up and frowned. It was still a fine garment. But she'd just have to sacrifice it if she were to clean up her room.

A few minutes later she was dressed for work, a kerchief tied around her hair, and in the kitchen demanding a broom, a mop, a bucket of hot water, lye soap, and a brush. When she emerged with her cleaning utensils and labored upstairs with them, it was to a chorus of insults and catcalls from Tuck Loudon, Buck, and their friends.

The task of cleaning just this one room was a rather daunting one. She had never done this sort of work at home. But she had watched servants do it and knew what must be done.

Getting rid of the verminous straw mattress was a puzzle, for it was very heavy, and Gretchen knew she'd never be able to drag it down the stairs. After mulling over this problem for a moment, she had an idea. Straining against the weight and bulk of it, but fueled by her determination to be rid of the bug-infested thing, she lugged the mattress to the window and shoved it outside, watching it tumble down the cliff, breaking apart before it hit the water. Other trash, including the filthy clothes, followed.

Later, having swept and concluded the rag mop was inadequate, she was on her hands and knees vigorously scrubbing the stained floor. She was extremely uncomfortable. Her knees were sore and her arms, shoulders, and back ached from her exertions. Worse, her hands and wrists were red and burning from the strong soap. But it was the only way, she told herself. She would not live in filth.

"Well, what have we here?"

She recognized the voice, heard the ridicule in it, but said nothing.

"Is this the way proper young ladies behave in Boston?"

"If they have to, Mr. Loudon." She did not look up. "Has no one informed you that a gentleman does not enter a lady's room without knocking?"

"I have been so informed, yes. I am standing outside in the corridor and have not entered. The door to your room is open."

She glanced up and saw it was true. "I can do something about that." Not without difficulty, for the pain in her lower back was intense, she rose, stalked to the door, and slammed it in his face. At once it was reopened and he was standing there chuckling.

"There are no locks on any of these doors, Gretchen—or haven't you noticed?" He laughed at her dismayed expression. "It should help you sleep with great ease at night."

She gasped in alarm and inspected the latch at once. It was true. There was no way to lock the door. "What am I going to do?" She wailed.

"You can spend the night with the Widow Sparrow, then return to Boston."

"You must know I will not." She stared at him a long moment, hands on hips. "I confess you are a thorough puzzle, Mr. Loudon. One moment you say you cannot resist me, which apparently gives you license to force yourself on me, and the next you are taunting me in front of your friends."

"All true, I'm afraid."

"As I recall you said you only wanted to help me. I fear I erred in believing that."

"Oh, it's true, Gretchen, every word. I am trying to help you by showing you how utterly impossible it is for you to operate the North Inn. In fact, if you think I've been unkind, I assure you it is nothing compared to what you'll encounter when this place begins to fill up a little later tonight."

"So you were helping me, were you?" She tried to insert ridicule in her voice, but with little success.

He grinned broadly. "I try to be of assistance."

"Then tell me what I am to do about locking my door."

"Let me see." Obviously enjoying himself, he made a fetish of rubbing his chin, as though deep in thought. "I know. You could wedge a chair against the door. Only you don't have a chair, do you?"

He was still laughing as he walked away. She slammed the door with even more vengeance this time.

An hour later she had decided the room was clean enough for her to abide. A good thing, too, she thought wryly. She didn't have the strength to do more. Standing in the center of the room, hands pressed against aching back, she surveyed her accomplishment. Yes, much better. Then she saw the window, streaked and yellowish. Tomorrow. She'd clean it tomorrow. Wiping a wisp of hair from her temple with her wrist, she picked up the bucket of dirty water and dumped it out the window. As the water dashed onto the ground below, Gretchen couldn't help but regret that Tucker Loudon was not standing under her window.

She carried her cleaning implements downstairs and was greeted by shouts from a now-sizable group of men accumulated in the tavern. Tuck Loudon's voice stood out. "Didn't I tell you she was a proper Boston maiden, men?"

She reddened under the taunting and looked down at herself. Her dress was wet and stained, her hands raw. Her hair and face were probably a mess, too. What did she care? These men were rowdies and utterly of no interest to her. But as she abruptly left the tavern on her next errand, she reminded herself that these people had to be of interest. They were customers at the inn, her only means of livelihood.

The late-afternoon air smelled fresh and clean, lifting her spirits a little—but not enough to keep her from muttering aloud, "Oh, Daddy, how could you do this to me? I thought you ran a wonderful place, not this. . . ." But she had no words to describe the establishment she had inherited.

Follen's General Store struck Gretchen as an oasis amid her feelings of desolation. It was clean and tidy, a *proper* store, filled with barrels and bins, bolts of fabric, and shelves laden with all manner of goods. It was a place to explore, and she remembered just how much she had always loved to shop.

"May I help you?"

To her right behind the counter was the shopkeeper, a woman in her early thirties, with a very ample, womanly figure. Two small, towheaded children, a boy and girl, clutched at her skirts, adding to her impression of motherliness. Gretchen smiled as she approached her. "Yes, please. I need several items."

The woman appraised her carefully and openly. "Are you new in town?"

"Yes, I just arrived today."

A lovely smile wreathed the woman's face.

"Welcome to Holyoke." She pronounced it properly and extended a hand. "I'm Esther Follen."

The fleshy hand was accepted. "And I'm Gretchen North. I'm—" She was interrupted before she had a chance to speak of her father and the North Inn.

"Our little village just seems to be growing every day." Mrs. Follen smiled. "You're so very pretty, such lovely hair. Are you married?"

"No, not yet." Somehow Gretchen always felt embarrassed to admit that. It was as though there must be something wrong with her.

"I'm sure our young men will be interested in that face." A gentle laugh made Mrs. Follen's ample bosom move. "How may I serve you?"

Gretchen hesitated. "What I need most of all is a . . . bed. Would you possibly have one?"

Esther Follen blinked. "A bed?"

"Yes, with a proper down mattress."

"I'm afraid we don't stock furniture." She gestured. "We're quite crowded as it is, but I think I can help you. We have a furniture maker here in town, Ezra Brown. He's a man of color, but you'll find his work adequate. He's all we have, in any event." She proceeded at once to give directions to the man's house, which was apparently at the edge of town.

Gretchen only half listened, for she was acutely disappointed. "But I must have something to sleep on tonight," she insisted. "I suppose I could use some straw, if it's clean, but—" At that moment an extremely slender man, little more than skin and bones, entered from the rear. She gathered he was the proprietor.

"Bill, this is Gretchen North. She's just arrived in town." Now she turned back to Gretchen. "My husband, Bill Follen." He approached, offering a hand—after wiping it on his trousers. "She needs a bed for tonight. Have you anything out back which she could possibly use?"

"Got some nice, fresh straw."

Gretchen sighed with relief.

"Come to think o' it, I do have somethin'. Had it made up fer a riverman. He never came back fer it. Come along, missy."

She followed the proprietor, marveling at how deep set the wrinkles were in his gaunt face. He led her through a storeroom piled high with barrels and boxes, then to a shed at the rear. After rummaging a moment he presented her with a simple wooden frame on legs, across which canvas had been stretched. He set it on the ground and tested the tension. It seemed quite tight. "Could you us somethin' like this, missy?"

Gretchen hesitated. It was hardly the sort of bed she was used to, but it was better than the hard floor of her room. "Yes, it will do nicely." Now she smiled. "If you have some blankets, I could make a sort of mattress."

"We got 'em, all right."

Back in the store, she selected four blankets. They were brown and made of coarse wool—really horse blankets, she suspected—but they were clean and would keep her warm. Spirits elevated by her purchases and warmed by the hospitable reception from the Follens, she again asked for directions to the furniture maker. Esther Follen said she saw Ezra nearly every day and would send him to her. Where she might get goose down for a feather bed was a more puzzling problem, but Bill Follen knew of several young women who might like to earn a little money doing cleaning.

Gretchen was positively glowing over her reception, especially when a couple of townswomen entered the store, were introduced, and chatted with her amiably, welcoming her to Holyoke. But it was nearly dark and she knew she had to get back. "Mr. Follen, is there someone who could deliver this bed? I fear it is too heavy for me."

"I'll do it m'self, missy, gladly."

"William," his wife butted in, laughing as she said, "I think you're much too eager to assist this pretty young lass."

"Wouldn't be much o' a man if I wasn't. Where ya live, missy?"

"The North Inn." Her admission was greeted by gasps, shocked faces, and stony silence. "Is something wrong? I said my name was Gretchen North. I've inherited the inn from my father, Winthrop North. Surely you knew him."

"Oh, we knowed him, all right."

Follen's tone affronted her. The reaction of these people was most unsettling, especially since they had seemed so friendly just minutes before. "I-I've come to run the inn—or to try. I'll need all the help I can get."

"I'm sure you will," Esther said coldly.

"And I can imagine just who'll give it to you."

"And why."

Those words were spoken by the two women customers, who put their noses in the air, turned, and walked out of the store. Gretchen looked after them dumbfounded, then turned back to Esther Follen. "I don't understand. What's wrong?"

The storekeepers looked at each other a long moment. Bill Follen opened his mouth to speak, but his wife shook her head to silence him. Finally he said, "It's only a short ways 'cross the green. I guess I kin carry this contraption fer ya, but I ain't goin' inside, hear?"

"Thank you," Gretchen said quietly.

In the deepening twilight she followed him across the green, carrying the blankets while he bore the bed balanced atop his head. Still greatly puzzled by the reaction she'd received, she said, "Mr. Follen, I really don't understand. What is wrong with my owning the North Inn?"

He was silent for a long time, trudging along under his burden. Gretchen began to fear he was never going to answer. But finally, he replied, "I just say this, missy. Ya musta seen the critters that go into the place."

"Yes, but I intend to change that."

"Humph! That'll be a cold day in hell—excuse the 'pression, missy." Then his voice softened a little. "Ya seem lika a nice 'nuff person, so I'll give ya a word o' advice. The North Inn ain't no fittin' place fer decent folk, let alone a proper lass like yerself. Ya just better go back where ya come from."

She stared at him in the near darkness. Here

was another person warning her to return to Boston. They arrived at the doorway before she could reply, however, and he quickly dropped the bedframe outside. "If you'll wait a moment, Mr. Follen, I'll get the money to pay you."

"It's five bob, missy, but I ain't waitin' fer it. Ya bring it to the store 'nother time."

With a sinking heart, she watched him walk away rapidly, indeed almost breaking into a run. Her heart sank with the realization that she was completely alone.

Chapter Five

As soon as Gretchen entered the inn, coming from the fresh air, her senses were assaulted. A smoky haze of rising wood smoke, cooking odors, and tobacco hung over the tavern. The place was crowded, almost every table filled, for it was the supper hour. Great platters heaped with fowl, venison, and pork had been set on the tables, along with wooden bowls of stew and vegetables. Patrons chewed on bones or slabs of meat, mostly eating with their fingers, but sometimes using a knife or spoon. It was all being swilled down with tankards of rum and ale.

The noise was deafening. Then an abrupt hush fell over the room as all eyes turned toward her. She was not made anymore comfortable at all by the voices which came after the silence: "This here's the new owner, gents. Ain't she the purty one?" "Wait'll ya see her in her fancy Frenchie clothes." "C'mere, lassie. Lemme git to know ya."

That brought laughter and shouts from other men who wanted to "get acquainted." It was an insufferable moment for Gretchen, but she stood her ground, looking over the room. To her surprise she saw several women, but they were like none she had ever seen, for they were coarse and dirty, their hair straggly and unbrushed. Likewise, their attire was disreputable, loose, and formless.

One woman stood up and looked at her with great intensity. She opened her mouth in a toothless smile, then rendered what could only be described as a cackle. "Yer gonna love it here, dearie. I'll even loan ya ol' Pudge fer a night. Do the ol' sot good." A new cackle was drowned out in a chorus of laughter.

Another woman joined in, saying, "Pudge wouldn't know what to do with ya, honey."

"But he'd die a-tryin'!"

Blushing, Gretchen turned away from the raucous scene and strode back to the taproom at the rear, where Timothy Wolf was busily filling tankards from barrels. A young woman stood at the counter waiting for the tankards to be passed to her. She had listless dark hair arranged in a bun atop her head. Though she might have been considered attractive, she was prevented any pretensions of comeliness by her heavily pockmarked complexion. Must have had the pox as a child, Gretchen thought. She wore a gray blouse, arranged to expose both her shoulders and upper arms, as well as an ample bosom beneath. Her skirt was a darker shade of gray. Both pieces of apparel were stained. But the girl's blue eyes were lively—Gretchen reflected that this young girl was the one spark of life in this dismal place. Gretchen smiled at her. "You must be Meg Gwynne, the serving girl." She couldn't bring herself to say wench. "I'm Gretchen North."

"So I heerd." Meg motioned with her head toward the tables. "Kinda ruff on ya, warn't they?"

"It wasn't very pleasant for me, I must say."

"Pay it no mind. They'll get used ta ya."

"I certainly hope so." Gretchen turned to speak to the barkeep. "Mr. Wolf, I've a bed just outside the front door. It's a little heavy for me. Would you be good enough to carry it up to my room?"

Filling a tankard, he glanced at her. Malevolence seemed to be the only expression he was capable of. "Too busy. Maybe later."

"It'll only take a minute, Mr. Wolf. It seems to me you could—"

Meg Gwynne interrupted. "Ne'er mind him. Lemme serve these drinks and I'll hep ya. The two o' us should manage."

Gretchen waited patiently for Meg to return, then together they carried the bedframe upstairs, not without hearing some lewd suggestions about the use to be made of it. When it was deposited in the corner of Gretchen's room, Meg said, "I heerd ya cleaned yer room by yerself. Ya did a real good job, Miss North."

"Call me Gretchen—and thank you. I've a long way to go to make it livable, but I intend to do it.

I'm going to fix up all the rooms and make the North Inn a proper hostelry for decent people."

Meg Gwynne made no comment, but the perceptible arch to her brows expressed her amazement at the whole idea. Gretchen turned to her bed and began to fold the blankets into a sort of mattress. Two made a thick padding; the other two would keep her warm at night. As soon as she could, she'd acquire some linens. This might make a usable bed, after all.

"Is this yer gown, Miss—I mean, Gretchen?"

Turning, she saw Meg fingering the blue gown which was folded neatly on her trunk. "Yes, it is."

"May I see it?"

"Of course."

Tenderly, as though in awe, Meg gently unfolded the gown and held it up in front of her. "I ne'er seed such a gown!" There was genuine wonder in her voice.

"It's the latest fashion—from Paris."

"Paris, France?" Meg's eyes took on a new brightness as she examined the garment. "I ne'er seed anythin' so bootiful." She looked at Gretchen, eyes still marveling. "This came all the way from Paris?"

"The gown didn't, Meg," Gretchen explained. "Dressmakers in Paris or London send over little dolls dressed in the new fashions. Seamstresses in Boston copy the designs and make the gowns."

"They do? Ladies in Boston wear dresses like this?"

"Oh my, yes," Gretchen assured her. "Every day."

"I ne'er!" She held the dress against herself. "Lordy, but it's purty. What do ya call this fabric?"

"It's silk, spun in France. The petticoat is made of muslin from India, and the lace is from Belgium."

"God almighty, it ain't possible!"

"I assure you it is, Meg. New England traders are sailing all over the world nowadays, bringing back the most fantastic goods." She longed to tell Meg about the life she had known, then realized it might sound boastful. She settled for saying, "Boston is a much different place than here."

"I should say so!" Meg clutched the gown to herself a moment, looking down at it, then abruptly handed it to Gretchen. "Put it on, Gretchen. I'd love to see ya in it."

Gretchen hesitated. "I fear it's not very practical here at the North Inn."

"Sure 'tis. Folks'll love it."

Gretchen shook her head, remembering her earlier experience. "I think not."

"Oh *please*! I wanna see ya wear it. It'll be nice."

A more vigorous head shake now. "I fear not." Gretchen told Meg about her experience in the afternoon. "Such gowns as this are very much out of place at the North Inn."

"No, it ain't—and don't pay 'em blokes no mind. Whaddo they know?"

Gretchen had to admit it was a good question, but still she hesitated.

"Ya sed ya want to make this into a nice place, dint ya? It's gotta start sometime, don't it?"

It was a persuasive argument. "I suppose I

could try." She wavered for one last instant, then agreed. "All right, Meg, if you think I should."

"Oh, I do, I do!" All delighted smiles—she did still have good teeth—the serving girl turned to go.

"How long have you worked here, Meg?" Gretchen inquired.

"Since my man went off soldierin'. He got hisself killed at Ticonderoga."

"I'm sorry."

Meg shrugged. "Don't matter none. He wasn't much ta begin with."

The brusqueness in her words affected Gretchen. "You've had a hard life, haven't you?"

Another shrug. "I s'pose. Most folk do. I kin take care o' m'self." She smiled. "Hafta. Nobody else goin' to."

Gretchen smiled. "I fear you're right. It's the same with me."

"You?" Meg's startled expression left no doubt she was shocked by the statement. "Yer so bootiful, ya got these fancy clothes, ya own this here inn. Whatcha talkin' 'bout?"

"I do own the inn, yes, but I'm not sure that's very much. Where do you live, Meg?"

"I gotta li'l place at the edge o' town."

Gretchen began to feel she was prying too much and changed the subject. "Do you know some people I could hire to help clean up this place?"

Meg hesitated. "I s'pose I could hep ya some."

"No, you work hard enough here at night. I was hoping to find some people to work in the mornings."

A puzzled expression crossed Meg's face. "I

dunno. Thass kinda hard." A dark expression flitted across her eyes. "I better git. Wolf'll kill me."

Gretchen had tried to read the expression in her eyes. Was it fear? "No, he won't. I'll not let him. Just one more question. What do you know about Tucker Loudon?"

"Tuck?" Meg thought a moment. "Not much to know. He's been 'round here a year or so, I s'pose."

"Where did he come from?" A shrug was her only answer. "What does he do—to earn money, I mean?"

"Now you ask, I don't rightly know. Ne'er asked. Don't pay to ask questions. Look, I gotta go. Can't hardly wait to see ya in that dress."

Then she was gone, leaving Gretchen with the feeling she'd had another strange encounter. But at least Meg Gwynne was pleasant and hadn't tried to get her to go back to Boston.

Gretchen hesitated again over wearing the blue gown, but she knew there wasn't anything much more modest in her trunk—and the dress she'd worn to clean in was hardly presentable. Perhaps it would be all right with the women downstairs. Meg had certainly liked the gown.

Not much more than a half hour later she had sponged herself—it felt heavenly to be clean— donned a clean chemise, snugged herself into her corset, and slipped on the gown. With only a hand mirror, fixing her hair was a chore, but she managed to braid it and pin it up in back, declaring the results acceptable, if hardly her best effort. Her last act in her toilet was to cover her shoulders and bosom with a pale blue silk scarf, which she tucked into the bodice of her gown. That should preserve her modesty—a wise act considering the noises emanating from below.

A hush fell over the revelers as she reached the bottom of the stairs. Everyone looked at her and Gretchen was embarrassed, although she had made many similar entrances, even in this same gown, without being so. Then Meg Gwynne came to her, eyes wide, and clasped her hands in front of herself, as though in prayer. "Lordy, it's bootiful!" Gingerly, she touched the wide lace ruffles at the sleeves, then felt the smooth silk of the skirt. "What makes it hang out so nice? Hoops?"

Despite her unease, Gretchen managed a sort of smile. "No hoops or farthingale, just the stiffness of the petticoats."

"My word!" Meg looked back at the crowd, searching. "Lemme show ya to Granny. She'll ne'er believe it."

"No, please," Gretchen protested.

"It's all right. C'mon."

She took Gretchen's hand and pulled her, however reluctantly, past several tables to a place near the center of the room. There sat someone Gretchen could only consider as an old hag. She was deeply wrinkled, with leathery skin, and white haired. A small pipe was stuck between toothless lips.

"E'er see anythin' like this, Granny?"

The old woman looked up at Meg. "Whassay?" She held a gnarled hand to her left ear.

Meg repeated her question more loudly, and the woman turned heavily hooded eyes on Gretchen and looked her up and down, much to her unease. Gretchen looked away and saw Tuck Loudon. There was an expression of vast amusement on his face.

"Whosis?"

"Granny, this is Gretchen North, Winthrop's daughter," Meg said almost at the top of her voice. "She just come from Boston."

Granny nodded her understanding. "Whassat she's a-wearin'?"

"It's the latest fashion from Paris, France, Granny. Ain't she bootiful?"

Granny never got a chance to reply, for several of the women had come up, seemingly awestruck as they touched the fabric and examined the dress, asking questions. Their comments were mostly favorable, on the order of, "Ain't that fancy" and "Sure is purty." It was comforting for Gretchen to realize that women on the frontier were just as interested in pretty clothes as the ladies in Boston, where the arrival of any new "fashion doll" caused a sensation.

"Ya gonna wear that out here?"

The question came from Granny. Gretchen raised her voice. "No. Meg asked me to wear it this once."

"Zat the same outfit ya had on earlier today?"

Gretchen turned to face the man called Buck, who had barged into the group of women. There was an immense leer on his bewhiskered face, and she was instantly uneasy.

"It dint look like this." In one swift movement he reached out and jerked the silk scarf from her neck, revealing her half-exposed breasts. "Now, thass more like it."

Gretchen was too stunned to speak.

Meg tried to grab the scarf from him. "Ya got no right to do that, Buck."

"Who sez?" He held the scarf away from Meg. "Thass the way she s'pose to look." He laughed. "Looks lots better to me." That brought a chorus of hoots and catcalls from the male revelers.

Gretchen found her voice. "Give me my scarf!" she demanded. She tried to grab it from him, but he held it away, then passed it to another man. Gretchen went to him, and tried to take it. "Please! It belongs to me."

"Do it, now?" The man tossed it to an adjoining table. Gretchen tried to catch it in midair, but missed. And she was too late to prevent it from being tossed again. Frantic, near tears, frightened by the men surrounding her, panic rose in her breast as she felt hands touching her. "Stop that!" She wheeled but could not see which man had fondled her. Then she squealed as someone pinched her bare shoulder, turning to see only a collection of ugly, leering faces contorted with laughter.

"Let Big John haf a good lookatcha."

She was pulled off her feet into a lap. She saw only a huge bearded face coming toward her.

"Give Big John a li'l—"

"Ya leave 'er be, John Clayton!" It was Meg,

pushing him away, helping Gretchen to her feet. "C'mon, lemme gitcha outta here."

Shocked and frightened, a grateful Gretchen was led away by Meg, but not before she saw her best silk scarf being grabbed and torn by men eager to possess it. Meg led her past the taproom and into the kitchen, sitting her at a table. Gretchen covered her face with her hands and groaned.

Meg patted her shoulder affectionately. "I know, they's ruff sometimes, but they dint mean no harm—just havin' a li'l fun."

Gretchen lowered her hands and raised her head. "You call that fun? It wasn't to me."

"I know, I know." Meg's voice was soothing.

"Someone pinched me! That horrid man tried to—" Gretchen broke off in embarrassment.

"Pay it no mind, love." Again Meg patted her shoulder. "Ya looks pale. Have ya et?"

The question distracted Gretchen. She shook her head in confusion. "I don't know. This morning . . . I guess."

"Thass yer trubble. Lemme fix that."

In a moment a steaming trencher was placed before her. It contained hard flanker bread made of barley, with a heap of venison stew covering it. It smelled divine. But Gretchen shook her head. "I'm not hungry."

"Yes, ya is. Ya'll feel better. Eat." She picked up a spoon and placed it in her hand.

Gretchen hesitated, examining the bowl of food, then spooned a tentative bite into her mouth, chewed, and swallowed. It was delicious. "It is good."

"A li'l food's all ya need, I told ya."

"No, it isn't." Gretchen looked up at the serving girl and saw her smiling benevolently. It didn't help. "I knew I shouldn't have worn this dress."

"An' why not? Yer bootiful in it."

"No, I'm not." She shook her head vigorously. "Why were those men so . . . nasty?"

"They dint mean to be. They was just havin' a li'l fun, like I told ya."

"It was horrid. Everyone tells me to go back to Boston. They're right. I don't belong here."

"Who tells ya?"

"Tuck Loudon—and the man at the store, Mr. Follen."

"Whaddo they know? Ya owns this place, don't ya?"

"Yes, but . . ."

"Gretchen, yer young, from Boston, and so purty. Yer the purtiest girl they ever seen. An' sure 'nuff, they ain't ne'er seed a dress like yer wearin'. Folk like Buck Shaw an' Big John Clayton is just seein' how fer they can go with ya."

"They went too far," Gretchen spat.

"Ya ain't hurt none, Gretchen." Meg smiled. "An' as soon as ya eat ya'll be fine. Ya liff the spoon and I'll look at the customers."

Meg waited until Gretchen began to obey before heading back to the taproom. At the tap counter Tuck Loudon approached her. "How is she?"

Meg looked at him closely. "Whassit matter to ya?"

"It matters."

"Do it, now? Ya bastards dint have to treat her that way. Ya had to see how young an' innocent she is."

"She's that, all right. How is she?"

"Upset, but she'll be fine. There's more'n meets the eye to her."

He nodded. "I know."

Meg picked up her tankards and walked away. A few minutes later she was back in the kitchen, noting with approval that the trencher of food was half-consumed. The color had returned to Gretchen's face.

"I can't eat any more."

"Ya did right well. Feelin' better?"

"I suppose." She sighed deeply. "I'm tired. It's been a long day. I think I'll go to bed."

Meg shook her head. "I don' think so. Ya can't let 'em think they's got yer goat."

"What will I do?"

"Come an' hep serve 'em."

Gretchen tried, summoning her courage, but every time she got near a table, the pinches started, leaving her squealing and jumping away. Soon she could bear it no more and ran up the stairs to her room, slamming the door behind her. Filled with anguish and humiliation, she leaned against it, and wept. She felt bereft, desolate, and her tears fell like a silent river down her cheeks, dropping onto her bare bosom. She made no effort to dry her skin or stanch the flow of tears. She felt incapable of any action.

Eventually the tears ceased, if only because the

reservoirs were drained. Slowly she began to undress for bed, eventually digging her warm woolen nightdress out of her trunk. Then she heard heavy boots on the stairs, along with loud voices and laughter, both male and female. The sounds became louder as they approached her room, but they turned off before reaching hers. She remembered there was no lock on the door, and fear stabbed at her. What to do? She looked around frantically. With effort she shoved her heavy trunk tight against the door. It would have to do.

She lay awake a long time, shivering in the darkness despite the warmth of her blankets, listening to the myriad sounds from the stairs and hallway. Many people seemed to be sleeping at the inn. Someone pounded loudly on her door and tried to open it, terrifying her, but her trunk held. What sounded like a man and woman occupied the room adjacent to hers. Through the walls she heard muffled voices and laughter and what sounded like squeals and grunts and moans.

Finally silence came to the North Inn and Gretchen slept her first night in her new home.

Chapter Six

GRETCHEN AWOKE EARLY, a little after first light, but remained in bed, waiting for the guests to depart the upstairs rooms. Sleep had not refreshed her, and her arms, shoulders, and back were sore from her exertions of yesterday. But that was not her most serious problem, she knew. She was emotionally drained, indeed numb, wholly discouraged, and unable to cope. Her situation seemed overwhelming. All she wanted was to remain abed and hide from everyone.

She did just that for a while, but inevitably the impossibility of hiding and the natural resiliency of youth asserted themselves. She rose, bathed, and donned her brown work dress. She felt anything but ready to face a new day, but at least she was moving in that direction.

The tavern downstairs was in total disorder, and there was no one around to do anything about it. Timothy Wolf had not come in yet. Miles Burnett was nowhere to be seen. Molly Dugan was at work in the kitchen, however. Gretchen's not-really-cheerful "good morning" was greeted by a non-committal "humph." Mary, the scullery maid, had not yet arrived. Gretchen helped herself to some of last night's stew—Meg Gwynne had convinced her of the need to eat—and carried it into the tavern, where she shoved aside some dirty trenchers and sat at the table to eat in solitude.

She had finished and was trying to decide what to do first when there was a knock at the front door. She opened it to face a man she had never seen before. He was well over six feet tall, with wide shoulders and a heavy body. His clear complexion was the color of cocoa and his dark eyes conveyed gentleness and intelligence. "Yes?"

"Would you be Miss North, ma'am?"

"I am Gretchen North, yes."

"My name is Ezra Brown, ma'am. Mrs. Follen at the store said you wanted some furniture made."

Gretchen blinked in surprise. She had not forgotten her conversation with Esther Follen, but she had assumed the woman was not going to help the owner of the infamous North Inn. That she had done so brightened Gretchen's spirits, and she smiled happily. "I do, indeed, Mr. Brown. Thank you for coming. Won't you come in?"

"I'd rather not, ma'am."

Gretchen sighed. Apparently the North Inn was off limits to anyone concerned about their reputation. "Very well." She stepped outside gratefully, for it was another sunny morning. "What a lovely day." She looked up at him, and he doffed his hat politely. "I have just moved here, Mr. Brown, to take over the North Inn, which my late father owned."

"I knew him, ma'am. God rest his soul."

Again she blinked. At least someone seemed to mourn her father. "Thank you, Mr. Brown. I have taken one of the upstairs rooms as my quarters. It is devoid of furniture. I need a bed, first of all, one suitable for a down mattress, then a proper commode, with a mirror, if possible, then a chest of drawers and a chair. Can you build all that for me?"

"Yes, ma'am. I've some walnut, maple, and cherry already cut and seasoned. It's fine wood, ma'am. It will make excellent furniture. Just give me a few days."

As Ezra Brown described the pieces he would build, Gretchen couldn't help but be impressed by him. He was courteous and accommodating, yet there was a certain dignity to him. And unlike many of the other townspeople she had met, his speech and accent were excellent. "You are well-spoken, Mr. Brown," she commented.

He nodded proudly. "Thank you, ma'am. I've have some schooling."

"I can tell. Where, may I ask?"

"In Connecticut, ma'am, a place called Hartford."

"I know of it, of course. What brings you to Holyoke?"

"Opportunity, ma'am, a better life for my family."

She smiled warmly. "I hope you succeed. Are you a freedman, Mr. Brown?"

"Yes, ma'am, my grandfather before me. I have the papers to prove—"

"That won't be necessary, Mr. Brown. I quite believe you."

"Thank you, ma'am." He displayed a certain awkwardness for a moment, then put on his hat. "I'll start to work at once."

"Thank you so much." Gretchen watched him stride away a few steps. Then a thought came to her. "Mr. Brown," she called, "perhaps you could help me with another matter."

"Yes?"

"I am hoping to fix up all the rooms in the inn. They all need suitable furniture. Would you be able to built it?"

"It will take some time, but yes, ma'am." He seemed pleased at such a large order.

"I will, of course, pay you appropriately."

"I understand that, ma'am. I'm grateful for the work."

"To create a better life for your family. I understand." She smiled. "And I'll need locks for the doors, Mr. Brown. Could you assist me there?"

He hesitated. "I believe Mr. Follen has a supply of locks. If not, they can be ordered from Springfield. But I could install them."

She was delighted. "That's wonderful! Could you put a lock on my door first thing today?"

"I can try, ma'am."

"Oh, thank you, thank you." Her glee came out as laughter.

A frown crossed his handsome face. "There's only one problem, Miss North."

"Yes?" He looked down at the ground, as though uncertain what to say. "You may speak freely, Mr. Brown."

After more hesitation, and still not looking at her, he said, "It's just that to install the lock I'll need to inspect the door and—" He had much difficulty going on. "It's just, ma'am, that the North Inn is . . ."

She pursed her lips firmly together. "I understand, Mr. Brown. You do not wish to enter the inn, because of its . . . reputation." He looked at her but did not speak. The answer was in his face. "Mr. Brown, I intend to change that reputation. But in any event, there are no patrons in the Inn at the moment. It will be safe for you to enter and make your inspections."

He studied her a long moment. "Very well, ma'am."

A few minutes later he had measured the door to her room for a lock, then at her request examined the doors to other rooms. Again the odors and filth affronted her. "I apologize for the . . . untidyness of these rooms, Mr. Brown. I'm determined to clean them all, but I can find no one to help me. Do you perchance know someone whom I might employ?" He seemed to bend overly long to his study of the door latch, and she sensed he didn't want to answer. "Do you?" she asked a second time.

Finally he stood up and looked down at her somberly. "I do, ma'am."

She waited expectantly for him to continue, but he did not. She now understood. Ezra Brown would not recommend anyone to work at the disreputable North Inn. "Mr. Brown, I am desperate. You see the conditions here. I cannot possibly do all that has to be done by myself. Yet no one will help me because of the very conditions which exist."

"I understand, but . . ."

"Will you please help me? The North Inn may be disreputable, but I assure you I am not. I want to make this a proper hostelry where decent travelers can spend the night in comfort. I cannot accomplish that alone."

He nodded his understanding, firming his lips into a hard line as he did so. Finally, he relented. "My wife and children could help you, ma'am, but I cannot in conscience let them enter. . . ."

She finished the sentence for him. "A place like this. I understand, Mr. Brown, and I heartily agree with you." She strode a few steps away from him down the hallway, thinking. Then she turned back. "Mr. Brown, as you see yourself, the inn is quite empty at this hour of the day. Perhaps Mrs. Brown and your children could work in the morning. No one will bother them. I give you my personal assurance of that." Just how she would protect them when she couldn't protect herself was a matter Gretchen chose not to think about.

He pondered her proposal for a long moment. "Very well, ma'am."

A half hour later she was standing in the open doorway to the inn, observing an amazing and blessed sight: Ezra Brown carrying a box of tools, leading a parade of children. She counted eight— three sons and five daughters. They looked to range in age from sixteen or seventeen to perhaps five. Mrs. Brown held up the rear of the column. She was a short woman of ample girth, wearing an apron and a bandanna on her head. She was obviously prepared for work. The children all carried brooms, mops, and buckets.

Gretchen felt she could weep with joy. "You have quite a family, Mr. Brown," she managed to say.

"Yes, ma'am, thank you." With obvious pride he introduced his family. They all had biblical names: Matthew, Jeremiah, and Joshua for the boys, Ruth, Esther, Mary, Sarah, and Martha for the girls. Mrs. Brown was named Rose. Gretchen smiled and greeted her warmly. "You have a lovely family, Mrs. Brown." And they were, the girls all slender and sloe-eyed, the boys strong and dignified like their father. "You must be so proud of them all."

"Thanky, ma'am. They'se good chillun."

She obviously did not have the schooling of her husband, but that was hardly unusual. "I can't tell you how much I appreciate your coming to help me."

"They'd best get started," Ezra Brown said. "I want them all out of here by noontime."

What happened then truly astounded Gretchen. The whole family set to with a vengeance, dumping the straw mattresses and litter outside, then sweeping, mopping, and scrubbing, two and three rooms at a time. Even Joshua, the littlest, fell to with a scrub brush at his mother's side. The oldest child, Ruth, worked downstairs with Gretchen, carrying the utensils into the kitchen, then scrubbing the tabletops and benches. She was a pleasant, gregarious girl, which made the work go easier. Ezra Brown had found locks at the general store and began to install them.

Into the midst of all this activity came Timothy Wolf, accompanied by Tuck Loudon. She had the impression they had been chatting amiably. Since she could hardly get more than a grunt out of Wolf, she concluded Tuck must possess some secret of communication she did not. It pleased her to see them both so obviously flabbergasted by the work going on. "I told you gentlemen that I intend to clean up the North Inn. As you can see, it is being done." She enjoyed uttering every word.

"Ezra Brown?" Tuck seemed to be in a state of shock.

"I've employed his whole family. I assure you they are very good workers."

He looked around and saw Ruth Brown scrubbing a tabletop. "Well, I'll be damned!"

"That is my most fervent wish for you, Mr. Loudon," Gretchen said cheerfully. She was in too good a mood to let him get the best of her.

"Upstairs, too?"

"As you can hear. Locks are being installed on the doors. Proper furniture will be made in due course." She turned away from him and went to the counter before the taproom. "I noticed you did a good business last evening, Mr. Wolf. I would like to see the receipts." She saw him glance over her shoulder at Tuck, as though for approval. "Tuck Loudon is not running this establishment, Mr. Wolf. I am. I wish to see the receipts."

Apparently he received approval from behind her, for he slowly, reluctantly, pulled out the cash drawer and placed it on the counter before her. She examined it, and saw to her dismay that it contained nothing so large as a pound note. Indeed, there were precious few shillings—mostly thruppence, pennies, and halfpennies, and a few farthings. She glared at the scar-faced barkeep. "Is this all, Mr. Wolf?"

"Ev'ry penny."

Gretchen couldn't believe it. "Mr. Wolf, I saw with my own eyes a great deal of food being served and generous amounts of spirits being consumed. This can't be all the money you took in."

"Is ya accusin' me o' cheatin'?"

"I don't know. Am I? All I know is that this can't possibly be all the money spent here last night."

Tuck came up beside her and leaned on the counter. "This is not Boston, Gretchen," he reminded her. "Cash money is in short supply out here. Folks pay when they can."

She looked at him sharply. "The North Inn offers credit?"

He glanced at Wolf, then looked back at Gretchen. "Something like that."

"Very well, may I see the list of who owes what?" she asked Wolf.

But it was Tuck who answered. "Everything is a bit casual out here, Gretchen. A lot of business is barter—you know, they provide something we need and take it out in food and drink."

"What sort of things do they provide us?"

A somewhat pained expression on his face, Tuck glanced at Wolf. "Oh-h, food mostly, you know, a deer they've shot, maybe a brace of pheasants, perhaps some fish. Oh yes, vegetables, too."

"Well, that's entirely reasonable. I can understand barter, something we need for something we have to offer. Tell me, what is the going rate for a deer these days?" She looked from one man to the other, sensing their distress. "How many tankards of spirits or trenchers of food is a deer worth, gentlemen—or a pheasant or a pig or a bushel of potatoes?"

Wolf shuffled his feet nervously. "It depends."

"Depends on what?" She watched him closely. He almost seemed to be suffering. "Do you have a price list?"

"Don' haf a list as such."

"Then what do you charge for your various spirits? Suppose I came in here and asked for a rum. What would I have to pay?"

"Ya wouldn't want that. Too strong fer ya."

"I might," Gretchen muttered. "What does a rum cost, Mr. Wolf?"

He glanced helplessly at Tuck. "Five pence."

"Very good. And a pint of ale?" Slowly, painfully, as though she were pulling teeth, she got Wolf to give the prices of the various wines and spirits dispensed. "And what do we charge for food, Mr. Wolf?"

"Food?" he asked stupidly.

"Yes, what people eat—and in a most unmannerly fashion, I might add. I saw huge amounts of it being consumed. What do we charge for it?"

"Don't charge. Folk 'spect to eat when they drink."

"Are you saying the cost of the food is included in the price of the drink? Regardless of how much they eat?"

"Thass 'about it."

Gretchen shook her head in disbelief. "And what do we charge for the rooms upstairs?"

"Folk 'spect a place to sleep."

Gretchen was dumbfounded, barely able to contain her temper. She walked away from the counter to try for control before she wheeled back to face them, anger burning bright in her eyes. "Let me see if I have this straight, gentlemen. We don't charge for rooms or for food. And we take in very little on drinks. Is that about it?"

She was delighted to notice that Tuck looked extremely uncomfortable. "Gretchen, there are things operating a place like this you don't understand."

"Oh, I understand, all right, Tuck. My comprehension is complete. What you two have been running is a public charity. You take in the rowdies, ruffians, and rogues of this world and feed, drink, and sleep them for nothing, or virtually so."

"Gretchen, listen to me."

"I've heard quite enough." She strode back to the counter, and confronted a somewhat cowed barkeep. "Miss Brown and I have done your housekeeping chores this morning—far better than you ever have. Therefore, you will have time to do something else. I want you to measure the liquid in each one of those barrels, Mr. Wolf. I want you to do it again tomorrow morning. I expect the cash drawer to have a sum of money equal to the amount of spirits dispensed."

"You can't do that, Gretchen!"

She turned to Tuck. "I can and I will. From now on the North Inn charges for all it dispenses."

"You'll lose all your customers," he warned.

"Then good riddance!"

"Be sensible. I told you people don't always have cash money."

"Then I'll accept barter at an established rate. I'll even give reasonable credit to customers who will pay," she proposed.

"God, woman!" Wolf complained. "I can't run the taproom and keep track o' all that."

She turned to him. "Obviously! You ineptitude is most apparent, Mr. Wolf. I'll tell you what. I'll take charge of the receipts, starting this very evening. All you have to do is dispense the spirits. I'll take care to see that every swallow is paid for."

"Lord, Gretchen, you can't!" Tuck explained.

Gretchen looked at Tuck's face a long moment. A mocking smile slowly spread her lips. "Oh yes, I can, Tuck. You just watch me."

She left them abruptly and went upstairs. The

strong odor of lye was pronounced, but it was heavenly compared to what it had replaced. Without the beds, the rooms were now largely bare, but they were blessedly clean. Ezra Brown spoke to her, saying he'd only be able to install half the locks this morning. He'd finish tomorrow. She'd receive the keys before he left.

Gretchen found the Brown clan at work in the last of the rooms at the end of the hallway. Rose Brown was on her hands and knees. "Having scrubbed the floor of my own room yesterday, I know how hard that work is, Mrs. Brown."

The woman turned her fleshy face upward. "I's used to it, ma'am."

"Please, call me Gretchen."

Rose Brown raised her heavy body to sit upright on her knees. "'Fraid I can't do that."

"Then Miss North."

"All righty, I kin do that," the older woman agreed.

"Have you a minute to talk?" Gretchen inquired.

"I s'pose." She labored to her feet, then motioned to her offspring to continue working as she followed Gretchen out into the hallway.

"I can't possibly tell you how grateful I am for all you've done."

"Glad to be o' hep, ma'am—I mean, Miss North."

"I can't believe how much you've accomplished, and how well. You have a wonderful family, Mrs. Brown."

"Thanky fer that. Sometimes it's hard raisin' eight."

"I'm sure it must be. What I wanted to ask you is if you know a seamstress hereabouts."

"I does some sewin', ma'am—I mean—"

"Miss North." Gretchen laughed mirthfully. "Is there no end to the talents of the Brown family?" She took the woman's arm and led her into one of the rooms. "I'd like to have curtains made for all the rooms, starting with mine. Nothing fancy, mind you, just some sensible curtains, perhaps with sashes, which could afford privacy and brighten up these rooms. Could you do that?"

"Sure 'nuff. Ya buy the material and I'll measure and sew 'em up as good as can be. Take no time a'tall."

"Thank you, thank you." Impulsively she hugged the woman. "What a God-send gift you all are."

Later, as the Browns were leaving, Gretchen fished into her purse and handed Rose two half-crown coins. "That's in payment for you and your children for your work this day."

Rose's eyes widened and she stared at the coins in disbelief. To her it was an immense amount of money. "I-I can't . . . 'cept this. It's too much."

"That is for me to decide, Mrs. Brown." She turned to Ezra Brown. "May I settle with you when your work is finished?"

He nodded with his usual dignity. "It is the proper way to do business, Miss North. If you wish, I can have my child Ruth come each morning to clean—as long as none of the . . ."

"I understand. She is a lovely young woman. I will look after her."

"My boy Matthew is big and strong," Ezra added. "He can fetch and carry if you need him."

Gretchen nodded. "I'm sure I will." She felt tears glistening in her eyes and she touched his arm. "I believe Providence sent you to me today."

He smiled a rare smile. "Perhaps so, but you have it backward. For folks just getting by, you are Providence to us."

Then he handed her the keys, all tagged, to the rooms he had outfitted. She clutched the one to her room and began to feel a little hope.

Chapter Seven

IN THE AFTERNOON, having measured the windows upstairs, Gretchen headed for Follen's store to buy material for curtains. As she crossed the green, she saw Tuck Loudon on horseback talking to two men who were also mounted. They were too far away for her to hear what was said, but the pantomime she witnessed struck her as strangely military. All wore civilian clothing, but the erect way they sat atop their mounts was something she associated with cavalry.

As she moved along, coming a bit closer to them, she saw them turn to look at her. They seemed to evaluate her for a moment, then spurred their horses and rode off.

Follen's store was populated by several women from the village, none of whom spoke to her.

Indeed, they all made it a point to ignore her, rather haughtily, Gretchen thought. She went to the rear of the store, where the bolts of fabrics were, and busied herself choosing one suitable for curtains. The selection was not nearly as large as she was accustomed to in Boston, but she did find a pretty blue-and-white calico. Fortunately, it was a large bolt, surely enough to cover the windows in the inn.

Passing on, she noticed some hooked rugs. That delighted her, for in her mind's eye, she envisioned the rooms as having a nice bed, proper furniture, perhaps a rocker, curtains at the window, a rug on the floor—the sort of place ladies and gentlemen would find homey and comfortable.

Finally the women departed and Gretchen was alone with Esther Follen. Gretchen looked at the buxom woman levelly. Her voice was civil as she said, "I thank you for sending Ezra Brown to me. Of whatever color, he is a gentleman and most helpful to me."

"They're good people," Mrs. Follen agreed.

"How well I know. Again, I thank you." She turned. "How much yardage is in this bolt?" Esther Follen answered and Gretchen calculated. "Then I will need the whole bolt."

The proprietress was clearly impressed. "All of it?"

"Yes. Mistress Brown has agreed to make curtains for the rooms at the Inn."

"I see."

Gretchen again studied her. "Do you, Mrs.

Follen? I am determined to make the North Inn into a proper hostelry." The woman's expression was noncommittal, even astonished. "And I will need a bolt of this material suitable for bed linens." She walked on a few steps. "How much is this hooked rug, Mrs. Follen?" She listened to the answer. "I will purchase it and the other three you have in stock." She glanced at her. "I will need a dozen more, if you can order them." Her tone was businesslike.

"I will order them." Esther Follen was clearly uncomfortable. "Miss North, I . . ."

Gretchen waited for her to continue, but she did not. "Mrs. Follen, I will say to you what I said to Mr. Brown this morning. The North Inn may be disreputable, but I am not."

"I can see that." The woman screwed up her face in a grimace, indicating her distress. "It's just . . ." She sighed and threw out her hands in a gesture of despair. "It's just . . . Miss North, things go on over there. You have no way o' knowin'."

"I'm sure I will discover one day." She turned toward the door. "Please add these purchases to my account, Mrs. Follen. You and your husband need not trouble yourself to deliver. I will have someone pick them up this day." The silence behind her was heavy.

"Miss North?"

Gretchen turned back to her.

"I—"

Gretchen waited, but no more words were forthcoming. She looked at Esther Follen seriously.

"Perhaps we will have a chance to chat another day. Would you be good enough to tell me again where the Brown family lives?"

A quarter of an hour later she approached the Brown home. It was neat and tidy, with a picket fence and a large, partially planted vegetable garden. But the dwelling was terribly small. Ten people could not possibly live there. In the rear of the yard was a shed. From it Gretchen could hear the sound of woodworking. Ezra Brown was already at work on her furniture.

As she approached the front of the cottage, the door opened and Ruth Brown emerged, her face wreathed in a smile. "How nice of you to visit, Miss North." Her accent was clearly influenced by her father, not her mother.

Gretchen returned the smile. "I've not come to call, Ruth, but to add to your labors—or your brother's."

"Yes?" At that moment Rose Brown appeared in the doorway behind her daughter.

Gretchen again smiled. "Mrs. Brown, I've found a bolt of suitable fabric at the store. If you will be good enough to have Matthew pick it up, I believe you'll be able to make my curtains."

Rose beamed with pleasure. "I'll send him at once."

"I've also purchased a bolt of material suitable for bed linens. Perhaps you can make them for me when you've finished the curtains."

"Oh yes, yes, I kin do that."

"Splendid." Things were going well at last! "Oh yes, there are four hooked rugs I also purchased at the store. Would you ask Matthew to deliver them to the inn? He may leave them at the door. There is no need for him to enter."

"Yes, ma'am."

"Miss North, remember—if not Gretchen." Another smile lit her face. "I see your clotheslines are full, Mrs. Brown. Do you perchance take in laundry?"

"Yes'm, my girls and me."

"Would you add the North Inn to your list of customers? Or would that be too great a burden?"

The reply came without hesitation. "I kin an' I will. Hard work ne'er hurt nobody."

Gretchen laughed. "Certainly not the Brown family. Thank you so much, Mrs. Brown." To Ruth she said, "Will I see you in the morning?"

"Bright and early, Miss North."

"Wonderful!" As she walked away she saw Matthew Brown running hard in the direction of the general store.

Gretchen took a circuitous route back to the inn, wanting to enjoy the spring afternoon and become acquainted with the village. Her spirits were high and she delighted in the beautiful scenery, the lushness of the fields. Gretchen had been raised in the city, but now she could see what had lured her father away from Boston.

Ahead she saw two men on horseback and recognized them as those she had seen earlier with Tuck. They were speaking to someone on foot hidden behind the horses. She assumed it was he, and her suspicions were confirmed a few steps later when she heard him say, "Yes, I'll take care of it." Then the men saw her and tipped their hats as they rode away.

Tuck was smiling broadly as she approached him. "How very good to see you, Gretchen. Have you come for a visit?"

"Hardly, Mr. Loudon. I'm just taking a stroll." To her left she saw a small, neat dwelling of split logs. "Is this your home, Mr. Loudon?" she asked.

"Where I live, yes. Would you like to come in for a cup of tea?"

"I'm afraid that wouldn't be possible," she said curtly.

"I thought we might declare a small truce."

She met his gaze levelly. There was warm amusement in his brown eyes. "Truce or not, it still wouldn't be possible, Mr. Loudon."

A look of understanding crossed his face. "I see. A proper maiden does not enter the home of a gentleman unchaperoned. That about it?"

"It is the proprieties, even if you are a gentleman—which I doubt."

"I said I can be a gentleman. I'd like the chance to prove it. Tell you what. I'll leave the front door open while you're inside. That should not shock the ladies of the village too much." At Gretchen's doubtful expression, he added, "Oh yes, I could return your father's painting. That would provide an excuse for your visit."

Gretchen relented. "Very well, Mr. Loudon. I would like my father's property back."

"Tuck, please. You have called me that before."

True to his word, he left the door open after she entered, creating a square of sunlight on the floor.

She was surprised by the interior of the cabin, for it was almost as attractive a room as one might see in Boston. It was warm by a fireplace, and filled with comfortable furniture, including a handsome chest and a writing desk. As soon as he entered, Tuck went straight to the desk and closed it, rather deliberately, Gretchen thought. There were shelves of good leather-bound books, and paintings on the wall. A hooked rug and calico curtains at the two windows added color.

"You look surprised, Gretchen."

"I must say I am."

He chuckled knowingly. "As I recall you declared me a rogue—and now you see, appearances can be deceiving."

She looked searchingly at him but did not speak.

"There are things about me you don't know, Gretchen."

There was a strange note in Tuck's voice that made Gretchen uncomfortable. "So it would seem."

"Here is your father's painting." He went to a far wall, took it down, and placed it in her hands. "Quite good, don't you agree?"

She studied the seascape. It almost looked real. A surge of emotion gripped her. "This was my father's?"

"Yes. I'm happy for it to be yours."

Her eyes glistened as she said softly, "Thank you. I'll treasure it."

"I know."

"It is quite good, isn't it?"

"I think so, yes," he agreed.

"Do you know where he acquired it?"

Tuck hesitated. "I'm not sure. There is nothing so fine as this to be had out here. Perhaps he brought it with him from Boston."

She looked at him, her eyes bright. "I prefer to think that he did, yes." There was a catch in her throat as she said, "That would mean this painting was my mother's. For that reason I'll treasure it all the more."

His smile was almost warm. "I get that impression. I'm glad I was able to keep it safely for you."

"Yes, thank you. I'm sorry I accused you of stealing it."

"I didn't take you seriously."

Gretchen made a face, then again held the painting out to look at it. "Where is my father's grave?" But when he did not answer she glanced at him in distress.

At length he spoke. "There is no grave, Gretchen."

She looked up in alarm. "Oh? How did he die?"

He seemed to hesitate before he answered. "He drowned."

"Drowned? But how?"

"No one knows for sure. He apparently went downriver alone. His boat must have overturned and he was lost. I'm sorry."

Gretchen swallowed hard. "His body was never found?"

"Some time later at the mouth of the river. Some fishermen buried him at sea."

"There is no doubt it was my father?"

"None, Gretchen. I'm sorry." To change the mood Tuck brightened his voice. "And now for that promised cup of tea."

"Thank you," she said quietly. Leaning the painting carefully against the wall, she again examined the room, acknowledging her amazement. This was a gentleman's home, there could be no denying it. But Tuck Loudon had not acted like a gentleman with her, not at all. This dwelling and the man she knew simply did not go together. Raising her voice so as to be heard in the kitchen, she asked, "Is this really your home, Mr. Loudon?"

"Tuck—and it most definitely is." In a moment he emerged bearing a silver tea service. "Please, sit down."

She gaped in wonder at the silver set. It could have been in one of the finer homes in Boston. Then she obeyed, taking the seat he indicated.

"I fear proper cakes are beyond my abilities. Will buttered bread suffice?"

"Of course."

He set the tray on a small table and moved it toward her. "Will you serve? A woman's touch is preferred in these matters."

She stared at him in utter disbelief for a moment, then began the service as she had been taught. Tuck sat opposite her, managing to balance both his tea and a plate with bread and butter on his knees. It might have been something he did every day.

"Surprised?" he asked.

"As you say, there are aspects to you with which I am unacquainted."

"Many," he said emphatically. "I'm hopeful you'll have opportunity to discover them." He swallowed generously from his tea. "Now, tell me about this good fellow you're running away from in Boston."

She wasn't sure it was any of his business, but she didn't want to be impolite, and she did long for someone to talk too. "I suppose he is a good fellow, as you put ·it, a gentleman of repute, circumspect, prosperous, a good provider."

"He sounds like a paragon."

"Perhaps he is," she acknowledged.

"But you did not wish to marry him?" She shook her head. "May I ask why?"

Gretchen paused. "He is older, a widower with two children, a boy and a girl." She looked at Tuck a moment and shook her head. "He is an austere man. I do not believe I could . . . come to love him."

"Squeeze the joy right out of you, would he?" Gretchen noted with annoyance his smile was one of unrepressed pleasure over her decision.

"So I fear," she allowed.

"One should always honor one's fears," Tuck declared. "Does the chap have a name?"

"Ephraim Waring. He is associated with my uncle's business." Noting a hint of recognition in Tuck's eyes, she asked, "Do you know him?"

"It has a certain familiarity, but no, I don't believe we are acquainted." Tuck looked at her somberly. "I'm glad you didn't marry him, Gretchen."

The intimacy of his words, the heat in his eyes, made Gretchen want to flee. She sought to change the subject. "I'm making great progress with the North Inn.'"

Tuck scowled. "Hang the bloody inn, for a moment at least. Let's talk about something else."

"I fear not." She placed her empty cup on the tray. "I must be going."

"So soon? But you just arrived."

She moved the table and tray away and rose to her feet. "It has been longer than you think, Tuck," she said pointedly.

He was on his feet, too. "They say time flies when you're enjoying yourself."

"Well . . . thank you." She smiled nervously and extended her hand.

The hand which clasped hers seems to melt her flesh, branding it into his own. She looked at their joined hands, then up at his eyes. They were filled with longing, and something more—something powerful and frightening.

He swept her into his arms in one smooth motion. His hot mouth devoured hers, breathlessly, open, moving, soon wet and ravenous for more, so much more. How could this happen? She pushed hard against him, moaning, as his sweet tongue electrified her. She was torn between a kind of panic and a growing need for more. Only the sharp forward thrust of his hips broke the mesmerizing spell. "Please . . ."

"You're so lovely." He touched her hair, her

cheek, her throat. His hand was warm, and even in that gentle touch Gretchen could feel the power behind it. Struggling for some semblance of control, she tried to be light. "Even in this attire?" To her dismay, her reply sounded flirtatious rather than casual.

"You would be beautiful even in sackcloth and ashes."

Stepping away from him, Gretchen replied, "If I don't leave here at once, that's what I may be forced to wear." As he reached for her again, she said, "The door is open. What of someone should pass by?"

"To hell with them." He removed her hand, kissed it hotly, then bent toward her.

But his mouth did not devour hers as before. His lips merely brushed hers, as in a caress, brushing along the sensitized surface of her mouth. She gasped.

Gretchen knew she was trembling all over, both from the sensation and the undiluted male passion which seemed to emanate from his very being.

Only the sound of footsteps from outside made Tuck release her at last. She leaped back from him, eyes wide with fear, hands at her mouth.

"Damn!" Tuck swore.

Gretchen removed her hand from her lips and smoothed her skirt, an act which helped bring her to her senses. A little louder than necessary she said, "Thank you for the tea, Mr. Loudon—and my father's painting." She picked it up and fairly flew out the door, leaving him standing there. Once outside, she realized the intruder was just a boy passing by, paying no attention.

Gretchen's every impulse told her to run away from his house as fast she she could, but she knew that would only attract attention. She settled for a rapid walk down the street and across the green. Her mind and body were in turmoil. Only when she was safely upstairs in her room, sagging weakly against the closed door, could she seem to catch her breath.

Still she trembled. Her whole insides seemed to be quivering. How could he do this to her? For one mad instant, she would have done anything he wanted. Something was wrong with her, terribly wrong. She simply had to stay away from him. This must never happen again.

Then a smile slowly spread over her face. Perhaps she wasn't the only one who couldn't resist. He'd admitted as much, hadn't he? Her smile widened. Perhaps she had some power over Tuck Loudon, after all. That could be useful.

Feeling better, though hardly herself, she had Timothy Wolf carry the hooked rugs upstairs. She didn't care how surly he was. When she had placed one on the floor of her room, she was delighted by the touch of hominess. Then she hung her father's painting over her bed, looking at it lovingly. It was back where it belonged. Aloud she whispered, "I'm going to make it, Father. You'll see. You'll be proud of me."

Feeling more cheerful, Gretchen turned her attention to unpacking her trunk and hanging her gowns in the now-clean closet. But as the afternoon wore on, her misgivings about Tuck Loudon returned. He was dangerous, and more than that, he was a mystery. Books, paintings, a full writing desk, even a silver tea set—those were hardly common sights on the frontier. But why was he out here, associating with the ruffians in the tavern, and acting like a rogue? There had to be some answer. She was just going to have to find out.

Chapter Eight

GRETCHEN DRESSED EARLY to go downstairs to the tavern for the evening. She consciously selected a modest gown, one with a high neckline. Part of her dreaded facing this unruly crowd again, but this was offset by her determination to make the patrons pay for their food, drink, and lodgings and turn the North Inn into a profitable enterprise. If she failed in that all would be lost. The purchases she had made at Follen's store, as well as her employment of the Brown family made a pay-when-served policy mandatory. The money she'd brought with her wouldn't last long. She had very limited funds already.

Meg was busy setting the tables with trenchers, knives, and spoons in preparation for supper. She again made a fuss over Gretchen's garment and was rewarded with a smile of appreciation. But Gretchen's mind was on business. "Meg, when you serve guests, do you collect money at that time?"

Meg shrugged. "Sometimes."

"Or do you keep account and collect at the end of the evening?"

"Sometimes," the girl repeated.

Gretchen looked at her and blinked. "What do you mean, 'sometimes'?"

"Folks give me money sometimes. Most o' the time Timothy takes care o' it."

"I see." Gretchen glanced over at the taproom. The burly barkeep was occupied with his barrels.

"Most folks just pay what they kin when they kin," Meg added.

"Which I gather is very little and seldom," Gretchen said bitterly. "Meg, it's got to stop. If I'm to fix up the inn, I must have some money coming in. People must pay for what they eat and drink. I'm asking you to help me."

The serving girl looked at her uncertainly, but agreed. "I'll do what I kin."

"That's all I ask. Meg, starting tonight I want you to collect payment when you serve people."

The very notion startled the girl. She shook her head, first in disbelief, then in denial. "Folks won't like it, Gretchen. There'll be lotsa trubble."

"At first, perhaps, but when they realize we can't just *give* away food and drink, they'll accept it," Gretchen reasoned.

Meg continued to shake her head vigorously. "I can't do it, Gretchen. I just can't."

"Why not?"

"Ya see how busy I am. It's all I kin do to serve folks—let alone argue with 'em 'bout payin' fer it."

Gretchen sighed. She had to admit there was truth to that. "Very well, I'll just have to collect what is owed myself." She left Meg and went in search of something to write on, finally locating a large slate and some chalk in a corner of the taproom. Apparently her father had used it at one time for just the purpose she had in mind.

Sitting at one of the tables she began to print in her neat hand: *Prices at the North Inn*. Underneath she listed the various spirits served, along with the prices Wolf had given her that morning. It was an impressive list. Food? No one had ever charged, apparently. Well, she was going to. Gretchen frowned. She really had no idea what to charge, but the way she'd seen the men eat, half a shilling seemed little enough. She wrote: Supper . . . Sixpence.

Shortly after she posted her notice, a handful of men entered, ordered drinks, and were served by Meg. Squaring her shoulders, Gretchen approached one of them, a small, mean-looking man wearing riverman's garb. "That will be thruppence for the rum, sir."

He glared at her. "Since when?"

"Since now." She pointed to the sign. "Three pence seems little enough for a flagon of rum."

"I ain't ne'er paid before."

"That is indeed remarkable, sir. Do you know of other taverns where they dispense spirits for free?"

He blinked stupidly. "Sure, lotsa 'em."

"I doubt that." Without missing a beat she took the tankard away from him.

"I ain't got no thruppence," he protested.

"Then I'm sorry. I fear thirst is not enough of a payment." As the men watched in disbelief, she started to walk away with the drink.

"All right, dammit." The man slapped a coin on the tabletop.

It was with a sense of triumph that she handed the rum back to him and picked up the coin. The other men grumbled volubly, threatening to leave rather than pay, but only one did. The others fished coins from their pockets. Back at the tap counter Gretchen said to Meg, "See, it will work. They have money. They just don't want to spend it."

Meg made a face indicating her doubt. "I dunno—maybe."

"At least point out my notice to them and see what happens."

"I'll try, but there's gonna be trouble," Meg warned.

As the tavern filled and platters of food were served and tankards fairly flew from the taproom, Gretchen heard grumbling and complaints, some quite vociferous. But to Gretchen's delight, many of the customers, perhaps even most, laid money on the tables. When Meg brought it to her in handfuls, it seemed to be a most impressive sum. In the meantime, Gretchen tried to keep a list of who hadn't paid. It, too, was rather lengthy, dampening her enthusiasm. And worse, the list included Buck Shaw, Big John Clayton, and Miles Burnett. She knew it would be an ordeal trying to collect from those men.

From her stool behind the counter where she guarded the cash drawer, she saw Tuck enter. He glanced at her, but then obeyed the summons from Buck Shaw to come to his table. It was a group who hadn't paid and just about the roughest in the place. Gretchen couldn't hear what was said, but from their gestures and expressions she had no doubt they were protesting her new policy. More than once she saw Tuck look over at her. At length he came to the counter, smiling broadly.

"You look very fetching this evening."

"Thank you." She saw his eyes lower, scanning her figure, and felt a hot flush of embarrassment as his eyes boldly took in her body.

"Another new gown?"

"Not new, but not worn here before," she answered primly.

"Most becoming." His eyes were so intense they seemed to bore into her. "I enjoyed our tea this afternoon."

She knew she was blushing, but she couldn't help it. "So did I—the tea, that is."

"I could tell. You thanked me most generously." His smile turned into a chuckle. "I can't tell you how much I regret that passerby. I should have closed the door."

"I would not have permitted it—and I was quite glad for the interruption."

"Funny, I didn't get that impression. Perhaps you'll come for tea another time."

"I doubt that." Gretchen glanced around nervously, hoping no one could overhear their conversation. If it were overheard, Gretchen would have no one to blame for the consequences but herself. But damn Tuck Loudon for pestering her so! His very presence unsettled her. She sought to change the subject. "I assume you've come for something other than tea."

"Indeed." He raised his voice. "I'll have an ale, Timothy, when you get to it."

When it was set before him, Gretchen said, "That'll be tuppence for the ale."

He looked at her a moment, squinting his eyes a little and shaking his head. "Are you really extracting payment for every drink?"

"And food."

"It won't work, Gretchen." His tone was serious now.

"I don't see why not." She opened the cash drawer. "It seems to be working so far. People have more money than you think. That will be tuppence, Tuck."

Still shaking his head, he laid the two coins on the counter and picked up his drink. "It's a mistake, Gretchen."

He left her, returning to Shaw's table. He talked to them in low tones, then Gretchen saw them smiling delightedly and laughing. With dread, she knew it was only a matter of time until she had to confront Buck Shaw and the others for payment. That was postponed for a while, however, for Meg was suddenly very busy. Supper was finished and patrons now settled into more serious drinking.

Gretchen decided to help her serve and also ask for payment. But as soon as she approached a table, the pinching and patting and fondling started. She squealed, squirmed, jumped away, even slapped the face of one man, but her actions only made the teasing worse.

"How's 'bout a li'l kiss, dearie?"

"Lemme see what's unner them skirts."

She heard her gown rip, but before she could react she was pulled into someone's lap, arms clutching her. She felt the man's hot breath and rough face as he tried to kiss her. She screamed, struggled, and finally freed herself, only to land in another lap, and then another, hands grabbing at her legs, hips, waist, and breasts. In a panic, screaming, helpless, surrounded only by laughter, noise, and clutching hands, she feared she might faint. When she broke free she ran, finally reaching the safety of the kitchen. Shaking with revulsion, she tried to control her roiling stomach.

A moment later Meg came in and put her arm around Gretchen's shoulders. "Ya don't haf to serve, Gretchen. I kin do it."

"They're so *awful*! Revolting!"

"I know. Come, sit. Ya ain't et yet."

"I couldn't."

"That's watcha said last night," Meg pointed out.

Gretchen obeyed her gentle shove toward the table, but turned to look at Meg as she spooned out a trencher of food. "They don't bother you, Meg. Why me?"

"They do some. But I'm used ta it. Been servin'

all my life, or so it seems." She finished serving and brought the food to the table. "'Sides, I ain't as purty as ya," she added. "Pay it no mind, Gretchen."

"How can I do that? You saw what they did." She shuddered from the memory.

"They's not bad folk, Gretchen—most o' 'em. They's just havin' a li'l fun. Now feed yer face."

Gretchen picked up the spoon but did not use it. "They don't do it to you, Meg. Why me?"

"'Cause ya lets 'em," Meg said simply.

Gretchen was shocked. "I do not! I hate it!"

"Which is what I mean by lettin' 'em. Ya let 'em get yer goat. That's all they's really after. The more ya' squeal and scream and get mad, the more they's gonna do it. The more they kin 'barrass ya, the more they's gonna try it."

"But what can I *do*?"

"Gif 'em back as good as they gif ya."

"What do you mean?"

"Like I say, they'll do it as long as ya lets 'em. If some bloke pinches me, I pinch 'em back. Maybe I'll jerk an ear or twist a nose. If it's bad 'nuff, I'll gif 'em a swift kick. If they sasses me, I sass 'em back."

Gretchen remembered seeing Meg do such things. "Does it work?"

"Sometimes." Meg grinned. "It sure do make a body feel better to fight back."

"But I don't know who's pinching me or—"

"Don't matter none. Gif it back to someone. Yer sure to get the right one sooner or later." She laughed. "I gotta get back to work."

Gretchen watched her leave the kitchen. There was no denying that Meg's advice made sense. The men out there were picking on her because she let them. Meg didn't. She knew what to do. But Meg had grown up out here; she knew these people and understood them. Gretchen shook her head, knowing full well she'd never be able to do the same. She hadn't been brought up that way. She didn't know any sharp replies. She was powerless to fight back as Meg did.

Gretchen managed to force down a few bites of food before going back to the taproom. As soon as she appeared a voice hollered, "Come back here, dearie. Ya's real soft to feel." The laughter scalded her. She sought out Tuck's face in the crowd. He seemed to be enjoying the scene just as much as everyone else. Gretchen's mistrust of him bubbled over into pure fury.

When interest in her had subsided a little, she picked up her piece of paper and stalked into the main room. Her mouth set in a grim line, she marched up to Shaw's table and said. loudly, "Let's see, Mr. Shaw, I believe you had supper and two rums. Sixpence, thruppence, and thruppence. You owe me a shilling.

"A whole bob? Yer outta yer mind!"

She pretended to consult her tally. "I assure you that is correct, Mr. Shaw." She pointed to the sign. "Those are the posted prices."

"I already paid," Shaw growled.

"Who did you pay?"

"The servin' wench."

"Meg says you never paid. I'm here to collect."

Gretchen turned to the huge man Clayton. "You had the same, Mr. Clayton. I'll take a shilling from you, too, please."

"I ain't givin' ya nothin'. I brung in a brace o' ducks and a couple of quail. That's worth a few bob anyway."

"Who did you give these fowl to?" she demanded.

"Ol' Tim over there."

"When was that?"

"The other day."

She turned back to the tap counter and saw Wolf watching it all, a bemused expression on his face. "Is that so, Mr. Wolf?" she asked.

"Sure 'tis."

"Did you write it down, who bartered what?"

"I don't write nothin'."

Then a voice called: "I brung in a deer." Another said: "I brung in a keg o' salt. I's still workin' on that." Soon it seemed that everything that the inn could possibly use had been supplied by its patrons. Then the voices turned ugly. "If they's not payin', I's not payin'." "I want me money back."

She waited it out, looking furiously at Tuck. There was a smirk on his face. Finally there was enough quiet for her to say, "I've no doubt this was all your idea, Mr. Loudon. Thanks a lot."

He pretended to look astonished. "I'm sure these gentlemen are all telling the truth, Miss North."

"So am I, indeed I am." She was seething with anger, and her voice was sharp as she turned to Shaw. "It is too bad there's no record of what you bartered. But it is not my fault. You should blame Mr. Wolf." She looked back at the barkeep. His amused look gave way to surprise. "Perhaps he'll make it right with you—out of his own pocket. Meanwhile, I'm sorry but I'll need a shilling from each of you—you, Mr. Shaw, and you, Mr. Clayton."

As if in response, Buck Shaw reached out and pinched her hard on the hip. Even through the layers of stiff petticoats, it hurt, and she jumped back, bringing laughter. "Gif o' Buck a kiss. Ya kin add it to my bill, iffen ya want," he said sweetly.

She looked over at Meg, read the concern in her eyes. Somehow it bolstered her courage. "Sure, I'll do that, Mr. Shaw." She kicked him in the shin as hard as she could. It hurt her toes, but it made him swear and bend over to rub his leg.

"Why did ya do that?"

"You said you wanted a kick, didn't you?"

"I said kiss!" But his reply was nearly drowned out in the laughter which filled the room. But now the laughter was directed at him, not at Gretchen.

She extended a hand toward Clayton. "I'll take that shilling now."

He grabbed her wrist, squeezing hard. "How ya gonna get it?" He was easily the biggest man in the room, and he knew it. "Fact tis, I think I'll haf another after this one."

"You want a drink, Mr. Clayton? Happy to oblige." In one movement she picked up his half-full tankard and tossed the contents directly into his face. It caused him both to release her and squawl as the fiery liquid burned his eyes.

Gretchen picked up another tankard and poured it on top of his head. "I'll keep this up until you pay what you owe," she threatened.

Her action brought stunned silence for a moment. Then there was a huge roar of laughter as she emptied a third tankard on Clayton. She sought another and it was placed in her hands. People were handing them to her to dump on Big John Clayton. He was drenched, rubbing his eyes and bellowing.

"Awright, awright! I'll pay."

"Now!" She watched him fish the coin from his pocket. She turned to Buck Shaw. "You want the same treatment?"

"No ma'am."

He paid; they all did. She was surrounded by raucous, almost deafening laughter, but she knew it was aimed not at her, but at these men she had cowed.

"I guess she showed ya, Big John," someone yelled.

"Give it to Buck. He needs a bath."

One of the women picked up a tankard and tried to pour it on Shaw, but he shoved her away with a growl.

In the crowd around her, Gretchen saw one face—Tuck Loudon's. He was laughing with genuine mirth. And in his eyes she saw something else. For all the world it looked like admiration. Then she turned, pushed through the people, and went behind the counter, watching the scene she had created. She couldn't stop shaking. Certainly, it had been satisfying to see Buck Shaw and Big

John Clayton looking so sheepish. But she feared the horseplay would grow violent. What if she couldn't control it?

Meg joined her, throwing an arm around her and patting her on the back. "Ya did wonderful, Gretchen."

"I did not." She might have succeeded, but Gretchen was not proud of what she had done.

"Ya did so. Ya show'd 'em. An' they paid up, didn't they?"

"I suppose." She turned inside Meg's arm and looked at her with troubled eyes. "But it was so awful. I hated doing it."

"No matter. Ya did it, that's all that counts. Ya fought back. Ya showed him who's runnin' this place. Ev'rythin' will be different now."

"Gretchen shook her head slowly. "Oh, I don't know."

"Yes, 'twill. Ya'll see. Just trust me." She squeezed her shoulders tighter. "I's so proud o' ya, Gretchen."

Meg's moral support did help, and a few minutes later Gretchen returned to the taproom. Timothy Wolf glared at her. "Ya had no right to tell 'em I'd pay."

She stood up to him. "Then don't lie for them, Mr. Wolf."

"I warn't lyin'—not entirely. Some do bring in game an' stuff fer barter. Where else ya gonna get all this grub?"

It was a good point, one she was not prepared to answer. She did not yet know enough about the operations of the inn. "I do not object to barter, Mr.

Wolf. If someone wishes to trade something we need or can use for food and drink, splendid. But I do not think it too much to ask that the trade be written down. We need to know who traded what and place a value on the trade."

"I ain't got time."

"Then I'll absolve you from the responsibility, Mr. Wolf. Henceforth, all trade will be approved by me." There could be no doubt of the hostility in his eyes. "I mean it, Mr. Wolf, every word of it."

She went to the cash drawer. It contents were most gratifying to her.

"Hey, dearie," a voice called, "ya dumped my drink on Big John. I ain't gonna pay fer it." A couple of others joined in.

"Fair enough. I don't expect you to." In a moment she carried over replacement tankards and was greeted by smiles. She sensed a new respect.

"Ya really showed Big John." "Take 'im a week to get the stink out."

But amid the laughter she felt a hard pinch and jumped. Almost without thinking, she reached out and gave a hard pull to a man's beard.

"Whadja do that fer? I dint do nothin'," the man cried.

"Someone pinched me."

"I dint, I swear. 'Twas Hank."

Gretchen turned to the man called Hank and saw the smirk on his face. "T'warn't me," he claimed solemnly.

Another pinch came from the rear. She recognized the game. But instead of squealing as she had before, she gave a harder pull to the beard of the first man. "It seems to me you'd better find out who's pinching me and stop it, or you're not going to have any hair left on your face." She was rewarded with a chorus of laughter as the man rubbed his sore chin.

It was near closing time and the crowd was thinning out when Gretchen saw two men and two women heading up the stairs. "The rooms are closed." She said it to Meg, who was standing at the counter. "There are no beds and I just had the rooms cleaned."

But as Gretchen came around the counter to go to them, Meg put her hand on her arm to stop her. "Let it be, Gretchen."

"I can't permit it."

"Ya can't stop it, Gretchen. It's always gone on."

"What do you mean, I can't stop people from using the rooms? What are they going to sleep on, the floor?"

"Prob'ly. Good a place as any to do it."

Gretchen stared at her. "Do what, Meg?"

Meg screwed up her face into a grimace. "Ya knows—don't ya?"

The sheepish expression on Meg's face didn't help Gretchen's understanding a bit. "No, I don't know." Then suddenly she did. Her eyes widened in shock. "You mean—"

"It's always gone on, Gretchen. Can't be helped none."

Gretchen was nearly speechless. "The women are . . ."

"They's gotta live, too."

Gretchen gaped at her in shock and disbelief, then slowly turned her gaze to the stairwell. Slowly, indignation and outrage built within her until she blurted, "Not in my place, by Heaven! Not in the North Inn!" But Meg restrained her.

"There'll only be trouble, Gretchen," she warned.

Gretchen pulled away. "You'd better believe it!" Snatching a whale-oil lamp from a table, she pounded up the stairs and stalked down the hall, throwing open the unlocked doors until she found the first couple. They were half-disrobed, itself shocking. But Gretchen was too furious to care. "Get out!" she shouted. "Both of you! Now!" She burst into other rooms until she found another pair. They were lying on the floor and in the lantern light Gretchen recognized Buck Shaw and a woman named Hannah. She saw what they were doing. Her scream was one of dismay and disgust.

Shaw did not even look at her, much less interrupt his task. "Get outta here. We'se usin' this room."

Shaking all over from what she'd seen, Gretchen turned back, pulling the door shut behind her. She saw the first couple hurriedly departing their room, still not fully dressed. Enraged, she followed them. "I won't have it, do you hear? Never again. I'm not running a . . . a brothel. My God!" She ran downstairs to the taproom and found a heavy stick which she knew was used by

Timothy Wolf to break up fights in the tavern. Still shaking with rage, she started for the stairs.

"Don't Gretchen!" Meg tried to stop her.

But Gretchen was already flying up the stairs.

"I have to!" She burst into the offending room, and in the semi-darkness provided by the lantern left in the hallway, she swung the rod as hard as she could with both hands across Shaw's naked back. He screamed in pain and rolled off Hannah. Gretchen hit him again, if only a more glancing blow, then raised the weapon over her head, glaring menacingly at Hannah. *"Get out! I won't Have it! Get out! Get out!"* Her eyes were wild with rage as she swung out blindly again and again with the heavy stick, fortunately hitting nothing. Only the arrival of Meg and Wolf, who finally managed to restrain her and take the weapon away, prevented a beating.

Meg led her out of the room, while Shaw and Hannah gathered up their belongings and ran downstairs, still half-naked, only to be greeted by hoots and hollers from the few patrons still in the tavern.

Upstairs, Gretchen's rage had subsided somewhat. Meg clucked her tongue. "Ya sure gotta temper, Gretchen." In truth, Meg could hardly hide her amusement at the episode.

"It was . . . *awful*. They were—"

"I knows what they was doin'. Ev'rybody does." Meg giggled. "Ya will yerself, one day."

"Never!" Gretchen said defensively.

Meg smiled, shook her head, and patted Gretchen's back. "Say one thing fer ya. I think ya puta stop to the usual nighttime goin's-on 'round here."

"I won't have it," Gretchen repeated.

Meg laughed again. "That's the 'pression I get, too."

Chapter Nine

A T BEST, GRETCHEN could give only a mixed review to her first week as proprietress of the North Inn, though she had to admit, many good things had happened. Ezra Brown's family was indeed a blessing. Ruth came early every morning and cleaned diligently. The place was spotless. And she even had time to help out in the kitchen, which Molly Dugan accepted, however grudgingly. There was also clean laundry, and Matthew Brown helped with the heavier chores.

But it was Ezra Brown himself who impressed Gretchen the most. The bed, chest, and rocker he made her were roughhewn and far from polished work, but compared to what she'd had before, they seemed almost elegant. He even brought her a feather mattress, and with the linens and curtains and the hooked rug on the floor, her room was cheerful and cozy.

One other room was ready for occupancy, and a second at least had a proper bed. At Gretchen's urgent request, Ezra installed a locked door at the foot of the stairs to prevent unauthorized entry and reduce the noise from the tavern below. Gretchen purchased some proper potter plates and cups from a passing peddler. She felt she would now be able to serve at least a few guests in proper style.

She bit her lip with worry. If only she had guests. Not a single wayfarer had stopped. Hers was still the domain of ruffians and rogues. It was disheartening to think that all her hard work and plans might come to naught, but with each day it seemed that her only customers would be the people of Holyoke—and they hardly appreciated her efforts.

At least, Gretchen reasoned, they now accepted her. Her nightly hours in the tavern were no longer a torment. Pinches and pats were now only occasional, and if the remarks of the customers were often offensive, she had learned to give back as good as she got, usually some insult no properly reared girl would think of uttering—or would ever have occasion to. But Meg was right. It did work. Gretchen was being treated more respectfully. She was better off than when she came.

Money was now coming in. Meg was collecting regularly, Timothy, too. Good thing, Gretchen thought wryly, for her outlays were considerable. She had ordered a wagon load of mattresses and other supplies from Springfield. And rather than engage in barter, she had begun to pay cash for foodstuffs—on the theory it made it easier to keep accounts. Besides, most of the money would be spent in the inn, anyway. She reasoned that if she got the place fixed up and if she attracted suitable people for food and lodgings, the North Inn might become a profitable enterprise. At the moment, though, she could do little more than hope.

Gretchen tried to put the best face on things she could, but in truth, she recognized she was disappointed and unhappy. Surrounded by people, she felt alone and isolated, without a real friend in the world. Timothy Wolf remained surly at best. Ruth Brown was pleasant, but very busy. Meg was helpful and supportive, but they came from two different worlds and had very little in common.

Worse yet, no one in the village was the least bit friendly. The Follens were civil to her—which they ought to be, considering the sums of money she spent there. But everyone else ostracized her. Even when she had gone to worship at the meeting-house on Sunday. The townspeople had snubbed her, their noses in the air. A couple of children who had spoken to her, admiring her gown, were snatched quickly away by their mothers. The circuit preacher had given a sermon on sin and consorting with evil, promising hellfire and brimstone would result. Gretchen had had an uncomfortable feeling he was directing his message at her. He didn't even speak to her when she left the church.

Her life was settling into a routine. She rose

early, supervised the cleaning, cooking, and ordering, kept the accounts in the afternoon, and worked in the tavern at night, retiring rather late. Perhaps she wasn't getting enough rest, she mused. Maybe that was the reason for her sense of dissatisfaction. She had believed coming out here would cure her restlessness. But it hadn't; indeed, it had become worse. There had to be more. Something was missing.

The nightly patrons in the tavern were uneducated and usually drunk, and she felt she was slowly but surely being brought down to their level. Is that what had happened to her father? At least she could understand how it could happen. Why hadn't she thought to bring some books to read? There seemed to be none in the village— except those owned by Tuck Loudon.

Gretchen frowned. Tuck Loudon had done nothing but torment her since her arrival in town. It was obvious he wanted the North Inn, and Gretchen knew now that he would stop at nothing to get it—including seduction. Twice she had foolishly allowed him to catch her off her guard. Gretchen vowed that he would not get another chance. For no matter how tiring the work, how cold the stares of the townspeople, the North Inn belonged to her, and now more than ever, she was determined not to give it up. Not when she had come this far.

She had been relieved to learn that Tuck had left Holyoke for several days, apparently with Shaw, Clayton, and some other men. Good riddance, she thought with satisfaction. She would not miss his smirks and taunts, nor his base attempts to send her back to Boston.

Idly, she wondered what had called him away. It unnerved her to realize that she had not a clue as to what had brought a man like him to the frontier. And what business had he with the likes of Shaw and Clayton? His choice of companions only increased Gretchen's already bad opinion of him. She'd be overjoyed if he never returned to the North Inn.

But in fact, Tuck Loudon returned that very evening. From her vantage point in the taproom, she saw him enter, and a wave of dread washed over her. He must have come straight from the stable, without stopping at home, for his clothes were dusty and his face was newly bronzed by the sun.

He caught Gretchen's gaze for an instant and winked boldly. The nerve of the man! Then he smiled his rakish smile and waved to a group of men at a nearby table.

"Looks like ol' Tuck is back."

Gretchen started. She had not heard Meg walk up beside her.

"Shore is handsome, ain't he?" the girl continued. "Don't ya think so?"

Gretchen looked at Meg sharply. "All I think about Tuck Loudon is that I wish he'd stayed away forever!"

As Tuck Loudon entered the North Inn, he had been aware of nothing but Gretchen—except perhaps the sense of anticipation and the stirring in his loins which the mere sight of her provoked. He had been away for several days—it had gone well; this business was finally coming to a head— hoping distance would rid himself of his longing for her. Now, he knew it hadn't worked. She was almost constantly on his mind, a vision of soft, ripe femininity which left him aching with desire. No matter how many times he told himself that it was impossible, he could not rid himself of the longing he felt. But it was preposterous, when her very presence was a menace to all his plans.

He knew his problem. As the fourth son of a minor baronet, really a country squire, in Devon, Tuck had neither title, land, or fortune to offer a woman. Lady Jane Townsend had made that abundantly clear. She had flirted with him, driven him wild with desire, even bedded him. Afterward he had proposed marriage, as he thought a proper gentleman should, and she had simply laughed at him. Marriage to the impoverished son of a country squire, a man without title or estates, was unthinkable. Humiliated, he had given up his life in England and accepted the only choice of a career open to him, ending up in the American colonies. Here, it was said, opportunities abounded for any man.

He liked his vigorous life here. He enjoyed the occasional danger of life on the frontier, and he believed he had convinced himself they more than made up for the absence of a woman in his life. Then, in this godforsaken place, he had met Gretchen North, more beautiful than he had imagined a woman could be, well bred, gentle, schooled, and so excruciatingly responsive to him. She was all he had ever wanted. And that made him denouce the Fates for bringing her to him now, here, when it was so utterly impossible. He could neither court her, nor stay away from her. Had a man ever been so cursed?

Still at the counter, Gretchen saw him turn to her and smile broadly. To her dismay, he immediately swung his long legs over the bench, stood up, and strode over to stand across the counter from her.

"You've been away," she remarked tightly.

"Yes, I went downriver, then westward—on business. Just returned."

Gretchen sniffed primly. "Yes, it is obvious you have been traveling."

He laughed. "Men here are not so concerned with their apparel as your dandies in Boston! But I must say you look most fetching, Gretchen." It was a faint description of what he really felt. She wore the blue gown she had worn her first night here and the exposure of her creamy breasts and the valley between was almost more than he could bear.

She was aware of his eyes boldly raking her body. Both her eyes and her voice were cold as she answered, "Thank you, but you've seen this dress before. Everyone has—all my gowns. They are no longer a matter of interest."

"I fear I cannot agree with that," he countered. "So, you're still here. I thought perhaps the North Inn had gotten the best of you by now."

"And I had returned to Boston—your most fervent wish? I hate to disappoint you, but as you can see, I remain. Actually things are coming along very nicely here." She related some details of her progress.

As he listened, he could not fail to notice the change in her. She was more self-confident, more poised, no longer the frightened young woman she had been a scant week ago. He had to admire her for that. At least that part of him which wanted her to remain did. But the fact was, she'd be a more formidable opponent now. "And you believe your drenching of John Clayton helped you?"

"Yes, that and other things. Manners have improved. I believe I've earned some respect.

"Taking the stick to Buck Shaw surely added to your respect, didn't it?"

She studied him a moment, trying to read his expression, but couldn't. "I had to, Tuck. I can't run a brothel."

"Ah, but the location is so convenient!" She was about to protest, but then Tuck's expression turned serious. He leaned closer to her and lowered his voice. "I must warn you to stay clear of Clayton and Shaw. You have made enemies of both—implacable ones, I fear—especially Shaw."

"But why?"

"You humiliated both in public. No man, particularly one like Shaw, will lightly accept a public beating, especially at the hands of a woman." He saw her draw back and blink her wide blue eyes. "I suggest you be careful with both men from now on."

"They humiliated me!" Gretchen countered. "They'll just have to get over it, that's all." "It is certainly to be fervently wished for."

Gretchen affected an indifferent stance, but Tuck's words made her most uneasy, particularly when, behind him, she saw both Clayton and Shaw enter the inn and sit at a table. She knew she had received good advice. "Thank you, Tuck. I'll heed what you say." She hesitated. "But why did you give it? I thought you only wanted to force me to leave and win your wager."

"Apparently I've lost that. It is now my wish that nothing untoward happen to you."

Gretchen regarded him doubtfully. But his words, the seriousness with which he spoke them, affected her. With surprise, she realized that she wanted to believe him. Perhaps it was the gleaming brown depths of his eyes, or the look of repentence and sincerity on his beautiful face.

Gretchen fell silent, awash in a sea of conflicting feelings. And she could not think clearly, for tonight, his strong, masculine presence—the long legs, broad shoulders, slim hips—was very nearly overwhelming. But all the while, she mentally whispered a silent warning. He was not a man to be trusted, no matter how attractive he was, no matter how her body yearned to be his.

He ordered an ale, paid for it, but remained at the counter, unwilling or unable to end this moment alone with her. "You seem changed, Gretchen," he said finally.

"In what way?"

He studied her a moment. "I'm not sure. You look a little tired, tense."

His perception impressed her. "Perhaps I am, a little. I've been working hard. The North Inn requires a great deal of attention, from early morning till late at night."

He appeared shocked. "You mean to say you remain here every evening?"

"Of course I do. Where else would I go?"

Tuck shook his head in disapproval. "No one, especially a well-bred woman such as you, can abide every evening in a tavern such as this. You must get away, have some fun, forget the North Inn for a time."

She smiled humorlessly. "And what would you suggest I do for fun—out here?"

"I don't know. Go calling, visit friends."

"I have no friends," Gretchen said flatly. "The people of the village ostracize me, even in church."

Tuck pursed his lips. "Yes, I can understand that." He paused. "I know! We could go horseback riding. The countryside is lovely in the spring. Do you ride?"

"I do, yes." The mere thought of it made her beam with delight.

"Then that's what we'll do—tomorrow. I'll arrange it." Before she could protest, he left her and went to sit with Shaw and Clayton to eat his supper.

Gretchen stared after him, knowing full well he had planted an invidious thought in her mind. The mere idea of fresh air and riding through the countryside filled her with longing. She suddenly hated the inn and everything about it—the smoke, the noise, the dreadful odors, the rough, rude talk. At once she scolded herself. It couldn't be helped. Wasn't this the life she wanted when she came west? No, by God, no, but it was all she had. She'd better make the best of it.

She tried, helping Meg serve, collecting for the cash drawer, speaking little to the customers, except to return the insults of some of the drunken men. But it simply wasn't working. She had no witty repartee. She found no humor in even inoffensive jokes. Everything was aggravating, and she felt weary, strained, able only to endure, not to cope. What was the matter with her? Hours ago she had been doing so well.

The worst came when she sought to serve Tuck and the others a new round of drinks. Clayton tried to ignore her, but Buck Shaw studied her with pure malevolence, making her a little afraid. Perhaps most perplexing was the completely disinterested look in Tuck's eyes. And she had wanted to show him how well she could handle the people in the tavern now.

"I seed ya give Big John a bath, but I missed ya takin' the stick to ol' Buck." It was Miles Burnett, speaking in his high-pitched, squeaky voice. "Hee-hee-hee. Musta been somethin'. Wish I'da seed it."

Gretchen sucked in her breath in alarm and shook her head at Miles to be quiet. He didn't

"War ya really nekked, Buck?"

Buck's only reply was a deep, growllike sound from his throat.

"I hear ya got marks on ya thass ne'er gonna

come out. Hee-hee-hee-hee. Musta been a sight fer sore eyes."

Buck started to rise, looking as if he were ready to kill the little man, but Tuck put a hand on his shoulder to restrain him. His eyes were on Burnett. "Miles, my good man, I suggest you keep your mouth shut. Otherwise Buck will make you into a wet spot on the floor."

"I dint do nuttin'. She's the one what whipped him. A purty lass like her. 'Magine. Wish I'd seed it."

Other voices now joined in, creating a cacophony of scornful jibes aimed at Shaw. "How'd it feel, Buck?" "How come ya letta girl whup ya?" "Always knowed ya wasn't so tough."

Rage seemed to rise in him like a flame under a bellows. He rose and shook his fist at the crowd. "That's enuff. I ain't gonna hear no more." Then he turned to Gretchen "No woman hits Buck Shaw. ya gonna pay fer it. Ya gonna pay real bad."

Bravely, Gretchen stood her ground. If she let Buck get the best of her, it would destroy all she had accomplished, and she would be back where she had started—an unwelcome newcomer surrounded by disrespectful, unruly men.

But before she could frame a response to Buck's threat, the burly man was on his feet. His eyes were menacing as he took one step toward her. Then without warning, his hand shot out and sent Gretchen reeling. She slammed into the table behind her, and this time, she knew she was no match for Buck Shaw. As the other men attempted to restrain him, Gretchen bolted up and hurried to the counter.

Tuck caught up with her there. Grabbing her hand, he whispered, "Let's get out of here."

"I can't. I have to—"

"Hang it all, Gretchen, listen to me. Buck isn't through. C'mon." He pulled at her again.

"I have to collect the—" she began, but Tuck cut her off.

"Timothy'll do it." He turned to the barkeep, told him to look after things, then put his arm around her and led her quickly out the door. She gulped in fresh air, but it didn't stop her trembling, nor did his enveloping her in his arms and leaning her head against his shoulder.

"That damn, stupid pipsqueak! If only he'd kept his bloody mouth shut!" He led her a few steps up the carriage way. "Let's go for a walk. You have to get away from here for a while."

"No, I—"

"Just do as I say, Gretchen. Let Buck cool off. He's very drunk and very angry, and it's best to leave him be. Come, let's walk."

She obeyed, knowing he was right. It was refreshing to be away from the tavern. It was a dark night with no moon. The air was crisp and cool, the stars so incredibly bright she felt she could almost touch them.

She didn't even mind Tuck's arm around her shoulders. Somehow it seemed so right and natural, so comforting, so warm.

He felt her trembling. "Don't be afraid. Forget what happened."

"I know. I'm just a little cold."

"How stupid of me." Tuck removed his coat and draped it around her shoulders. "That better?"

She looked up at him, although she could scarcely see his face in the darkness. "Yes, thank you." Expectancy was ripe within her. "Where are we going?"

"Just walking."

Soon they were crossing the green, the earth soft and moist beneath her feet. His arm felt so good around her shoulders, and she did not mind that he held her so tightly their legs touched as they walked, his stride matching hers. She looked up at the stars. "It is a beautiful night."

Tuck stopped and turned her within his arms to face him. His voice husky, he whispered, "That's not what's beautiful."

The kiss came as before, a scintillating wisp of sensation as he brushed her lips, parting them, followed by gentle pressure and the repeated search for the perfect fit. He found it anew, drilling sensation into her, causing her to gasp into his mouth, to moan and clutch his head as she leaned hard against him. His coat fell from her shoulders, but she was no longer cold.

"Gretchen, my darling . . ."

Gretchen felt dizzy. No previous kiss had been like this, so deep, so exquisitely intimate. Perhaps it was the darkness, the night air and the stars, the sense of being alone in the universe. But maybe it was his hand cupping her chin, surrounding their wet, eager mouths, creating a tunnel through which their passion poured. She could only trem-

ble and cling to him, especially when his tongue
joined hers, so sweet, so terribly needed, making
her sag weakly against him, little sounds of pure
rapture emanating from her throat. When he
moved his hand, she thought it was going to end.
But no. Slowly he caressed her cheek, her eyelids,
her ears, down the ivory column of her throat, his
hand so smooth and strong, and everywhere he
touched seemed to come alive, tingling with sensation, adding to the havoc his lips and tongue
created.

She felt his hand slide down from her throat.
She wanted it to, and she moved back to give him
access, knowing where he was going, eager for the
arrival. As his fingers found her breasts, the valley
between, she could only moan under the intimacy
of it and the ache he caused within her.

Passion a storm within him, he wanted more, so
much more, but her chemise, her corset, denied
him access. For a moment he tried to content
himself with that small portion of her he had, but
the knowledge there was more drove him wild. He
broke away. "Not here, come."

They walked more rapidly now, so much so she
had to run a little to keep up, stopping only once
for more feverish kisses and caresses. She knew
where they were going, perhaps even what was
going to happen when they got there. Passion
flooded her body, and she did not protest.

Chapter Ten

TUCK'S HOUSE WAS warm, lit only by the flames of a log in the fireplace. She smelled the masculine odors of tobacco and leather, saw a huge flickering shadow of him on the wall. If some native caution stirred within her at that moment, it had no chance to surface, for in an instant she was swept back into his arms, his passion propelled into her mouth, melting all resistance.

Tuck had the scent now. He wanted her; he wanted her desperately. But he was not mindless. In his heart he knew this was a mistake, a gross mistake, every kind of mistake there was, but he was powerless to stop himself. He simply had to have her, at whatever cost. And his mind now accommodated him with a rationale. If he took her, deflowered her, surely that would drive her back to Boston.

Gretchen was not uninformed about what went on between a man and a woman. All her friends were married; some were mothers, and their prattle, frequently taking the form of boasts or complaints, were sometimes improperly spicy and explicit. If she was unaware of the specifics of what took place, she certainly had heard of a man's "needs." They were something to be "taken care of."

But what surprised her were the needs she encountered in herself. She was consumed by his passion, overwhelmed by his masculinity, helpless to resist her own cravings. His mouth was heaven, his hands paradise, and when he held her head and smothered her face—her eyes, her ears, her throat—in little kisses, she felt she couldn't breathe. When he slid his lips down her shoulders and onto her breasts, finally nestling into the valley between, she cried out from the sheer intimacy of his touch. When he returned to her eager, open still-wet mouth, it was a form of exquisite torture, filling a need while creating a greater one. She felt the hard, spasmic thrust of his hips against her, knew what it meant, and held firm against him.

"I want you so," he whispered.

She looked into his eyes, shining now with reflected firelight, and knew she couldn't deny what she felt any longer. "Yes," she said softly. The single word was a commitment. There would be no turning back, even if she could. Her time had come.

For a moment, she was shy. She didn't know what to do, except to stand there, looking at him, quivering with anticipation. Then his hands came to the front of her gown, fumbling clumsily with the tiny buttons. "Let me," she whispered and took over the task.

He watched each unfasten as a revelation, a harbinger of what was to come. There was a roaring in his ears, and he bent to devour her upturned mouth as her fingers feverishly worked the tiny buttons. Still clinging to his lips, slowly turning her head to soak up the sensation, she slid the gown from her shoulders, knowing that without his kisses, his constant touch, she would not be able to reveal herself to him.

She felt him tremble just before he stood back to look at her in the warm, glowing firelight.

"Oh God, Gretchen!"

She was still wearing her chemise, corset and petticoats, but no man had ever seen her thus. If she had shyness, perhaps revealed in her small hesitant smile, it was lost in the wonder in his eyes. He leaned over her, immersing his face in her half-exposed bosom, passing his lips and smooth cheeks over her breasts, and nestling his chin between them, bringing an aching fullness.

"Your skin is as soft as down."

She knew only that the sensation of his hot breath against her skin thrilled her—but the intimacy of his action affected her all the more. Still it wasn't enough. She reached behind her and began to untie her petticoats.

He watched in awe as she stepped out of the lace-trimmed outer garment, then another, and still another. The sight enflamed him, for he had never seen a woman remove her petticoats. To his mind, they had always been like a shield. Like most men, he had never seen a woman naked. With every woman he'd had, it had been darkness or nearly so, a quick attack among a maze of skirts and petticoats, met with coquetry, giggles, and halfhearted protests. Now, when at last he glimpsed stockinged legs and smooth, creamy thighs, he knew the wonder of it all. He fell to his knees and embraced them.

Above him she trembled, so much so she had to hold on to his shoulders. But when he released her and looked up at her, and she saw the awe and amazement in his eyes, she had doubts. "Is this not what I'm supposed to do?"

He swallowed hard against a dry throat. "Yes, yes, it is."

"But you are not undressing."

He looked down at himself in confusion. "Oh God!" The mere thought of what was happening made the blood pound in his head. "I will, I will." He stood up and began to hurriedly fling off his clothes as he watched her unfasten and step out of her stockings, then unknot the ties to her corset.

With all the purity of innocence, she had per-haps more aplomb than he did, although watching him unbutton his underwear and slide it back to reveal strong shoulders, a hard chest, and a tightly muscled stomach excited her beyond anything in her experience. He paused, the red garment at his waist, gaping not at her but at the chemise she wore. His eyes seemed to burn into her. Both stood there a moment, a moment torn and isolated from time. It was she who went to him, reaching out a tentative hand to touch his chest. "You have so much hair," she marveled.

He couldn't speak.

"It is very soft." That reminded her, and she reached up and quickly undid her own hair, letting it fall to her shoulders and back, a golden rain, the ultimate act of intimacy.

"Oh, Gretchen!" He was spellbound. Slowly, he reached out and touched her hair. A low groan escaped her lips as he ran his fingers through it. When he clutched a handful of it, she gripped his hand, binding him to her, and she turned to kiss his wrist. "Oh, Tuck, this is . . . so . . ."

"Yes."

She wanted him to kiss her, hold her deep within his arms, but he did not. Releasing her hair, he slowly slid her chemise from her shoulders, unmasking her breasts. He did not speak or even make a sound. He did not have to. His eyes told all. It was as if she had given him a gift, one more precious than jewels. When he raised his eyes and looked into hers, she recognized gratitude amid the wonder. She had a sense of total womanliness—and also of power. When his gaze returned to her breasts, as she knew it must, she slowly removed the chemise and she was naked.

His eyes viewed what his mind had only imagined. In the soft, flickering light, his eyes measured slender thighs, toured a golden meadow, witnessed diminutive hips, a tiny waist, and fragile shoulders. But it was her breasts that leaped toward him—snowy, engorged, opulent with reddish-orange nipples, hard and flowered like buds about to bloom. With effort, he raised his eyes to hers. "How beautiful you are," he whispered.

His words only added to the sense of wonder she felt, increasing her longing for him. Slowly he reached out a hand and touched her waist. Then the hand slid upward, cradling one breast, cupping, squeezing gently. A small groan escaped him as a second hand joined the first, gently kneading the soft flesh. Then his thumbs whispered over her tender, distended nipples, shooting a bolt of sensation through her, making her quiver. Glancing up at her, he repeated the exquisite movement, heightening her pleasure until she couldn't bear it and had to close her eyes.

He fell to his knees before her, his arms around her hips, his face embedded in the golden field.

She trembled all over, unable to control her body, and had to grip his shoulders just to stay on her feet. His head was at her woman's place, as she thought of it, and she could feel his hot breath as he rolled his face through it. And she felt his hands sliding over her buttocks, molding the halfmoons, his fingers arcing jolts of pleasure through her. Then his hands were at her inner thighs, stroking her tenderly, making them ache. She felt each movement of his fingertips, shuddering, moaning as they separated, separated, found, found. She gasped and gasped again. She couldn't breathe.

She felt him rising up to her waist, his head moving from side to side. She knew where he was going, and she was eager for the arrival. Once more, he buried his face in her breasts. She moaned as she felt his mouth slide to her nipple. She cried out with unbearable pleasure as he began to roll his head from side to side, rendering sweet, tender little bites with his teeth, laving with his tongue. Now he found her other breast, magnifying her pleasure. And all the while his hands were incessant, propelling. She shuddered under an onslaught of pure animal pleasure.

"Oh, please, I cannot bear more." Her hands already held his head, having been his guide, and now she gently pushed him away from her and bent to kiss his wet mouth. He swept her into his arms, giving her a kiss like no other—sweeter, made electric by nakedness, flesh against flesh, hands moving over smooth skin, increasing the sensation which radiated through them. Both were trembling, gasping, moaning, feverishly trying to withstand what was happening. Then suddenly she was floating through the air into a cooler, darker room and deposited on a bed.

In the dim light she was aware that he was standing above her, removing his undergarment. She reached out her arms, not wanting to be apart from him, and he bent to kiss her, returning that font of passion to her. One hand found her breasts, teasing her eager nipples, the other found her thighs and parted them, inflicting exquisite sensations that left her moaning from the throbbing ache of want. He knelt above her, widening her thighs with his knees. She felt a hard probing, then a hot stroking brought a sharp rise in her throbbing, making her moan anew. Another probe. She gasped. Another. Then she felt an exquisite stretching and she cried out from a sudden sharp twinge of pain.

"Did I hurt you?"

She could not speak, only shake her head beneath him, moaning her pleasure. Tuck moved again, and she was filled, stretched to her limits. Somehow he had entered her and become part of her. Shuddering, unable to breathe, she felt him rise up, as though planning to separate from her. She could not bear to lose him and thrust her hips upward to contain him. Then he thrust down at her, hard, almost savagely, and she cried out in ecstasy. She felt him rise up and descend into her again. She was helpless, her whole being lodged in one enflamed area of her body, a place deep within her, known only to her, discoverable only by him.

"You're so hot! You're on fire!"

Her whole body seemed centered where he filled her, throbbing, pulsating. As he thrust into her again and again, ever more rapidly, a terrible tension rose in her, building and building as though it would never stop. It was as if there was some great wave far from shore, coming toward her. It would move forward, then recede, leaving her to cry out at its loss. Again it came but did not reach her, and she cried out once more, desperate for relief. She opened her eyes to see him looking at her in amazement. She clawed at his outstretched arms, raised her head, found his mouth, consumed it. The wave swelled, rose hugely, seemed to hang there a moment so close to her, then crashed thunderously upon her, taking her breath away. Mindlessly she lay beneath him, her body writhing, her head rolling from side to side, moans and cries of rapture coming from her open mouth.

Tuck stopped in amazement. Never had he witnessed such a reaction, or even known it was possible. But he paused for only a moment. Truly maddened now, he thrust into her anew.

Slowly her senses returned, and she knew he was still within her, moving rapidly through the sweet, lingering sensations which still swept her. With every thrust, she sensed his power and strength. She clutched at him with her thighs and wrapped her legs around him. She had a sense of ultimate rhythm; they were as one, and she was accompanying him wherever he went. She heard him moan, gasp, increase his tempo, swell within her. She felt his muscles harden. Something was happening to him. She knew it, marveling at the wonder of it. Then he moaned more loudly, thrust harder into her, and cried out. So intent was she on what was happening to him, she was almost unaware of the renewal within herself. Even as she felt a great eruption inside her, a new devastation bore down on her, so sudden, deeper and stronger than before, leaving her writhing beneath him as he emptied his passion into her.

He rolled onto his back and she lay beside him, tucked within his arm, her head on his shoulder, her arm clasping his chest, her legs entwined with his. She felt deliciously lanquid and the sense of nearness and intimacy was overpowering. With it came an array of other feelings—contentment, inner peace, great relief, womanly knowledge, ultimate fulfillment, and yes, triumph. He had delighted in her, and she had thrilled him as he had her.

Sweet sensations still lingered inside her. It was as if her whole body were sighing. And she could feel wetness where she never had before. He must have done that. How mysterious it all was—and not at all what she had expected. Her friends had made it sound awful, something to be endured. But it wasn't, not at all. She had loved every moment of it. How strong he was, how masculine, how powerful. Yet now he was tender and gentle. She'd had no fear, not for a moment—only an overwhelming need. She would never forget the look in his eyes when he had seen her naked. He had seemed so surprised, awestruck, almost shy. It was strange; he had always seemed so bold to her, so sure of himself. Obviously, there were things about him she didn't know.

But as her breathing returned to normal and her mind began to clear, she was plagued with an awful sense of guilt. After all, she was unmarried, and much worse, she hardly knew this man. Indeed, she wasn't even sure she liked him. Certainly she had no idea of his intentions toward her. He was her adversary! He had not courted

her, declared his undying love, or even hinted at
marriage. Utterly unbelievable! How could she
have done this, why did she feel such desire for a
man who was intent on destroying her life? Oh,
she couldn't think of that now. All she knew was
that she had needed him, and it was too late for
regrets.

Tuck's thoughts were equally troubled, but for
different reasons. He was torn between his two
natures, an effect she usually had on him. Part of
him was captivated by her, awestruck, humbled,
grateful, and somehow privileged. It was all
etched in his memory, never to be forgotten, only
cherished, her undressing, revealing herself to
him—God, how beautiful she was!—giving herself
to him, wanting him, then writhing, clutching,
and crying out, wild with passion and enjoyment.
Every other woman he'd know had simply wanted
to get it over with as quickly as possible. He
couldn't begin to understand what had happened
to her, what she felt, but her reaction had only
increased his own pleasure until he was crazy with
need, unable to hold himself back.

But it was madness—utter folly. Tuck reminded
himself that her very presence here was a near
disaster. She could ruin all he'd worked so hard
for. He'd tried everything to drive her away. But
his weakness for her beautiful face and luscious
body had distracted him from his task. First those
stolen kisses, now this. What a fool he was! He
mentally railed at himself a moment, then abandoned that to think of what he must do now.

She was never going to leave. Unbelievably, she

was making a success of the North Inn. Yet every moment she remained posed a risk she would discover what was going on. Damnit all!

He felt her stir, raise her head from his shoulder. She had sensed his mood. "Is something wrong. Didn't I do what I was supposed to?"

He sighed in memory and shook his head. "You were wonderful."

She raised her head higher, trying to see him in the darkness. "You liked . . . what we did, didn't you?"

"You know I did." A desperate thought came to him. It might work. "Now you know what a rogue I am—hardly a gentleman."

"So that's it." She laughed lightly and snuggled her head back against his shoulder. She mustn't let him sense her fears.

"No gentleman takes such advantage of a lady. You must know what a true cad I am." He tried to say the words with real conviction.

"Oh, you're that, all right." Again she giggled and turned on her side, moving even closer to him. She kissed his shoulder.

"I mean it, Gretchen. You should leave, have nothing more to do with me."

"Still trying to get me to go back to Boston, are you? I must say you have the strangest way of going about it." She shuddered from the memory.

He misunderstood. "Are you cold?"

"A little, yes," she admitted.

He rolled away from her, got to his feet, and padded across the room. It hadn't worked. Nothing ever did with her. Why had he bothered to try?

He was never going to force her to leave—and he didn't want to. That was the real problem. He lit a candle and turned back to her. What he saw in the better light startled him. She was naked on the quilt, so incredibly lovely, so exquisitely tempting, her golden hair framing her face, breasts gaudy with deep pink flowers, the golden meadow, the luscious thighs. Incredibly, she appeared to have no embarrassment. Any woman he could imagine would have covered herself. He didn't understand her at all. "Gretchen, you're so lovely," he said aloud.

She was also really seeing him for the first time, so slender and lean, yet with such broad, strong shoulders. "You are, too." His hips, she saw, were almost as narrow as hers. "You're small now," she observed curiously.

"You had something to do with that."

She really didn't understand, but smiled shyly. Pulling back the covers, she scampered under them and held them out for him as an invitation. "We'll be warm and cozy now."

He wavered. The temptation she offered seemed irresistible, but no, he had to think, decide what to do. And there was no possible way to think when she was around. "I'd better take you back."

"Back?"

"We only went for a walk, remember? It's going to be hard enough to explain why we've been gone this long."

Realization took a moment for her, and then she sat bolt upright. "Oh, Lord! Everyone will know, won't they?" She threw back the covers, flew out of bed, and ran to the other room for her clothes.

He followed at greater leisure, having donned his underdrawers. She was dressing frantically. "Take your time. It'll be all right," Tuck assured her.

"No, it won't! Everyone will know! We've got to get back!"

In some amusement he went for his britches. By the time he finished dressing, she had donned her gown, worked the exasperating buttons and smoothed her skirt. "Have you a mirror?"

"In the bedroom. I'll get it."

He held it for her. She saw in dismay her red, puffy lips, then cried out, "Oh no, my hair! Have you a brush?" She did the best she could, hoping no one would notice the change. "It will have to do. Let's go."

She both walked rapidly and ran through the cool night air, Tuck striding more languidly beside her. He knew she was only right to hurry back. Every man in the tavern lusted after her, and she had kept them at bay only by having nothing to do with any of them. If these men, especially ones like Shaw and Clayton, knew Tuck had bedded her, they would expect to do the same. She'd be in great danger. He wondered if she understood that—or was she simply worried about her reputation, what others would think of her?

Halfway across the green, he stopped her, his hands on her shoulders. "You can't go in there like this, Gretchen. Wait, catch your breath, relax. We've just been for a stroll, remember?"

Despite her agitation she knew he was right. "Yes, I'll try." She sought to calm her heaving chest, her rattling nerves.

"Act natural. Nothing has happened."

Gretchen gazed at him for a long moment. "Maybe not to you, but a great deal has happened to me." She took a deep breath. "Come, I'm ready now."

Chapter Eleven

JUST OUTSIDE THE door to the inn, Tuck said, "Walk in like you're angry." When she hesitated, he said, "Go on, do as I say."

Gretchen obeyed, stalking rapidly toward the taproom. Behind her she heard Tuck's voice, loud and angry. "You have to be the most exasperating female who ever lived. It's bloody stupid to think you can run this tavern by yourself. Go back to Boston, where you belong!"

She stopped dead in her tracks, bristling with sudden anger. But when she wheeled to face him she realized what he was doing. They'd been quarreling, not making love. "I'll thank you to keep your opinions to yourself, Tucker Loudon. I am not going back to Boston, and I *am* operating this establishment—very nicely, I might say."

"Nonsense. The place is falling down around your ears."

I am doing far better than when *you* supposedly ran it."

"No, you're not. You're driving all the customers away. Nobody wants to drink in a tea parlor," he sneered.

She looked around. The place was largely full, but she was pleased to see Shaw and Clayton had left. "Who are all these people, Mr. Loudon? Ghosts?" That brought a chorus of laughter from the patrons. One man declared he was no ghost. "Hear that, Mr. Loudon? He looks real to me, drinking his ale and, I assume, paying for it."

"He only came in because you weren't here."

"Then I thank you for that—and for the very pleasant stroll. You were your usual overbearing self."

He doffed his hat and bowed, making an exaggeratedly wide sweep with his arm. "You bring out the best in me, Miss North."

With that, she turned away from him, went past the taproom, and into the kitchen, where she could be alone—necessary for she could barely suppress a sigh of relief. Everyone's attention had been focused on their quarrel. No one paid any attention to her appearance or wondered why they'd been gone so long. She let out a giggle now. Just wonderful! No one suspected. He had helped her get away with it.

Meg Gwynne entered at that moment. "Whasso funny?"

Gretchen struggled to suppress her mirth. "Oh, nothing. I was just thinking how absurd that man is."

"Tuck Loudon? I ne'er heerd nobody use that word fer him."

"Well, that's what he is—truly bizarre." She knew Meg was looking at her closely. Did she suspect something?

"Ya was gone a long time. I thought maybe you and he was—"

"Don't be silly, Meg." Gretchen hoped she wasn't blushing.

"It ain't silly. He's sure a handsome devil. If he'd look at me, I'd—"

"He's all yours, Meg. I can't stand the sight of him."

"Really?" The girl looked at her employer queruously. "Here I figgered you and he was makin' eyes at each other."

"Not on your life, Meg. I can't bear the man!"

She abruptly left the kitchen, for fear her face would reveal the truth to Meg. In the taproom now, she felt a strange sense of excitement despite her misgivings. They had done a forbidden thing, taken a great risk, and gotten away with it. They were sharing a secret, fooling everyone. She felt very conspiratorial as she approached Tuck and asked if he'd paid for his ale.

"It's not ale, but rum."

"Even better. Thruppence, please." She extended her hand.

"I'm not paying." He glared at her, but there was amusement in his eyes. "Putting up with you on that walk ought to be good for something."

"You should pay for my company, you insufferable clod. Thruppence—or would you like a real drink?" She picked up his mug and held it over his head. She heard others urging her to dump it on him.

"All right, all right." He reached in his pocket. "But one day you'll get yours."

"I've already had mine, Mr. Loudon," she said sweetly.

She busied herself with her duties, or tried to, but her mind remained on him. She didn't dare think about his lovemaking, all they had done, for fear it would show on her face, so she restricted herself to thoughts about the many contrasts she had observed in him—rough frontiersman enjoying the company of even rougher men, yet gentle, loving, even shy; her brusk tormentor, holding her up to ridicule, then helping her escape what could have been real harm. She felt it was a secret known only to her. Indeed, there seemed to be a whole secret side to him. He wasn't what he seemed.

But what was he? She had one answer. Obviously, he was an adept liar. His performance when they returned to the inn left no doubt of that. Could she believe anything he said? She must forget that tonight had ever happened. It would never happen again, she promised herself.

She watched him get up and leave, and in spite

of herself she was hurt when he didn't even glance back at her.

The patrons thinned out, and she said good night to Meg and Wolf, finally bolting and barring the door a little after eleven o'clock. The tavern was empty and quiet, and she felt strangely alone. There was not a single lodger. Would any ever come? She attended to her closing chores, turned out all but a single lamp on low wick and made her way upstairs to her room. She was not as tired as she usually was. Indeed, she was wide awake. But it was bedtime and she prepared for it.

As she unbuttoned her gown she realized it was the second time she'd done that this evening. Oh, how passionate he had been! She shivered a little from memory. As she undid her petticoats, then her corset, she kept remembering that look of wonder in his eyes. She slid her chemise slowly from her shoulders as he had done, revealing what he had seen and loved. And when she was naked, she stood there, quivering even now from the memory of all that had happened. She cupped her breasts as he had done, sliding her thumbs over her flowered nipples as he had, memory bright within her.

"Stop it!" The sound of her own voice awakened her from her reverie, and she began to bathe.

Later in her nightdress, her hair plaited, she turned down the lamp, but sleep eluded her. She was too excited, too full of all that had happened, too restless. She went to the window and opened it, throwing out the shutters wide. The cool air was clean and refreshing. As she had once before this night, she looked up and saw the stars shining brightly. Still there was no moon, not even a waning sliver. Below her she could just make out the river, shining in the star light. It seemed to her she could hear voices far below. The rivermen must still be up.

"Gretchen, is that you?"

The voice below was a hoarse whisper, but she recognized it. "Tuck?"

"I need to talk to you."

She looked down but couldn't see him. "What do you want?"

"Let me in. I have to see you."

"Now? I'm ready for bed."

"Put on something and come downstairs," he urged.

Gretchen bit her lip. She didn't want to see him or even think of him, but if he continued to call up to her, someone might hear. "Very well. Give me a minute."

She hurried downstairs, turned up the lamp, and greeted him at the door wearing a warm, dark blue, wool robe. "Oh, it's you. I thought it was Romeo," she mocked him.

"I must say you make a lovely Juliet," he returned.

Gretchen held the door for him to enter, then closed it and stood there looking at him expectantly.

"I'm sorry to keep you from your sleep," he said at length.

"I doubt if you're very sorry. In fact, I'm beginning to doubt everything you tell me."

He blinked. "Why is that?"

"Your little performance this evening, our fake quarrel. You were most convincing."

"So were you." He laughed. "It worked, didn't it?"

"Oh yes, and I thank you for it. But I believe you meant those things you said."

He ignored that. "Well, your reputation remains intact." He looked toward the taproom. "I'd like a drop, if you don't mind." He headed for the barrels. "Can I get you something?"

"I don't drink."

"Some wine, perhaps. It will help you sleep."

"Very well, a little," Gretchen agreed.

They sat opposite each other at the end of the table nearest the taproom. As always, she had a powerful sense of his masculine presence, so much so it made her feel uncomfortably warm. Her skin was tingly. His eyes on her were too intense. She looked down at her wine, raised the glass and sipped. Without looking at him she said, "You said you wanted to talk to me. What about?"

Away from her he'd had a chance to think, to calculate what he must do. He decided that if he couldn't make her leave the inn with all the danger she posed to his plans, there was only one thing for him to do. He would distract her, keep her from discovering what was really going on at the North Inn. He had come to begin the process. "I need to know if you have regrets about this evening—what we did. I'd hate it if you do."

"I thought that might be it." She raised her eyes, studied him a long moment. She knew what she must say. "I know I should, but—" she sighed—"I don't, I can't. It was too . . . too . . . everything." He opened his mouth to speak. "Let me finish. I'm eighteen past. I should be a wife, a mother. What we did should have happened to me long ago. I'm glad it finally did—and so wonderfully. I can think of others with whom it might not have been so . . . pleasurable."

He smiled, reached across the table, squeezed her hand. "Oh God, I'm so glad to hear it. Are you sure?"

"I'm sure." She nodded. "You said life is different out here on the frontier. I know that now. We have to make our own rules as we go along, don't we?"

"Yes, Gretchen."

He half rose from the bench and leaned across the table to kiss her. But she moved back so he couldn't reach her. "I do have regrets, Tuck, if not the ones you worry about." He sat back down, his expression changed. "I gave myself to a virtual stranger. I don't know where you come from, anything about your family, how you came to be here, and what you're doing here. I have no idea of your intentions toward me, what I mean to you, what will happen between us. I don't even know if I'm supposed to love you."

"You must know my intentions are honorable. I wouldn't be here now if they weren't."

"Perhaps, although I can think of another reason why you came." She shook her head slowly. "I don't understand you at all. You seem like two people: one a gentleman, the other a—"

"Rogue?" he finished for her. "Perhaps I am." In truth, her perception of him came as a surprise. She was a most insightful person, one to handle with great care. He reached across the table with both hands, took hers between them. They were so soft and small and delicate. "One day you'll learn all about me. Everything will be clear to you." He squeezed her hands. "Meanwhile, can't we simply enjoy each other."

His hands felt so good, but she said, "I must know *something*. Your accent is English. Where are you from?"

"Devon."

"And you are well-spoken. I associate your accent with the peerage."

He smirked. "Hardly the perrage. My father has only a small estate."

"A country squire?" Gretchen guessed.

"One might say that, I suppose, yes."

She looked at him intently. "You seem most guarded in what you say. Is there some secret in your family? Do you wonder that I don't trust you?"

"There is no secret, Gretchen. I have a father, who is up in years now, a stepmother who raised me, three brothers, all older. It is extremely ordinary. I hide nothing."

She smiled. "That's better. How did you come to be here in Holyoke?"

"That, too, is familiar. The American colonies are supposed to be the land of opportunity, or so we are led to believe in England. Since, as the fourth son, I will have little or no inheritance, I came here to make my fortune."

"And have you?" Gretchen inquired.

He grinned. "Hardly, but I remain optimistic. There is time."

"You live well. Your home does not suggest poverty."

"Oh that." His laugh was a shield against his mounting nervousness. "Most of those things belonged to my mother."

"What do you do to support yourself—while you earn your fortune?"

"So many questions!" He released her hand and rubbed his chin, a gesture she had seen before and associated with nervousness. "I do a little trading, furs and such." He smirked playfully. "Until you came along I made a little money at the North Inn."

"I doubt if very much was made." She knew he was not telling the truth, at least not all of it. Now he was looking away, lifting his tankard. His evasive behavior only added to her suspicions.

"That's all there is, Gretchen. Believe me."

"Then why did you just say everything will be clear to me eventually? What will be clear to me?" Her voice was insistent.

"I've a rather large business deal pending," Tuck explained. "It could make me a handsome profit. But I can't talk about it just now."

"What sort of business deal?"

"Some trading," he said shortly. He shook his head, enveloped her hand again. "I simply can't say more at the moment, Gretchen. Is it possible for you to trust me for a few days? You will know everything then."

She looked at him a long moment. He was being evasive, not telling her the truth. But he'd asked for trust, a reasonable request. She'd let him believe she trusted him—while seeing what she could learn on her own. A smile slowly brightened her face. "Very well. I'm sorry. I have no right to pry into your affairs."

"It's not prying. I should have told you all this before." His grin reflected his inner sense of relief. She had accepted his story. How he rose and came around the table to sit beside her. His arm circled her shoulders. "I still plan to take you riding tomorrow. Do you want to?"

She'd planned to refuse, but now she realized the day might provide an opportunity to divine his secrets. She smiled with delight. "Oh yes, very much so."

"At midmorning, then."

"Fine." His proximity was overpowering, and the heat in his eyes was as she had seen before. When he tenderly kissed her temple, she shivered.

"You asked my intentions," he reminded her.

"You said they were honorable." Her voice sounded strange to her, a little throaty, perhaps.

"They are. There is no woman on earth like you. I can't bear the thought of losing you."

He had said it before in the heat of passion, but she still thrilled at the words. Yet, they seemed too powerful. "I'm sure not," she hedged.

"When you revealed yourself to me, I felt I had received a priceless gift. I will cherish it always."

She felt her resolve slipping, and tried to fight it. "I'm sure all women are much the same."

"Never. There is no one so lovely as you—or so responsive."

She didn't understand. "What do you mean?"

"You enjoyed it, didn't you?"

"Oh yes, yes." She shivered. "Doesn't everyone?"

"You must know they do not."

Remembering, she smiled. "Perhaps I do." Her smiled extended into a light laugh. "My friends in Boston do not speak of their men in the manner I now would." She was a little embarrassed to say such things to him, but added, "Why is that so?"

"I do not know what you felt—only that it was pleasurable for you."

"Oh yes, extremely so."

"What did you feel?" Tuck wanted to know.

"You don't know?"

"How could I? Tell me, please."

She swallowed. "I can't. It's too . . . too intimate."

"Oh, please, I must know," Tuck insisted.

She swallowed again. "It is hard to explain. It was as though . . ." She looked away from him, remembering, envisioning. "I felt this great ache, a sort of . . . longing, a terrible tension. I couldn't bear it." She struggled for words. "Then came this great—I don't know, a heavenly release, a wonderful sensation . . . over and over. It wouldn't stop, not for a long time—nor did I want it to."

He kissed her then, and his mouth on hers was full of passion, achingly so, and without willing it she was on her feet, pressed against him, feverishly clutching at his shoulders, turning her head in desperate craving. It was as though there had been no interruption from their previous desire. She twisted her mouth away and said breathlessly, "How can you . . . do this to me?" Her answer was a renewed, melting, dizzying submersion of her lips. Unable to bear more, she stepped back from him, wide-eyed and gasping. But she found no surcease. His hands slid inside her robe, unbuttoned her nightdress and found her breasts, kneading, stroking, cupping, gently pinching, sending jolts of sensation from her nipples into her body.

"I must have you," he murmured.

She heard the throaty words and knew he spoke the truth. She brought her hands to her breasts, tried to still his. It didn't help. She looked around desperately, disoriented. "Not here," she said.

She led him up to her room, which was warmed

by a small fire. She sensed no shyness in him this time, no hesitation, only boldness as he opened her robe and unbuttoned the remainder of her nightdress. He bent from the waist and buried his face in her breasts, laving, biting, sucking her deep within his open mouth. Only distantly did she hear him moan, for he created a havoc within her, especially when his hands found her, one stroking her derriere, the other at her woman's place, sliding smoothly, separating, finding, entering.

It was not as it had been before. Gone was the sense of discovery, replaced now by certain knowledge of where all this would lead. There was familiarity, to be sure, but also anticipation and marvel that it could happen again. She moved back from him, slid the robe and nightdress from her shoulders and arms, and became naked. Again she felt his eyes devouring her.

His hands circled her waist. "How tiny you are. My hands almost reach around you." He molded her hips, then rose, cupping, enveloping. "I love your breasts."

She had a sense of total womanliness. "Yes." She smiled a little. "I can tell."

"I've wanted you all my life."

She loved his words, but she could not reply, for he again fell to his knees before her, pressed her breasts together with his hands, and levied pure pleasure upon her, rapidly sweeping his mouth from one distended, eager nipple to the other, making passion ravenous within her.

"Oh please! No more!" She pulled free of him

and stepped back, looking at him with longing. "You still have your clothes on." Frantically, he at once began to disrobe. She went to her bedside and lit the lamp, bathing the room in light. When she turned back to him, he seemed startled by the light, yet his eyes feasted upon her nakedness.

"You are beautiful."

She was basking in his gaze. There was no shyness in her, only assurance—and pride. She looked at him and rendered a small smile. "You will be, too, if you remove your drawers." When he hesitated, she murmured, "I want to see you, too, Tuck."

"You already have."

"No, it was dark and I was too busy." She couldn't help laughing, and then she went to him, unbuttoning his drawers, sliding them from his body, past the strange bulge arching in front. Surprised, she stood back, looking at him boldly. "Is that what you put in me?"

"Yes." He seemed most uncomfortable. "Gretchen, I—"

"It is too big. You couldn't have." Now she smiled. "I guess you did." She came closer, stroking his chest, sliding her hands over his muscled waist. Then she hesitated, her eyes fixed on his as though mesmerized. She lowered her hands to caress his flat hips and rock-hard thighs, then moved inward, clasped his swollen member, and fondled it.

He gasped, then gasped again. In his previous experience no woman had ever touched him. As far as he knew none had even looked at him. To have this most beautiful of woman touch him, stroke him, hold and caress him, was simply unbelievable.

"You have a beautiful body, Tuck. You are beautiful, too." Because he had done it to her, she fell to he knees before him and took him in her hands, holding the hard cylinder against her cheek, feeling its throbbing heat. It almost seemed to have a life of its own. She began kissing the length of it.

"Oh God, Gretchen!" her cried.

She felt him trying to pull her up, but she stopped him. "I want to know you, too." She slid her hand along the length of him. Above her she heard shortened breath and halting gasps. Soon she heard him moan, felt him shake, lurch spasmodically, and knew she was pleasuring him, as he had pleasured her. That knowledge excited her even more. Still holding him, she leaned her head back and looked up at him.

He gripped her shoulders and pulled her to her feet. He carried her over to the bed and laid her down gently. In an instant her thighs were parted and his head submerged between them. Nothing in her existence had prepared her for the pure sensation that came from his lips and laving tongue at her most intimate place. She gasped, moaned, began to writhe, then cried out as the heavenly release came to her, crashing through her so suddenly, deadening mind and body, so much that she had no awareness of being moved, his mounting her, entering, the stretching and filling, his powerful thrusts only adding to the ecstasy she felt. Again it happened. It was as though her body had broken into tiny, disintegrating pieces, leaving only rapturous sensation.

For a moment it all seemed to come together for her, re-creating her, then she was gone again, propelled by him, and she had a sense only of brilliant light, thunder, scintillating sparks, and total abandonment.

Chapter Twelve

IT WAS REACHING out and finding an empty bed that awakened Gretchen early the next morning. She felt a sense of loss, for sleeping with him, being held, cradled within his arms had been so heavenly. She opened her eyes, saw first light, and realized he had been wise to leave her. She smiled. What would people think if they knew?

Now she laughed. There was a lot to know. Oh my, yes! Memory flooded her. A night of love. She really couldn't remember its ending. She must have fallen asleep. Then later, he had awakened her. That was best of all, so sweet and langorous . . . precious sensation finally overriding sleep, slowly, coming from so far away, then rising sharply, carrying her to paradise.

She lay there assessing this new person she had

become. It had happened so quickly, almost over-night. Yes, a morning ago she had been an inno-cent girl who knew only dreams of love. But never had she dreamed such wonders. Her hands moved under the covers and discovered her own nakedness. She had never slept nude—and with a man! Her hands lowered and found wetness at her woman's place. He had done that. Stretching lan-guidly, she discovered soreness in her muscles. Small wonder. Oh, the things he'd done—they'd both done.

She knew she had better get up and start the day. But she couldn't move—not yet, anyway. There was so much to think about. So much had happened to her in less than a fortnight. She had wanted an adventure, but had not imagined such a marvelous one. Did she love him? She must. She couldn't have done all this if she didn't. But what was love? She shook her head. She didn't know. Was it this terrible craving to be with him, have him touch her? It must be, for if he were here now she would only open herself wide to him. Did he have the same cravings? Yes, yes, she knew he did. His kisses, his touch told all, his clutching her even as they slept. Their bodies, at least, seemed made for each other. But in her heart, Gretchen knew that that was not true love.

Darker thoughts intruded. Why did she have this uneasiness about him, this feeling she couldn't quite trust him, that she shouldn't? Why had he asked her to trust him? What was there about him that required trust? There had to be something. And could she love a man who asked for blind trust? It came naturally, didn't it? She now sat up in bed. There was only one thing to do—she had to learn more about Tuck Loudon, starting today.

She was wearing her riding habit when he came for her a little before eleven o'clock. The horse Tuck brought for her was beautiful, a sorrel, outfitted with a sidesaddle, and it had some spirit, which delighted her.

They set out along a road that led away from the town.

"You ride beautifully, Gretchen. I'm impressed."

"I'm full of surprises. There is much about me you have yet to learn," she said, turning the tables. Perhaps she could distract him.

"I only look forward to it."

He spurred his horse from a canter to a gallop and she followed, loving the thrill of the wild ride. He seemed to be testing her, but she knew she was equal to the challenge.

He pulled up and patted his animal's neck. "You have no fear." There was admiration in his eyes.

"Not of horses, anyway." She shook the reins and moved on ahead of him.

They passed through rolling countryside, lush with primeval woods, flowering trees, and burgeoning wildflowers. Everything was magical to her, all sun and blue skies and the loveliness of nature. Except for an occasional farmhouse, a hunter or two, she felt alone in the universe with him.

But she was aware of the time. "Shouldn't we be turning back?"

"Soon. I want to show you something."

But it was not soon. It seemed to Gretchen they had gone several miles when he plunged his horse up a hillside and through the woods. He stopped, reached over, and took her reins. "Close your eyes. I'll guide you." She hesitated. "You won't be disappointed." In a moment he stopped again. "Now, open your eyes."

She stared in wonder. Below her in the distance the Connecticut River cut through the land like a silver-blue ribbon, making a series of turns like a corkscrew. "It's lovely!"

"I thought you might think so."

They rode a bit farther, feasting their eyes on other views of the panorama. "Thank you for bringing me here, Tuck, but shouldn't we get back?"

"There's no hurry."

"People come to the inn at midday," she reminded him. "I need to be there."

"Stop worrying about the inn. Enjoy yourself." He got down from his horse. "Speaking of midday, I brought us a meal—of sorts, anyway."

She watched him open his saddlebags and extract some bread, cheese, cold meat, and a flask of wine. "Really, Tuck, I think we should get back."

"The horses need a rest. Besides, I'll bet you haven't eaten."

"That's true." Reluctantly she let him help her to the ground and lead her to a small meadow full of daisies. The food he offered was delicious, and the view from the hillside could not have been more spectacular.

"Are you tired?"

"A little." She gave a wan smile. "Someone kept me from my usual sleep."

He leaned over and kissed her tenderly. It was sweet, lingering, but lacked the passion of the night before. That surely was a good thing. "I will remember last night above all nights of my life."

She smiled at the loveliness of his words, but she had no chance to reply as he gently pushed her to her back on the ground and propped himself up on one elbow beside her, looking down at her. He kissed her anew, as though savoring her, seeking and finding that precious joining of their lips.

In a moment he picked a daisy and put it in her hair above her ear. "The flower is nice, but you exceed it."

She smiled her pleasure. "My, aren't you the romantic one." He kissed her again, then sighed, rolling onto his back beside her, looking up at the sky as though lost in thought.

"Tell me about Devon, Tuck. Is it like this place?"

"Now that you mention it, there is a certain similarity. Perhaps that's why I like it here."

He spoke of his home, his childhood, growing up. She gained a sense of him as a lonely child, a dreamer. Yet it seemed such a contrast to the man he was now that she felt she had learned little about him.

He rolled to his side and looked down at her again. "Enough of the old times. They are gone forever." Tenderly he caressed her cheek with his fingertips, traced her lips, and kissed them softly. "I love you, Gretchen."

The confession both startled and thrilled her.

"Whatever happens, know that I love you."

"What can possibly happen?" The question seemed to unsettle him. "What worries you, Tuck?"

He moved away from her sharply. "Nothing, except something always does, doesn't it?" He sat up beside her. His mood had changed.

"There's something you want to tell me, but feel you can't, isn't there?"

He stood up and extended a hand down to her. "Maybe we should think about getting back."

She didn't accept the hand. "Is it what I'm supposed to trust you about?"

He hesitated, then smiled. "I think you should trust me to find our way back home." Now he laughed. "I'm not sure I can."

Gretchen finally let it go, but stored the incident away for further thought. Letting him help her to her feet, she said, "We can always follow the river."

"You are a regular pioneer. Is there no end to your surprises?"

"Not with you, apparently."

It was well into the afternoon by the time they approached the North Inn, and Gretchen was a bit irritated with him. "Why do I have the feeling you've dawdled getting me back? Did you want to keep me away for some reason?"

Her question unnerved him. How perceptive she was, almost impossible to fool. Then, ahead, he saw a heavy wagon pulled by a team of oxen. It was just pulling away from the front of the inn. His timing was perfect. "What possible reason, Gretchen? I just thought you'd enjoy the ride and an afternoon away from this place."

She, too, saw the wagon, and spurred her horse a bit. "That could be someone wanting lodgings. You know how much I've looked forward to guests."

"Not hardly, Gretchen—just a farmer with his load of hay. Probably stopped to quench his thirst."

"The wagon seems awfully heavy for just hay," Gretchen pointed out.

"Hay weighs more than you think."

They stopped at the hitching post in front of the inn. "I'm sorry the ride took so long. I hope it didn't spoil it for you."

She studied him a moment, questioning his sincerity. "It didn't. I'm sorry. I'm just tired from the long ride. It was very nice, Tuck. I thank you."

"I wanted it to be so." He helped her dismount, then led both horses away.

Gretchen had just finished changing from her riding habit into a gown when Timothy Wolf knocked at her door. She wasn't about to let him enter, but she heard him call, "There's somebody downstairs. They's a-wantin' a room fer the night."

At last! Her first guest. Wildly excited, she answered, "I'll be right down."

Her surprise was boundless when she saw the person standing just inside the door. A woman! She was short and plump and of an age Gretchen considered elderly. Gray hair showed beneath her bonnet. She wore a dark wool suit. A cloth bag resided at her feet. Gretchen could only stare at her. An elderly woman was the last person she expected as a first guest.

"Do you offer lodgings, my dear?" the woman inquired.

Gretchen swallowed hard. "Y-yes, we do."

"Then I will spend the night, if I may." She smiled, and Gretchen warmed to her instantly. "Don't be so surprised, child. Women have been known to travel alone."

Gretchen began to recover. "Yes. I did so myself, very recently." She smiled and extended a hand. "How do you do? I'm Gretchen North, proprietress of the North Inn. I bid you welcome."

"You're not, my dear!" Obviously it was the old woman's turn to be surprised. "A young woman like you, running an inn, out here?"

Gretchen was now on more familiar terrain. "It is a bit unusual, I suppose. Let me have your bag and I'll show you to your room, Mrs. . . ."

"It's Miss, my dear, always has been. Miss Alma Smallwood."

"From Boston. I hear it in your voice. I, too, came here recently from Boston. I don't believe we've ever met, though."

"What did you say your name was?"

"North, Gretchen North."

"Any relation to John North, the merchant?"

"He's my uncle. Come, let me take you upstairs." Gretchen showed her the room next to her own and heard it declared most comfortable. Alma Smallwood struck her as energetic, pleasant, and good-natured.

"Are you really John North's niece, the one declared the most beautiful and sought-after girl in Boston?"

Gretchen blushed. "I don't know about the latter, but I am his niece."

"What on earth brings you out here to—"

"Holyoke. It's quite simply, really," Gretchen explained. "My father was Winthrop North. He died and left me the North Inn. I came out here to claim my inheritance and operate this establishment."

"All by yourself?"

"Yes."

Alma Smallwood touched Gretchen's hand. "My dear, what courage you have! How very splendid! How I envy you!"

Gretchen stared at her. "Envy?"

"Oh, how I wish I'd had such an opportunity when I was young—to be in charge of my life, test my mettle."

"I-I never thought of it that way."

"Well, you should, my dear. I"m positive you'll do an absolutely splendid job," she declared.

"Thank you." She hesitated. "Perhaps I should warn you, Miss Smallwood. You will not find this at all like the better inns in Boston. The patrons below can be . . . boisterous at times. May I recommend you take your supper in your room?"

"Of course." Alma Smallwood did not appear surprised.

"But have no fear. There are locks on the doors."

"At my age I have nothing to fear." The older woman laughed. "I will be most comfortable here for the night. Will you have someone look after my horses, please?"

"Horses?"

"Yes, I travel with two: one to ride, the other to bear my luggage and necessaries. With the abominable state of the roads, I find it much easier to travel by horseback." She chuckled. "Some of the places I go could simply never be reached by carriage or other conveyance."

"Are you really traveling alone?"

"Oh, indeed. There is no other, although persons sometimes traverse a distance with me from time to time. I have met the most delightful people that way."

Gretchen was amazed by her. "May I ask where you are going?"

Alma made a small, fluttery gesture with her hand. "Oh, at my age, I thought it imperative that I see some of the beautiful countryside. I have hardly been disappointed in that. Then it seemed to me so much of my family, so many of my friends had moved elsewhere. I decided to pay them a visit. Tomorrow I hope to be in Springfield, then to Hartford, New York, Philadelphia—a great city, I hear—and Baltimore. Then, if the Lord is willing,

I will visit my niece Caroline McLeod in South Carolina. Poor child lost her family in an Indian raid and I raised her in Boston. Couldn't love her more were she my own daughter. She's recently married a gentleman named Randall McLeod." and returned to South Carolina."

"Your niece will be as glad to see you as I am." Gretchen turned toward the door. "You must be tired after your journey."

"Not a bit. I travel slowly. One sees more that way. But I will freshen up before dinner. Will you join me? I do so dislike dining alone."

"I'd love to."

Gretchen spent much of the evening with Alma Smallwood, enjoying herself immensely. It was not just that Alma was a woman from Boston, educated, well-mannered, and cultured, but that she was such a kind and sympathetic person, not at all cold and stiff like her Aunt Sarah. Indeed, Alma Smallwood was much like the mother she always wished she'd had, and Gretchen found herself sharing secrets she would not have with another.

"Ephraim Waring? How could John North ever think of betrothing a sweet person like you to that cold fish?"

Gretchen could not help laughing. "An apt description, I fear."

"You did absolutely the right thing in coming out here to escape him. He would have bled the life right out of you, my dear."

"Are you sure?" Gretchen was thrill to find someone who approved of her course.

"Of course I am—although I'm not sure you've come far enough to entirely escape your uncle or Ephraim Waring," she added.

"I know." Gretchen frowned worriedly. "I'll just have to face that problem when it comes."

Alma patted Gretchen's hand. "I have every confidence you will do what needs to be done. Don't you ever marry Ephraim Waring. I refused such a man when I was young, and I've never regretted it for a moment. Her face softened in memory. "Of course I wasn't as beautiful and sought after as you. My dear, you truly are lovely—a beauty, if I may say so."

Gretchen blushed. "Thank you, but—"

"Surely you have caught the eye of other, more suitable young men."

Gretchen looked at the floor. "Oh, there is one, perhaps. I-I met him recently."

"Out here? Splendid! There are real men out here in the west; independent, hardworking, self-reliant, not the poppinjays I see so often in the city."

Gretchen laughed delightedly at the apt description, then sobered. "I'd hardly call Tuck a poppinjay, although I'm not at all sure what I would call him."

"You will be, my dear. You strike me as a young woman who quite knows what she's doing."

Later, when Gretchen returned downstairs, Tuck suggested coming to visit her again after closing. "It's impossible, Tuck. I've my first lodger. A Miss Alma Smallwood, from Boston. She's in the room next to mine."

"Come to my place, then," he urged.

"I had better not."

"Damn!"

She shook her head. "I need a good night's sleep, and so do you." It made her feel good to realize how eager he was—and how disappointed.

"I'll see you tomorrow, then. I've a surprise planned."

"A surprise?" She raised her brows. "What kind of surprise?"

"If I told you, it wouldn't be one." He winked. "Just pack a little lunch for two."

"Are we going riding again?" Her curiosity was piqued. "I have to know what to wear."

He hesitated. "Very well. We're not going riding. That's all I can tell you." His laughter trailed after him as he ambled away from her.

In her room after closing, Gretchen had trouble falling asleep, despite her fatigue from her long horseback ride. In part she was stimulated by the arrival of Alma Smallwood. Such a fascinating woman, outspoken, independent, yet caring. Her approval of Gretchen's operating the inn had meant so much. Her first guest. Gretchen could only hope that more would follow.

But what really kept her from sleep was that there seemed to be much more noise than usual from the river below. She could even hear voices. She got up and looked out the window. She couldn't see much, but she noticed there were a lot of torches and lanterns bobbing back and forth through the black night. As her eyes adjusted to the darkness, Gretchen realized a boat was tied to the wharf. It hadn't been there earlier. And men were off-loading it, carrying crates and barrels up the steps. How very strange. Why do this work at night?

Chapter Thirteen

IT WAS MIDMORNING before Alma Smallwood was set to depart. She dawdled over breakfast, talking to Gretchen, who insisted on packing her a boxed meal for her journey. Indeed, Gretchen hated to have her leave, for she had brought such pleasure into her life during her brief stay.

Alma had mounted her horse and tethered the pack horse to her saddle when Tuck Loudon approached. Gretchen introduced them, and Tuck expressed his amazement that she was traveling alone. He offered her advice about the road ahead, all the way to Hartford, New Haven, even to New York, explaining how to avoid certain pitfalls she might encounter.

When Gretchen said her good-byes, Alma

leaned over and whispered, "Is that the young man of whom you spoke?"

Gretchen smiled and whispered back, "Yes."

"My, he's extraordinarily handsome—you could do much worse, my dear."

"The thought has occurred to me. We shall see."

Standing in front of the inn, Gretchen watched and waved till Alma was out of sight, then turned to Tuck. "How do you know so much about the roads to the south?"

"Oh, I get around," he said evasively. "Are you ready for your surprise?"

"It depends on what it is."

He gave an exaggerated sigh. "I suppose I can tell you now. We're going canoeing on the river."

"Oh, Tuck, I don't know."

"Why not? It's a perfectly splendid day. The river is lovely. You'll enjoy it."

Gretchen screwed up her face in an expression of doubt. "I have so much work to do. And, as you know, I don't swim."

"The work will keep, and you won't wet a finger, let alone have to swim. Come, time's a-wasting."

The idea did appeal to her. "Will we be gone long?"

"Only as long as you want to be. Come."

She sighed, relented, then grinned her pleasure. "Just give me a minute to get ready."

A little while later he was leading her down the steps toward the river. She was glad to take his hand, for the steps were just split logs thrust into the earth, and the hill was steep. There was no railing. She had elected to wear nothing fancy, just a skirt and a bright blue blouse. Her hair was tucked into a straw bonnet, and she carried a small basket of food. "I've never been down here before. Is all of this part of my property?"

"No, the North Inn ends at the bluff."

"Then who owns it?" Gretchen wanted to know.

Tuck shrugged. "Hard to say. It's here. Everyone uses it."

"There was a lot of activity last night. It kept me awake."

He glanced at her sharply, but said, "Doesn't seem to be anything special now."

It was true. The boat was gone. There was only the usual ferry and the canoe they were to use. "I saw men off-loading. Why would they do that at night?"

Another elaborate shrug. "Beats me. Probably had to be somewhere else today." Tuck stepped into the canoe, steadied himself, reached up for the basket, and then for her.

Gretchen hesitated. "I don't know, Tuck. I've never been in a canoe before. It looks awfully unstable."

Tuck grinned. "It'll be fine. Just step in and have a seat."

A little fearfully, she leaned into his outstretched hands, squealing as her balance teetered a moment. Then she was seated forward, facing him. Soon they were away from the wharf and floating downriver.

"Just relax. Enjoy the ride."

She tried, but she couldn't stop herself from holding on to the sides tightly and looking around apprehensively. But when nothing untoward happened, she began to relax, encouraged by his obvious competence with the canoe as he guided it across the river, closer to the far shore.

"If you fall in now, it's shallow. You'll be able to wade out."

"I thought I wasn't going to get wet."

"You won't. Trust me." He grinned. "I thought a little reassurance might help you enjoy this more."

Soon she was captured by the beauty of the scenery for it was a perfect day, the breeze soft and warm for May. The sunlight glistened on the water as they passed under the shadow of trees, maples mostly, but also pines, chestnut, and acacia. Dogwood flowered on the shore and wildflowers cast their blooms upward. "It is lovely, Tuck. Thank you for making me come."

"It's the quiet I like the most. Just listen to it."

"Yes." She was surprised by what she heard—the gentle lapping of the water, the rustle of leaves, the extravagant songs of birds. "It's like there's no one in the world but us."

"It may well be true," Tuck agreed.

It wasn't quite. They passed an occasional riverboat, slowly forcing its way upstream, and they waved and exchanged greetings, but mostly they had the river to themselves. Again Gretchen felt she was seeing another side to him, a romantic, pastoral side. He liked nature and found beauty in it. Such a quality seemed wildly at odds with the man she'd known a week ago.

Eventually it seemed to her they had gone a long ways. "Won't you have trouble rowing back upstream?" she asked.

"It'll be more work than this, that's for sure," he agreed.

"Then perhaps we should turn back," she suggested.

"Soon. There's a little white water ahead. I thought I'd give you a little thrill, then we'll stop to eat."

"White water? You mean rapids?" At once she turned to look ahead.

"Careful, Gretchen. Don't move suddenly, or you'll upset us."

She twisted farther and saw rocks ahead, and spray as the current took on speed. She felt a frisson of dread. "Oh, I don't know, Tuck."

"Just sit still and hold on. It'll be all right." But she remained twisted sideways, strangely fascinated by what lay ahead. "Don't do that, Gretchen. Face me." Tuck released one hand from the paddle and reached out toward her.

Perhaps his movement was too abrupt, for the equilibrium of the canoe suddenly shifted. Gretchen lurched, cried out, tried to hold on. It only made the rocking worse, and she squealed as she was thrown into the water.

The river was not shallow as Tuck had promised, but over her head. She screamed, swallowing water as she did so, and thrashed about wildly as her heavy skirts dragged her downward. She went under, came up, and saw Tuck paddling frantically toward her. She knew he was calling something she couldn't hear. It seemed to take forever for him to reach her, for she was being swept ever more rapidly downstream. Then finally he was there, reaching over the side of the canoe with the paddle. She clutched it, lost her grasp, struggled toward him, then took firm hold of the paddle. She felt herself pulled toward him. Close now, she flailed out with one hand, grabbed the side of the canoe, and tried to pull herself up.

"Don't do that, Gretchen!"

Tuck's warning came too late. The canoe over-turned. Now they were both in the water. She went under a moment, then broke the surface of the water, coughing and sputtering, waving her arms and legs wildly, careening downstream. She bumped hard against a rock, felt a sharp pain, but the collision turned her to face downstream. Ahead she saw another rock, and reached for it with both hands. She held on for dear life, cough-ing as hard as she ever had in her life.

"Hold on! I'm coming!"

In a moment he was there, his arms around her, leading her, half carrying her through the rocks. Finally she collapsed on the bank, coughing as he patted her back. Finally her coughing subsided, but she lay there exhausted, both from exertion and fright.

"Are you all right now?"

She lay facedown against the grassy slope, panting. Finally she managed to say, "Do I look all right?"

Tuck's eyes danced with laughter. "I told you the water wasn't deep. You could have walked out."

"I could not!"

He rolled her to her back and laughed out loud now. "You look like a drowned rat."

"I am drowned—thanks to you."

"You're the one who overturned the canoe." Smiling, he reached down, took her hand, and pulled her to her feet. He helped her stagger up the bank to lie in a sunny clearing. Looking down at her, he laughed again. "My, that was fun, wasn't it?"

She sat up but wouldn't look at him. "I'd hardly call it fun." She began to squeeze water out of the hem of her skirt. "I was scared to death and now I'm freezing."

"Better get out of those wet things. Lay them in the sun to dry. I'm off to see if I can recover the canoe."

She watched him stride away, then stood up, knowing he was right about her wet clothes. She started to undress, then realized she had nothing to put on. Frantically, she looked around. No one else was near. Still she hesitated, then she shrugged. What choice did she have?

It seemed to her Tuck was gone a long time, and she was beginning to get concerned. What would she do alone out here? Her chemise was beginning to dry against her skin, and her hair was very nearly dry, when she saw him approach, his head nearly hidden inside the canoe he carried over his shoulders. In a moment he dropped it to the ground. "Found the canoe straight away, but I had the devil's own time with the paddle. Got soaked all over again."

She watched him start to disrobe, then turned her face away. "Are they damaged?"

"Damn lucky there, no. We'll get home safely." He took off his boots, dumped water out of them, wrung water out of his socks, then unbuttoned his britches. "Sorry about our dinner. Couldn't save it."

"That's all right." In dismay she watched him start to remove his underdrawers. "Do you have to do that?"

"I do. They're sopping." He looked at her quizzically. "You've seen me before."

She looked away. "But not in daylight—in front of God and everyone."

He chuckled as he slid the wet drawers off his legs. "There's no one around, and I'm sure God knows what we look like."

"And here I thought you were shy," she joked.

"I am, but I also don't want to catch my death wearing wet clothes."

With what appeared to be perfect nonchalance, he busied himself wringing out his drawers—a great deal of water was expunged—hanging them on a limb to dry, then perching his shirt, britches, and socks. He said nothing, nor did he even glance at her. For a secret moment she feasted her eyes on his lithe body, watching his muscles follow his movements. It was exciting. She felt a little breathless.

"Your clothes dry?" he called.

"Coming along." Her voice sounded strange to her.

"They'll dry faster on a limb." He went to where she had spread them on the ground, picked them up, and hung them. That's when she saw he wasn't quite as nonchalant as he acted, for his manhood had begun to swell. In fascination she watched it lengthen and harden until it arched in front of him.

"Is your chemise dry?"

She realized then that he knew what she was looking at, and she blushed. "Almost."

"Let me see." He came to her and felt the straps at her shoulders. "Still damp." He slid them down. "You'd better get out of this."

She stopped the movement with her hands. "I don't think so." She knew she was trembling.

"Are you sure?"

His hands came to her face, bending it upward as his descended. His lips were hot and dry on hers, caressing the smooth surface, sending jolts of sensation through her. Her lips parted in surprise. Soon they were wet and she was in his arms, pressed against him.

"Oh please, I can't—not here."

"There is no better place," he contradicted.

"What if . . . someone comes . . . sees us?"

He slid the chemise from her now. "There is no one but us."

She really had no chance against him, or herself, once she felt the heat coursing through her veins. Once she accepted what was happening, there was something about the boldness of it all—

outdoors in a grassy meadow in daylight, warmed by the sun, stillness all around—which heightened her pleasure. Her skin was exquisitely alive to his. His every touch thrilled her. And he was so strong and energetic, rolling with her over and over through the soft grass, laughing. Indeed, they were like children at play. Joining in the laughter, she spun away from him and ran.

He caught her from behind, filling his hands with her breasts, truly tormenting her. She bent over and reached between her legs, determined to torment him, too, and she felt she succeeded. He fell backward, pulling her down with him, amid squeals and laughter. He bent his head to kiss her, but she spun away. He crawled after her on all fours, pretending to growl like an animal. Feigning fright, she tried to get away, but he was too quick for her. He lay on top of her, but she held her legs tight together, teasing him, until at last she could bear no more of this exquisite torture. She accepted him, eyes closed, the sun forming brilliant colors against her eyelids, and as he plunged into her wetness again and again she reached total fulfillment, a disintegrating burst, a cataclysm of nature, rolling through her, making her cry out in ecstasy.

Then, to her surprise, he pulled her atop him. Her breasts filled his hands, her mouth covered his, and she lowered herself onto his erect member. It was slower now, and Gretchen reveled in the sensation of their joining, giving him all of herself, faster and faster, until they both cried out in mutual abandon and delight.

* * *

Gretchen knew she must have fallen asleep, for when she opened her eyes, she was still lying in the grassy field. Tuck was dressed, looking down at her, his eyes bright.

Feeling as relaxed as she was satisfied, she stretched and lazily sat up, accepting the hand he extended toward her. "I suspect you deliberately overturned the canoe just to get me out of my clothes."

Tuck's eyes twinkled with mischief. "The thought did occur to me."

It was a long, arduous paddle upriver. She knew Tuck must be tired, but he did not complain. It was late afternoon when they finally arrived back at the wharf. When they had climbed the steps and entered the inn, Gretchen found three well-dressed men who desired overnight lodgings. But she was not as pleased as she might have been. One of the men was Ephraim Waring.

Chapter Fourteen

GRETCHEN KNEW HOW she must look. Her clothes were dirty and wrinkled from her dip in the river. Nervously she touched her hair. It had fallen to her shoulders, dirty and matted, for she'd had no brush or comb.

"Gretchen?"

"Ephraim's dark eyes were upon her, looking her up and down, clearly disapproving. Tall, rail thin, there was an ascetic look to him, perhaps because of his gaunt, pinched face. His mouth was nearly lipless and his eyes deep set above a rather large nose. He was anything but handsome, and there was no evidence of warmth or humor in his tone or bearing.

"Ephraim," Gretchen returned quietly.

"What has happened to you?"

He looked so severe, more like an asutere father than an eager suitor. Nervous, wanting to avoid his eyes, she looked down at her shoes and flared out her skirt. "Oh, this? Tuck and I—I mean, Mr. Loudon and I—were canoeing on the river. I'm afraid we overturned . . . fell in." Her laugh began nervously, then turned into genuine mirth. It was suddenly very funny to her.

"Are you hurt?" The anxious question came from one of the other men.

"I'm fine—only disheveled," she assured him. "Mr. Loudon was quite gallant in rescuing me." She turned to look at him. He stood a little behind her, and Gretchen was surprised to see a most serious expression on his face as he eyed the visitors.

Her question intruded on Tuck's thoughts, making his reply nervous. "I don't know how gallant, but we did get out of the water and save the canoe."

Ephraim cleared his throat and looked at Tuck sternly. "I assume it was your fault the accident happened." His tone was entirely accusatory.

Tuck bristled. "I assume responsibility, of course, but it was an accident."

"And no harm was done." Gretchen smiled, ignored Ephraim, and extended a hand to the man beside her. He was young and quite good-looking, with blond, curly hair and brown eyes. But there was an effete quality to him. His attire, although sensible for travel, was of a quality and design seldom seen in the colonies. "I'm Gretchen North, proprietress of this establishment. Do you seek lodgings for the night?"

"I do, we all do." He bowed, accepted her hand, kissed it in courtly fashion, and smiled graciously. "I am Clive Hopkins. This is Mr. Ian Pemberton and—" He hesitated. "I gather you and Mr. Waring are already acquainted."

Gretchen made a mental note that Hopkin's accent was clearly English—very well bred English. He was not from the colonies. "We are." Still she did not look at Ephraim.

Hopkins now turned away from her. "If you are Tucker Loudon, then you are one of the men we've come to see."

"I am," Tuck acknowledged.

"Is the shipment ready?"

Gretchen saw him glance at her warily, then smile broadly at the men. "One should never talk business over a thirst. Let me buy you gentlemen a libation."

Hopkins and Pemberton followed Tuck to the counter of the taproom. Ephraim Waring remained behind, his eyes intent on Gretchen. "I have come to take you back, Gretchen—where you belong."

"Have you, indeed?" Her impulse was to argue with him, but she restrained herself. "We'll discuss it later, Ephraim. I must change now—and prepare your lodgings."

She walked sharply past him and upstairs to her room. Inside, she muttered aloud, "Of all the rotten, bloody luck!" She inspected herself in the mirror, discovering she looked worse than she feared. Her hair was truly a mess and there were smudges on her face. How shocked he must be! At least she consoled herself, he surely would not want her now.

When she was undressed to bathe, she discovered pinkness where there had never been any before. Sunburn! She smiled in memory of their frolic in the meadow. She tried to imagine Ephraim ever gamboling naked in the woods. She simply could not, and laughed at the very thought.

As she began to dress, Gretchen tried to divert her mind to more comforting thoughts. The presence of Clive Hopkins was surely good news. Such a gentleman! So well mannered! She wouldn't be surprised if he was titled. Imagine! A member of the peerage at the North Inn. Gretchen took extra care in dressing, washing her hair, and brushing it dry till it shone. Without hesitation she chose her blue gown with the extravagant bodice. She gave no thought to covering herself with a scarf. Mr. Hopkins would be pleased. Doubtlessly he saw many women so attired in London. Ephraim would not be pleased. But perhaps it would show him what he was missing. There was no possible way she would return to Boston with him. She checked her available rooms. Only the three next to hers were ready for guests. She made a mental note to put Ephraim in the one farthest from hers.

Downstairs she saw the three men huddled at a table with Tuck. Shaw, Clayton and a couple of other men had joined them. Their conversation was involved, and they did not notice as she passed by toward the taproom. It seemed an utterly incongruous gathering: three well-dressed gentlemen, one of whom worked for her Uncle John, deep in conversation with hooligans like Shaw and Clayton. And why was Tuck there? Hopkins had said they had come to see Tuck, and asked about a shipment. But what sort of shipment? And why had Tuck acted so strangely? He'd glanced at her nervously, then changed the subject and led the men away. It was as though he hadn't wanted her to know or hear.

"I must say, you look no worse the wear for your canoeing mishap, Miss North."

She turned to face Clive Hopkins, who had approached the counter. His face was wreathed in a smile and his eyes were bright as he surveyed her gown and what was revealed. She felt no shyness, only pride. "Thank you, Mr. Hopkins. I'm afraid I was a fright when you first saw me."

"One so beautiful is never frightening." He laughed gently. "At the risk of rudeness, may I say how delightful it is to discover so charming, stylish, and obviously gentle a woman as yourself"—he made a small gesture with a delicate hand—"well, shall we say, out here, so far from civilization?"

She beamed. "You may. Again, I thank you."

"May I also say I find it unfathomable? What brings you here, Miss North—not that I am not grateful."

"I told you. I am proprietress of the North Inn."

"How did that come to be?" The man's puzzlement and disbelief was most apparent in his face.

"My father, Winthrop North, bequeathed this place to me. I came here to run it."

"My dear, you aren't!" He seemed genuinely shocked. "Such places as this, especially out here, are often—"

"I know exactly what they are, Mr. Hopkins. I'm determined to change that, to make this a proper inn for wayfarers such as yourself. I'd like to think I am succeeding." She saw him shake his head, still clinging to his disbelief. "As proof, may I serve you supper?"

He seemed to ponder her a long moment, smiling at what he witnessed. "Only if you will join me, Miss North."

She hesitated for only a moment. "I believe I can join you. It would be my pleasure."

A few minutes later she was seated across from him at a small table in a corner farthest from the taproom. Meg Gwynne, on Gretchen's instructions, served them with the newly acquired pottery. But it was only slightly improved from her usual service. Gretchen reminded herself to later instruct Meg in how to serve guests properly. She also made a mental note to build a separate room so guests could dine away from the tavern patrons.

If Hopkins was appalled at the service, as Gretchen knew he must be, he was too much of a gentleman to comment. She was grateful for that—and for the attention he lavished upon her. "May I ask what brings you to Holyoke, Mr. Hopkins?"

He dismissed the query with a wave of his hand. "It's very mundane, my dear—and boring. It would not interest you. Business is most dreary."

"I thought it might be business. I heard you ask about a shipment. Are you in trade?"

His glance was wary. "In a manner of speaking. I represent a company interested in some of the . . . products available out here." He smiled. "Does that satisfy your curiosity?"

"Not quite." She smiled. "What does Mr. Loudon have to do with your enterprise?"

"Him? Oh, he's making arrangements for us."

"And Mr. Shaw and Mr. Clayton? They hardly seem the sort of persons a gentleman such as yourself usually deals with."

Clive Hopkins laughed generously. "One must accommodate one's self to all types of people in this world."

At once he changed the subject and began to regale her with news from London. She was not surprised to discover he was a viscount, but when she tried to refer to him by his title, he demurred, explaining that titles were often a handicap to those traveling in the more egalitarian colonies. Although she realized he had said almost nothing about what brought him to Holyoke—indeed, he seemed to evade her questions—she quickly became enmeshed by his bonhomie. Clive Hopkins surely was amusing—and enticingly wicked as he related the latest court gossip. Gretchen had not enjoyed such civilized conversation since leaving Boston.

But Gretchen, while enjoying herself, was not captivated by him. He was certainly handsome, utterly suave and urbane, thoroughly attentive and flattering, but hardly irresistible. Her impression was of shallowness and flash. His charm seemed too practiced, as though he used it often and felt assured it would work to perfection with a girl "far from civilization," as he put it. In truth, she began to dislike his aura of arrogant superiority.

These were entirely her private thoughts, however, as she gave the impression of being enchanted by him, smiling, laughing, seeming to flirt with him. Occasionally she glanced across the room. She met Tuck's eyes once. They were serious, but she could not read anything in them. There was no such problem with Ephraim Waring. He looked at her frequently, eyes full of distress and hostility. This caused her to intensify her attentions to the urbane viscount. Let them both wonder, she thought angrily.

Ultimately, though, she rose from the tête-à-tête, saying how much she'd enjoyed herself, but regrettably she had duties to attend to.

Clive Hopkins also rose. "I still find it incomprehensible that you operate this inn by yourself. May I see you later? We still have much to . . . discuss."

She understood his meaning, but considered it only flirtation. "I will be here all evening, Mr. Hopkins. I have no place to go."

Shortly thereafter, Ephraim Waring approached her, as she knew he would. "I must talk to you, Gretchen. Is there someplace where we can be alone?"

She was not about to take him to her room. "That is very difficult"—she gestured to encompass the room.—"as you can see." She hesitated. "We could step outside a moment, if you wish."

"Very well."

She went for her shawl, resigning herself to getting this over with, and followed him outside. It was very dark, for which she was grateful. Not seeing his face would make this much easier.

Ephraim wasted no time on pleasantries. "Your uncle has sent me to bring you home. He and your Aunt Sarah are most distraught by your disappearance."

"I have not disappeared, as you have witnessed, Ephraim. I left them a note telling them where I was going and why."

"Nonetheless, they are most upset. You are to return with me at once."

Her eyes had adjusted to the darkness, but she still had only the faintest glimpse of him. "I'm afraid that won't be possible, Ephraim. This is my home now. I am creating a life here."

"You call this a life—associating with rabble, rascals, scalawags?"

"You need not raise your voice, Ephraim. I hear you just fine."

He did make an effort to restrain himself. "You should have seen yourself this afternoon when you returned with that . . . that disreputable man Loudon."

"I'm sorry if I shocked you, Ephraim," she said seriously. "But it was an accident and couldn't be helped."

"An unacceptable excuse, Gretchen. No proper

young woman puts herself in such a compromising position. What will people think?"

Gretchen shrugged, affecting nonchalance. "They will think I fell into the river and half drowned myself."

"Make light of it if you wish, but your conduct is most improper. And just now you were behaving most outrageously with that Hopkins chap."

"He is charming, Ephraim, and I was simply being a polite hostess. I assure you it was all quite harmless."

"I warn you to be careful with him."

"I have every intention of being careful—with everyone. But thank you for your concern. Is that all you wished to say to me?"

"You know it is not." He paused. "Gretchen, we are betrothed."

She had been expecting this, but that made it no easier. "I know of no such arrangement, Ephraim," she hedged.

"Your uncle promised you to me. We made an agreement."

"One I am not party to! You have never sought my hand, Ephraim, therefore you have no claim on me."

"I will do so immediately," he declared.

"Please don't. I will refuse you."

He sucked in his breath audibly. Clearly, he was shocked. "*Refuse* me?"

"I'm sorry, but I must."

"I-I have everything to offer you."

"I realize that, Ephraim, and I don't wish to hurt you. You are a fine man and will be an excellent husband—to someone. But I fear we are not . . . *suited* to one another. I will not bring you happiness."

"You will, you will!" He grabbed her shoulders and roughly pulled her against him. "I must have you!"

His outburst startled her. She had no idea he was so impulsive—or that he possessed such physical desires. She turned her face to avoid his clumsy attempt to kiss her, and felt his hot breath against her cheek. Flustered, she backed away. "This is unseemly, Ephraim. I'm surprised at you."

"You are mine! You were promised to me!" He pulled her back to him.

His mouth clawed at her. She struggled. "Stop it! I say!" At last she managed to physically push him away. "I'm ashamed of you, Ephraim. For your sake, I will pretend this never happened."

"I want you. I deserve you." A sound escaped him. It sounded like a sob. "You . . . you have no idea what I've done . . . just to have you."

She sensed all the fight had gone out of him, for his tone was nearly plaintive. "What do you mean? What have you done?"

"I've risked everything for you."

Gretchen was confused, and curious. "I don't understand, Ephraim. What sort of risks?"

He hesitated a long moment, then blurted: "You'll find out one day. I'll make you rich."

"I don't care about being rich—only happy." She turned away. "I must go back in now."

"It's that scoundrel Loudon, isn't it? You've given yourself to him."

She stopped in midstride and searched for his face in the darkness. "What I have or have not done is no affair of yours. And I hardly think you are qualified to judge Tucker Loudon as a scoundrel."

"Oh, but I am, Gretchen. If you knew what he's up to, you'd—"

"Exactly what is he up to?" She waited for an answer, but heard only Ephraim's heavy, agitated breathing. "Do you have some involvement with him? Is that really why you're here in Holyoke? Is he the risk of which you speak?" She could not hide the anxiety behind her questions.

Ephraim was silent for a moment, then he stalked past her toward the door. "You'll find out, damn your soul in hell."

She hung back, greatly puzzled. At least she'd have no more trouble with Ephraim Waring. But his mention of Tuck fueled doubts she had foolishly ignored.

A short while later Ephraim approached her in the taproom. "Miss North, if you will show me to my room, I will retire now."

His eyes were terribly cold, his manner entirely stiff and formal. She had hurt him, she knew, and she regretted that. There was nothing wrong with Ephraim Waring, besides the fact that she didn't want to marry him. "Of course, Ephraim," she said kindly. Ian Pemberton also decided to retire, and she showed both men to their rooms, Ephraim first, then Pemberton.

As she left to go back downstairs, Ephraim waited for her in the doorway of his room, looking at her coldly. She knew she had to say something. "I'm sorry, Ephraim. My refusal of your offer of marriage does not mean I do not have regard and respect for—"

Ephraim interrupted her. "I don't care what you think, Gretchen. As soon as I return to Boston, I am going to report your disreputable behavior to your uncle. I'm confident he will take appropriate action to save you from this place."

Gretchen's annoyance resurfaced. "I don't need saving, Ephraim." She shook her head. "What's the use. I'm sure you will do what you must."

"Indeed I will. You may be certain of that."

He stepped back and slammed the door in her face. Gretchen stood there a moment, looking at it, feeling miserable. Why did he have to act this way? Suddenly she felt very dejected and extremely weary. The whole day seemed to have caught up with her.

Slowly she made her way downstairs. With the departure of Ephraim and Pemberton, the business discussion seemed to have broken up. Shaw, Clayton, and the other local men had left, leaving only Tuck and Hopkins. The viscount invited her to join them, but she declined. At length, though, Hopkins came to her, exuding charm, telling her stories she felt were a trifle ribald and risqué—more then a trifle. She laughed and tried to act amused, but in truth, she wasn't. It was obvious that Clive Hopkins was more than a little tipsy. All she wanted was to be rid of him, to be rid of the lot of them.

Tuck, who she had been watching, came to her rescue, buying Hopkins a drink, glad-handing him in a broad sort of way, leading him back to the table. Later, when Hopkins staggered to the privy out back, Tuck came to her side. "You look exhausted, Gretchen."

She sighed. "I am very tired, Tuck. It's been a long—" she managed a wan smile—"and most unusual day."

"Hasn't it? Did you have trouble with Waring?"

"Yes," she said dully. "He proposed marriage. I refused him. He did not take kindly to it."

Tuck laughed. "I can imagine. Look, Gretchen, why don't you go to bed—while Hopkins is gone."

"I can't. I have to—"

"I'll get Hopkins up to bed and close the place for you."

Once again, he was trying to get rid of her. "No, it's my—"

"I know how to close, Gretchen. I've done it many times." He took her arm and led her toward the stairs. "Just listen to me for once." Still she hesitated. "I will not help myself to the cash drawer. Trust me."

"It's not that. I—" She heard Hopkins fumbling at the door, singing a little, and dread won out over suspicion. "Very well. The bed will feel good."

"Be sure to lock your door."

She had no idea how long she'd slept before she was awakened by a rapping at her door. It was not loud, but insistent. Finally she rose and spoke through the door. "Who's there?"

"I haf to talk to you."

Despite the slurred speech, she recognized the voice of Clive Hopkins. "I'm in bed. I was asleep."

"Put somethin' on. I mus' speak to you."

She hesitated. What could he possibly want? It must be something important. Perhaps he would tell her about his business with Tuck. "Very well." She turned up the lamp, put on her robe, and let him in. At once she knew it was a mistake, for he was leering at her, obviously drunk.

She backed away. "It's the middle of the night! What is so urgent that you must speak to me at this hour?" Hopkins kicked the door closed and stood there with a silly grin on his face. Suddenly she knew what he wanted. Fear gripped her and she backed away a little more. "It's improper for you to be here, Mr. Hopkins. Why don't you go to bed?"

"I'm a-goin' to bed, all right—with the bes' li'l tart I've seen in a long time."

To her horror he started toward her, then stumbled, falling against her. Before she knew what was happening, she was thrown back on her bed and he was on top of her. "Don't do this! I'll scream!"

"I like it when they scream."

She tried to shove him off, but he was too heavy, too strong. He tried to find her mouth with his, but she fiercely turned her head from side to side. "Stop this at once, I say!" she muttered.

"You know you wannit!"

"No!" She tried to scream, but his hand clamped over her mouth, reducing the sound to a heavy moan through her nostrils.

"A fighter, are you? All the better!"

She struggled with all her might, but even fear did not give her enough strength. She sensed she was losing, for his weight had thrust her legs apart, and she felt him opening her robe, fumbling with her nightdress, pulling it up.

"You'll like this, believe me."

She intensified her struggles, beating his back with her fists, but it was no use. She felt a hard probing, and fear gave way to panic.

Then came a loud pounding at the door. "Whass ya doin', Clive ol' chap?" More pounding. "Hey, lemme in."

It was Tuck, and he sounded very drunk. But his persistent pounding and shouting caused Hopkins to stop his efforts, although he still held Gretchen tightly.

"Go 'way. I'm busy," he called out.

"Naw, yer not. C'mon, I gotta talk to ya." Tuck's slurred words were accompanied by an even harder pounding on the door.

Gretchen thought it would break. Wide-eyed, she watched Hopkins, as he wavered in indecision. Finally he shouted, "All right, all right, I'm comin'." To Gretchen he said, "Don't go 'way. I'll be right back."

He crawled off of her. She watched, still in terror, as he buttoned his britches and opened the door. Tuck was there, leaning against the jamb, looking terribly drunk. Without even a glance at

Gretchen, he grinned stupidly at Hopkins and threw his arm around his shoulder. "We didn't finish our rum, ol' chap. Thass bad luck, ya know."

Gretchen watched him lead Hopkins away, still without even noticing her. She jumped up and locked the door, then stood there trembling.

Chapter Fifteen

WAKING CAME AS a surprise to Gretchen. She
had lain in bed a long time, trembling
with fear that Hopkins would return, certain
she would not be able to sleep. But obviously
she had, although she had been troubled by
bad dreams. The sun was already well risen,
but she still couldn't get out of bed and face the
day.

What had possessed Clive Hopkins? He was a
gentleman, a peer, yet he had attempted to rape
her. How could he? Drunkenness was no excuse.
She had seen other drunken men, none of them
gentlemen, yet they had not acted as he had. And
Tuck? He had come just in time to save her, but he
had been so drunk, too. He hadn't even looked at
her, asked if she were hurt, offered to help. All he

cared about was Hopkins. Obviously he cared nothing about her. That was what hurt the most. Tucker Loudon had showed his true colors. He was embroiled in some scheme; he had been using her! What a terrible mistake she'd made.

Only because she knew she had to—Ezra Brown was already at work down the hall—Gretchen forced herself out of bed. When she opened her shutters, she saw Tuck and the three guests going down the steps toward the river. Where were they going so early in the morning? Across the river? About halfway down the steps, she lost sight of them behind an outcropping of rock. She watched for some time, but they never came back into view. Where-had they gone? She waited and waited, finally giving up. At least she wouldn't have to face them downstairs.

Ultimately she did, however, for all returned wanting breakfast. Hopkins looked the worse for wear, apparently from his excesses of the night before, yet he acted as though nothing had happened. He was his usual insouciant self, attempting to cajole and flatter her. Such arrogance dumbfounded her.

Ephraim was insufferable. "It seems you entertained visitors last night, Gretchen."

Gretchen glanced at him in shock. His expression and voice were filled with pure mockery. Before she could reply, however, Hopkins said, "What are you talking about, Waring?" That truly amazed her. The man acted as if he didn't know.

"I distinctly heard a lot of shouting, pounding"—Ephraim snickered—"and other noises."

"You must've been dreaming, Waring," Hopkins snorted.

"It was no dream, Sir Clive. In fact, I distinctly heard your voice—and Loudon's too."

"My voice? Look here, Waring, I don't care much for—"

"Don't take offense, Sir Clive. No one could blame you for an interest in Miss North's charms. I only wish I'd partaken myself."

"Really, Waring, that's uncalled for!"

It was Ian Pemberton coming to her defense, but Gretchen did not wait to hear more. She ran to the kitchen and stayed there, even after the three visitors saddled up and rode away.

She was extremely depressed. Everything had gone so badly. Ephraim now hated her and had acted unspeakably bad. He'd probably tell Uncle John and Aunt Sarah lies about her, and they'd come to take her back to Boston, which they had every legal right to do. Uncle John was her guardian, she his ward. Clive Hopkins had seemed charming and amusing at first, then attempted to take advantage of her, scaring her half out of her wits, and ended up pretending to know nothing about it. Worst of the lot was Tuck. He'd offered her no help or sympathy. He didn't care what happened to her. She should have known all along.

Tuck had sensed Gretchen's mood. He knew Gretchen was avoiding him. He also knew why, and mentally cursed his bad luck. Nothing had worked, and he'd had to make the Devil's own choice about what to do. Hopkins's intentions toward Gretchen had been obvious to him. He'd tried to ward it off by sending her to bed, then staying up with Hopkins to get him drunk enough to pass out. But he had misjudged the foppish peer's capacity. Instead of going to bed he'd invaded Gretchen's room. Tuck had heard him and rushed upstairs. His impulse was to break down the door and knock the brains out of the man. But he couldn't. Everything he'd worked for would be lost. He simply had to cajole Hopkins and the others awhile longer.

He sat in the tavern drinking coffee, which he really didn't want, watching her walk past him several times as though he didn't exist. Finally he said, "Apparently Hopkins was so drunk last night he doesn't remember his little escapade."

She still did not look at him, but she did speak. "You may call it little and an escapade, but I do not."

"He didn't really hurt you, did he?"

Now she glanced at him sharply. "I doubt if you care whether he did or not."

"I do care, Gretchen," he insisted. "Did he hurt you?"

"Of course he hurt me. He attacked me, held me down, tried to force his way with me. How could he not hurt me? Are you a fool?" she cried.

"I thought I got there in time," Tuck said quietly.

Gretchen blinked. "What do you mean?"

Tuck looked at her earnestly. "I was afraid something like that might happen. I stayed with him, hoping to get him drunk enough to go to bed." He shook his head. "Apparently he wasn't as drunk as I thought."

Gretchen's eyes widened in surprise. "You did that deliberately?"

"I did. I even stayed downstairs, waiting till I was sure all was quiet. When I heard noises I came as quickly as I could."

"And did absolutely nothing!"

"I got him to stop, didn't I? What else could I do?" He saw her disdain. "I know, you wanted me to knock him silly. But you must realize I couldn't do that."

"Because he's a man, your good friend, your drinking companion." Gretchen's voice dripped sarcasm. "What does it matter what happens to me?"

"I saw you weren't really hurt," Tuck defended.

"You didn't even look at me!"

"Yes, I did." He sighed in frustration. "Gretchen, he's an important man with powerful friends. I couldn't make an enemy of him."

"Regardless of what happened to me." She stared at him with contempt. "You worried about being a cad, Tuck. Perhaps you are, but that is not your worst fault. You are a coward. There's not an ounce of chivalry in you."

Tuck met her gaze and his eyes turned cold. "Think what you wish, Gretchen, but I am not a coward." He hesitated, searching for words. "I believe it was Shakespeare who wrote that the better part of valor is discretion. I could not attack Hopkins, however much I wanted to."

"I don't believe you *did* want to!"

"I did—more than I can tell you."

She looked at him a long moment. "Why is this man so important to you?" She noted with satisfaction that Tuck looked extremely uncomfortable. Obviously he didn't want to reply. "Have you some sort of business dealing with him? I heard him ask you about a shipment. What is that all about?"

Tuck coughed. "You heard that, did you?"

"Ephraim said something about taking a great risk for me. I got the impression that risk involved you. What is that about?"

He gave no answer.

"This morning I saw the four of you walk down toward the wharf, at least partway. What is going on, Tuck? Does it have something to do with me and the North Inn? I have a right to know that much, at least."

"It has nothing to do with you, Gretchen," he insisted. "Pay it no mind."

"You said you had a business deal pending, one which would make you a profit," she continued. "Ephraim also said he was going to make me rich if I'd marry him. What is this all about, Tuck?"

"If you must know, yes, it is my business deal," Tuck answered guardedly. "I hope to do very well with it. It should be over soon."

She didn't believe him, and her skeptical expression showed it. "Ephraim Waring and that man Pemberton are also involved?"

"Yes."

"Also Shaw, Clayton, those other men?"

Damn her inquisitive mind! "Yes, them too."

"There must be a large profit to share with so many."

Tuck's smile masked his inner feelings. "We hope to do well, yes."

She studied him a moment, then shrugged and started to walk away. Then she stopped and turned back. "Ephraim Waring is an associate of my uncle. That must mean he is a party to your business venture," she guessed.

Again, Tuck mentally swore. If he wasn't careful, she would figure out the whole thing. "I hadn't realized that. I suppose John North is involved—from a distance, of course. He is a merchant, isn't he?" He sought to distract her. "I thought Waring's remark most uncalled for." He looked concerned. "I gather the man isn't too fond of you at the moment."

"Hardly," Gretchen sniffed.

"No man likes to be refused—especially by a woman as attractive as you. But he'll get over it. He's not for you. You're better off rid of him."

Gretchen was not convinced. "I only hope I am."

"Aren't you?"

"He has threatened to tell my uncle about my very scandalous life here," Gretchen told him.

"So?" Tuck appeared unconcerned.

"I am his ward. Uncle John and Aunt Sarah have every right to take me back to Boston, whether I want to go or not."

"Will they?" Tuck wanted to know.

"I don't know. They wanted to be rid of me, I'm sure—even if it meant marrying me off to a man I didn't care for. I can only hope they'll write me off as good riddance."

"As they did your father. Is that what you want, Gretchen?" He bent to look into her eyes. "I gather anything is better than Waring—even me."

Gretchen rose abruptly. "I'm not at all sure of that."

Tuck watched her leave him and enter the kitchen. If he could have read her thoughts, he would have discovered that Gretchen was far from convinced. She simply had too many questions. Why was Tuck so secretive about his business dealing? There must be something improper or dishonest about it. Why else would people dissimilar as an English peer just over from London and a ruffian like Buck Shaw be involved? And her uncle? John North traded in goods brought into Boston and other ports. What could he possibly want from out here? Was her uncle getting into some kind of trouble? She ought to find out and warn him. She owed him that much, didn't she?

She tried to tell herself to pay it no mind, as Tuck so often urged. Just operate the inn and stay out of what didn't concern her. In other words, mind her own business. But the more she told herself that, the more she realized that was exactly what she wasn't going to do.

Rather early that afternoon Gretchen left the inn and started down the steps toward the river, trying to act nonchalant, as though she were only going for a stroll. She saw activity on the wharf below, but no one else was on the steps. She had chosen a good time.

A couple of times she glanced back at her window high above, trying to judge the spot where she'd lost sight of Tuck and the others that morning. It had to be right about here. Just then she noticed a well-worn path hacked out of the side of the bluff. That must be it. She turned onto it, mindful of how narrow it was and of the sharp drop to the river below. It made her palms sweaty, and she forced herself not to look down.

After a few steps, the path turned inward to the bluff around a promontory of rocks, and she confronted the entrance to what looked like a cave. A dark, dirty piece of canvas hung over the entrance—obviously to conceal it from anyone looking up from the river. A person passing below wouldn't even know it was there. A secret cave—how strange!

She hesitated, a little afraid. But she had come this far, hadn't she? Bolder now, she pulled back the edge of the canvas and peered inside. At first she could see nothing, so bright was the sunlight outside. Then she recognized the glow of lantern

light and stepped inside behind the canvas. After a
moment her eyes adjusted. It was not a big cave,
perhaps only a dozen or fifteen feet wide and
maybe twenty feet or so in depth. It was packed
to the roof with boxes and barrels and bales, a
narrow aisle down the center. She passed along
the aisle, deeper into the cave, her astonishment mounting. There were a great deal of goods
here. Why was it being kept in this cave—a secret
cave?

She passed all the way to the end. All this stuff!
What was it? Everything seemed to be sturdily
packaged in heavy crates or tightly-bound bales.
Then she knew where she had seen things like
this before—in Uncle John's warehouse. This was
the sort of material that came off trading ships.
Holyoke was far inland; there was no ship or
ocean port for maybe a hundred miles. What was
this material doing here? And where had it come
from?

Thoroughly curious now, she took a lantern
from overhead and brought it down so she could
look more carefully at the crates. She saw no
labels or identifying marks, at least none that had
meaning for her. But when she rubbed some dust
off, she found some faint writing which she
couldn't read. It looked Oriental to her. How
could that be? She returned to the front of the
cave, examining containers, learning nothing.
Then her attention focused on a pile of long,
cylindrical objects, tightly wrapped in heavy,
oiled paper. Oriental markings were clearly
visible on the sides. The shape of the packages

suggested bolts of fabrics. They must be intended for Follen's store. Yet Follen's had only a limited selection, and there were so many here.

So deep was her concentration that she did not hear the voices until they were just outside the cave. Fear gripped her, for she recognized the voices of Shaw and Clayton. They must not find her here. Looking around desperately, she saw a narrow space between some boxes. She had no other choice. With effort, sucking in her stomach, flattening her bosom, she managed to squeeze into the slot just as Shaw and Clayton entered the cave.

"Whass that lantern doin' in the aisle?"

She recognized Shaw's voice, and saw in horror the offending lantern where she had left it.

"Is somebody in here?" Shaw called.

Clayton answered, "Naw, just some damn fool. I'll gittit 'fore some bloke kicks it o'er and starts a fire."

Gretchen held her breath—not that she had much room to breathe, anyway—as she heard the heavy steps approaching. From the corner of her eye she saw Clayton pass within an arm's length of her, bend over to pick up the lantern, then hold it high and look around.

"Smells like ladies' p'fume in here."

Shaw laughed from the front. "Ya got women on yer brain, John. It's just them spices we brung in yesterday."

"I guess yer right."

To Gretchen's great relief, he hung up the

lantern and passed by her toward the front. For a moment she thought they'd left the cave. Then she smelled the unmistakable aroma of pipes being lit.

"What did ya think o' them three blokes?" Shaw asked.

"I don't think 'bout 'em a'tall—just their gold." Clayton laughed.

"Yeah, but it's not very damn much fer all the risks we's took."

"It's still more gold than I'll ever see."

"It ain't right." Shaw was silent for a time. "What gits me is Tuck. He ain't dun nuttin' fer his share."

"He put the deal together, Buck. We couldn'a done it wit'out him."

"Still ain't right. I got half a mind to—"

"Get rid o' him?" Clayton gave an evil laugh. "Can't say it ain't 'curred to me, too."

A long silence followed. "Won' be easy, but if you an' me was to put our minds to it, we oughta be able to think o' somethin'."

Clayton laughed again. "I'd rather think 'bout that hussy up at the inn."

"Yer first after me. I's gonna fix her ass good—soon as 'em wagons come an' take this junk away."

"An' enjoy doin' it. Bet she's gotta tight li'l—"

"Maybe not. Tuck's prob'ly been inta it—which is 'nother reason to git rid o' him."

Gretchen listened in horror, both from the way they talked about her and the thought of what they wanted to do.

"C'mon, Big John, le's shove off."

Despite her great discomfort, Gretchen waited a long time before daring to leave her hiding place. Only slowly, checking carefully to see that no one was around, did she leave the cave and head back to the inn.

Chapter Sixteen

GRETCHEN RAN STRAIGHT to her room and leaned against the door, trembling. All she could think of was that Shaw and Clayton planned to kill Tuck and do great harm to her. She had to stop them, but how? What could she do against them? She ought to tell the authorities, but there were no authorities out here. Who could she go to? Tuck. She must warn Tuck.

A short while later she was at the door to his cottage, having forced herself to amble naturally across the green, as though she were simply out for a walk. She knocked on his door. Even under her gentle pressure it came ajar, for it was not latched. Opening it wider, she called his name. No answer. After a moment's indecision, she stepped inside. If his house was unlocked he couldn't have gone far. He wouldn't mind if she waited here.

She called his name again and glanced into the bedroom, then the kitchen. It looked as if he had just left and would be back soon. Tea was steeping in a pot; a cup and saucer were laid out. Beside the kitchen doorway, his desk was open, his quill in the inkwell.

He had been writing something. Gretchen hesitated, not wanting to invade his privacy. Then she remembered how he'd closed the desk during her previous visit to keep her from seeing his work. Perhaps, she reasoned, it would provide some clue to the strange business he was involved in.

But when she studied the paper there, she was amazed to discover what looked like poetry. And obviously, Tuck had been well schooled in penmanship.

Any concern Gretchen might have had for Tuck's privacy disappeared when she read the title: "To My Fair Love." She began to read. Such lovely phrases: "eyes of heavenly blue," "hair of Angel's guise," "object of Aphrodite's envy." Who was he writing about, so passionately and beautifully? Then she knew. "A wood nymph who graced fair meadow." He was writing about her! The words leaped to her eyes: "an opening well," "desire's fruition," "longing's requital," "passion's fulfillment," "an eternal gift of the Gods to the undeserving." The words thrilled her, so much she had trouble breathing against the lump in her throat. Did he think her this beautiful? Could he love her this much? No, it wasn't possible.

"I wish you hadn't seen that."

So intent was she on Tuck's verse, she hadn't heard him enter. He stood just inside the open doorway, his expression sheepish. "You wrote this, didn't you?" It was a foolish question. Of course he had. "I didn't know you were a poet."

"It is just a hobby—something to while away the time." Tuck hesitated, looking down at his feet. "You weren't . . . supposed to see that."

She sensed his embarrassment. "It's a very beautiful poem, Tuck."

Tuck's mischievous grin returned. "Thank you."

"It's about me, isn't it?"

He sighed in resignation. "I intended to call it 'To Gretchen,' but"—he looked at her now and smiled shyly—"it is hard to rhyme with Gretchen."

"You cannot think this of me. You cannot mean it."

He held her with his eyes a long moment, then said, his voice little more than a whisper, "I have no words to express . . . how I really feel."

His voice, the passion of his words, made her want to weep. "Oh, Tuck, I am not worthy of such love."

Then she was in his arms, totally enveloped by him, her lips drenched in passion, clinging to him, all thought lost from her mind but of this man who loved her so beautifully. No words were said; none were needed. He simply shut and barred the door and led her willingly into the bedroom. Clothes were discarded and bodies intertwined, raising passion that needed no encouragement, intensifying already-limitless desire. Doubtlessly because of what she had just read, Gretchen felt wholly beautiful, desired, and loved, and she abandoned herself to this man who cherished her.

"I love you, Gretchen, always and ever more."

His penetration was an ultimate joining, a welding until they truly were one, and she let herself go, becoming part of him, he of her, rapture uniting them, floating them away in togetherness.

Afterward she lay within his arm, folded over him, filled with sweet tenderness and fulfillment. How wonderful it had been—he had been.

Tuck broke the silence. "I meant what I said. I love you, only you, always."

She smiled. "I believe that's a line from your poem. If it isn't, it ought to be." She kissed his shoulder, and tightened her arms around his chest.

"I still wish you hadn't seen that bloody thing," Tuck groaned.

"Why not? It's lovely." She raised her head to look at him. "See the effect it had on me? I just melted."

"You did feel like you were on fire." He laid her head back down, and caressed her cheek. "Why did you come? Just to read my poetry?"

"Oh, no!" Memory shocked her and she sat bolt upright. "You made me forget everything. Tuck, you're in danger. I came to warn you."

She sat above him, legs tucked under herself, utterly unmindful of her nakedness. But Tuck wasn't. She had never looked lovelier. "About what?" He smiled complacently as he reached out to fondle her breasts. "I need no warning about you. I'm already captivated."

She blinked in confusion, then took his hand away. "I'm serious, Tuck. I overheard Shaw and Clayton talking. They plan to kill you."

He returned his hand to her breast, luxuriating in the softness. "Do they, really?" he drawled disinterestedly.

She couldn't believe him. "Aren't you concerned?"

"Not a bit."

"But they are very evil men," Gretchen protested.

"Yes, they are," Tuck admitted. "But wanting to kill me, even planning to, is far different from doing it. I know what they have in mind. I can take care of myself."

She looked at him. He seemed so unperturbed, so sure of himself. "Perhaps you can, but what about me? I heard them say what they are going to do to me." She shuddered. "It wasn't very nice."

He squeezed her breast. "Is that what you're worried about? Don't be. Shaw and Clayton will not touch a hair on your head."

Gretchen was far from convinced. "How can you be so sure?"

"Because I won't let them."

She pursed her lips. "I want to believe that, Tuck, and I am sure you do. But"—she sighed—"I don't know. I'm terribly frightened."

"You're being silly, Gretchen." He moved his hand to her other breast. "Where did you hear this conversation, these threats?"

She hesitated, certain he would disapprove of her finding the secret cave. "In the cave." She had not misjudged him. He drew his hand away and his expression turned somber.

"You found that, did you?"

"Yes." She told of seeing him and the others going down the steps and disappearing into the bluff. "I went looking this afternoon. That's when I found the cave." She explained how she had hidden from Shaw and Clayton.

Tuck's next words were stern. "Stay out of there, Gretchen. I mean it." His voice was firm and dictatorial.

But Gretchen could not let it go unexplained. "What's all that stuff in there?"

"Just stay out, Gretchen," Tuck warned.

"What is it? Why is it being hidden?"

Abruptly, Tuck twisted off the bed, padded across the room, and began to dress. She followed him with her eyes, turning in bed to face him. "Shaw said he wanted to kill you because you had done nothing to earn your share of the gold. Clayton said they couldn't have made the deal without you. Tuck, you are involved, aren't you?" He didn't answer. His mouth firmed into a harder line. "You say you love me. Then why are you shutting me out of this part of your life?"

"Because I have to." He really was angry with her. Why did she have to discover the cave and meddle with all this? But he knew being angry would only make it worse. "It will all be settled tomorrow, Gretchen. Then you'll know everything."

"What do you mean, settled?"

"Wagons are coming in the morning. Everything in the cave will be taken away."

"I see," she said, though in truth she didn't understand at all. "Is this the business deal you said you had pending?"

"Yes, it is." He tried to force a smile. "Tomorrow's my big day. I'll have enough money to ask for your hand in marriage." He hoped that might distract her. It did, for her eyes brightened, and she squirmed off the bed, came to him, and on tiptoes kissed him lightly.

"Is that a proposal?"

"Not quite. I'll do it on bended knee tomorrow."

She felt his hands at her waist, then rising to cup her breasts. "I'll have to think about how I might want to reply."

"Do that." He kissed the tip of her nose. "I hate to bring up unpleasant subjects, but don't you think maybe you ought to get dressed? I'm expecting some visitors."

She basked in his gaze, not at all embarrassed. "Since you enjoy looking at me so much, perhaps others will, too." He aimed a swat at her behind, which she managed to dodge, giggling. As she began to dress she thought of how very nice this was, so intimate and natural, just how it would be when they were married. Yes, she did want to marry him. Somehow she'd known it from their first meeting at the river. She smiled in memory of that first kiss.

He had left her, and now he brought back tea for both. Nearly dressed now, a thought came to her. "Since I am my uncle's ward, won't you have to ask his permission to marry me?"

"I wouldn't think that necessary."

She doubted that, but accepted his word. "And if I'm married, I won't have to worry about his coming to take me back to Boston, will I?"

"No."

She smiled. "Now, that just might persuade me to accept you."

"I hoped it might."

She was in his arms then, kissing him lightly, affectionately, for their passion was spent. Picking up her tea, she walked into the parlor. "How do I look?"

"Like a woman who's just made passionate love."

She made a face at him. "I was afraid you'd say that." She took a sip of tea. "Why do you have to hide your shipment in that cave?"

The question startled him. He thought she'd forgotten all that. He didn't know how to answer and stalled for time to think. "Why do you suppose?"

"I don't know. Are you doing something illegal? Smuggling, perhaps?" She heard him laugh, but the sound seemed nervous, forced.

"Do I look like a smuggler?" he queried.

"I don't know what smugglers look like. It seems to me Shaw and Clayton surely do. But why hide the shipment in the cave, Tuck? Why is no one supposed to see it?"

"My, but you have a suspicious mind. Remind me never to try to get away with anything around you." He came to her and put his hands on her shoulders. "There is a very simple reason for the cave, my darling Gretchen." His smile could not have been broader. "To keep someone from stealing it."

She blinked. "Oh, I guess I should have thought of that."

"I think so. Are you now convinced I'm not a smuggler?"

"I did so hope you were," she teased. "It would've been so romantic."

But Gretchen wasn't convinced, and as the day wore on she became less and less so. It began with her observation of how nervous and hesitant he was under her questioning. He was hiding something from her; he was not telling her the truth. The more she tried to talk herself out of that feeling, the more insistent it became. He was telling her whatever he thought he could make her believe. But why? If it was a straightforward business transaction, why not simply say he had acquired such and such goods and was selling it at a profit? Some of them, she knew, were being sold to Ephraim Waring, who represented her Uncle John. He was a merchant, in the business of trade. Why act so secretive about it?

And why would Tuck say he wouldn't have to ask her uncle for permission to marry her? Of course he would! She had some sort of dowry. Surely he would want that. Did Tuck know her uncle, after all? Was there some type of relationship between them? And, come to think of it, hiding the boxes and barrels in the cave would not prevent theft. All manner of river people traversed those steps every day. Surely they must know about the cave. The path was well worn and obvious. Anyone could steal from the cave anytime they had a mind to.

As the evening wore on, Gretchen's mental turmoil worsened. She scolded herself for mistrusting the man she loved and planned to marry. But he wasn't being truthful with her. And what sort of marriage was built on lies? She sighed. Plenty of them. Most wives had no idea what their husbands did, nor did they give a thought to whether they were dishonest. But she couldn't be that way, she knew. If Tuck were smuggling, she couldn't abide it.

Do I look like a smuggler? She remembered his words. Of course, he didn't. And what would he smuggle? She remembered what she'd seen. It looked like bolts of fabric with Oriental writing on them. And Shaw and Clayton had referred to spices. Those came from the Far East. What would they be doing in a cave on a bluff in Holyoke, Massachusetts?

She had no answers, but there was a way to find out. She would have to go back to that cave and see what was really there. It would settle once and for all her traitorous doubts about the man she loved.

After closing the inn for the night, she made her way down the steps, using a shaded lantern that cast only a small sliver of light in front of her. At the path leading to the cave she almost turned back. She did not want to believe that Tuck was lying—but it seemed obvious. What a fool she had been to trust him again and again. She wavered over the problem, then made up her mind. She would inspect the cave more closely. If Tuck was proved innocent, she would ask God to forgive her for mistrusting him. If he was guilty—which more and more Gretchen believed he must be—she would know the truth at last.

Where would that leave her? Gretchen wondered. Much as she had tried to deny it, she was in love with him. If he were a smuggler, could she turn him over to the authorities in Springfield? Without him, Holyoke was a joyless place. Even her success at the inn meant nothing if she could not share it with him.

But could she live with a man who was a liar, who had deceived her for his own gain? Unhappily, Gretchen knew what her answer must be. Even if she proved herself to be an utter fool, she must know the truth—and face the consequences.

Inch by inch, trying not to think of falling, she made her way to the cave entrance, slid back the canvas, and peeked in. It was dark. She opened the shade on her lantern for greater light.

Resolutely she made her way to the rear of the cave, where she'd seen what she suspected were bolts of fabric. Using a heavy knife she'd brought from the kitchen, she carefully slit open one of the rolls and felt the fabric inside. She lengthened the slit and pulled out some of the material. Her eyes widened in disbelief. Silk, the richest and most beautiful she had ever seen. But out here in Holyoke? Who could afford it? Where would it be worn? She opened a second roll. More silk, and even more beautiful. It had to come from the Orient, possibly China. But how did it get here?

She slit open another bolt. What she pulled out was an even greater surprise—cotton muslin, the sheerest and softest she had ever seen. How prized it would be in Boston, and how valuable! The niece of a merchant, she knew where muslin came from—India. Wielding her knife, she found fine linens and imported calicoes, even the most exquisite cambric.

Wholly curious now, she moved on to the larger containers. The barrels revealed their contents by odor—spices. She smelled ginger, cloves, nutmeg, black pepper. All of it came from the Orient. Using her knife, she pried open a large barrel. Sugar! Soon she made another discovery. A leaking barrel revealed its sticky contents: Madeira wine, the favorite drink of the wealthy. Her Uncle John imbibed nothing else.

She stopped her search now, looking around dumbfounded. What was all this valuable merchandise doing here in a secret cave on the Connecticut River below a frontier village? There could be only one answer. These luxury goods were not intended for Follen's store or any other store along the frontier. They were intended for Boston and other cities along the coast. But why bring it here, so far inland? Why not take it to Boston, Newport, or some other port? Carry-

ing this overland to Boston would surely be difficult.

Then she knew. Over dinner some months ago
she'd heard Uncle John complain bitterly about the
new, heavy customs duties imposed by the
Crown. He'd complained the most about a large
duty imposed on Madeira. Apparently the English
government wanted to force the colonists to drink
port wine made in England. He had also men-
tioned sugar. The tariff had been increased on
sugar, but lowered on molasses produced in the
British West Indies. Uncle John had been particularly incensed because the higher customs fees had
been imposed on most luxury imports, the very
things he traded in. She looked around the cave
wide-eyed. The items taxed were the very ones
hidden here.

More snatches of overheard conversations came
to her mind. The British were determined to collect
these new duties to defray the costs of the French
and Indian War. New tax collectors had been sent
over and ten thousand British redcoats were to be
quartered in the colonies to ensure that the taxes
were paid. She even remembered hearing Uncle
John say that if the Crown kept this up, they were
headed for trouble in the colonies.

She had paid scant attention to all this at the
time, but it was now suddenly clear to her. This
cave contained illegal contraband destined for Uncle John's warehouse. It was being smuggled in to
avoid customs. But why from Holyoke? Suddenly
she knew the answer to that, too. All the regular
ports were watched by customs officials and sol-

diers. They were effectively closed to smugglers. But cargo could be unloaded from ships anywhere along the coast, then brought upriver, and, yes, hidden in this cave. And wasn't Holyoke closer to Boston by land than any other place along the river? Yes, it was. She was sure of it.

Gretchen felt the world disintegrating around her. Tuck *was* a smuggler! Despite all his denials, that was exactly what he was doing. Everything was so clear to her now. He had been so dismayed by her coming; he had done everything he could to force her to go back to Boston—so she wouldn't learn what was really going on. And he'd been so mysterious, never talking about himself and what he really did. A big business deal! Trust him! Trust him, my eye, Gretchen thought.

Anger and shame began to boil inside her. What a fool she'd been! He had made love to her, made her fall in love with him just to keep her from seeing what was really going on. That endless horseback ride had been nothing more than a ploy to get her away so she wouldn't see the shipment. But she had—that heavy wagon she'd seen pull out as they returned. Contraband hidden under hay. And he'd tried to tell her hay weighed a lot. It would be funny if it weren't so . . . so *pathetic*.

The canoe trip had been another excuse to get her away. He'd probably overturned the canoe deliberately so she'd be gone longer. Maybe he had even hoped she'd drown.

Hot tears filled her eyes. *Oh, Tuck. Why did you have to do this?* In her anger, disappointment, and frustration she pounded her fists against one of the crates. How blind she had been! Uncle John, Ephraim Waring, everyone she knew was a party to this. A sob was wrenched from her. Had her father been, too? Probably. No wonder he didn't want her to come to live with him. And the English peer Hopkins. He was involved in all this somehow.

Mostly, though, her anguish was reserved for Tucker Loudon. Did he have to do this? Was money so important to him that he had to smuggle, turn to crime, consort with the likes of Shaw and Clayton? Wasn't her love enough? Couldn't he have found happiness with her? Apparently not. What a fool she was, trusting him, believing him, giving herself to a scoundrel. He didn't love her; he never had. All he cared about was his precious shipment and gold. But she had been so lonely, so hungry for him. She had played right into his hands.

Despite her distress, Gretchen knew she must think. Tuck had said wagons were coming in the morning and all this would be taken away. Over her dead body! She would find some way to stop it. But she didn't have much time. Agitated now, full of determination, she started for the cave entrance.

She never got there.

"My, ain't we the nosy one."

The sight of Shaw and Clayton standing at the entrance, leering at her, filled her with fear that even her anger couldn't overcome. "I—I wasn't . . . doing . . . anything."

Shaw moved toward her. "'Course ya warn't. Just out fer a li'l stroll, was ya?"

She stood there a moment, frozen with terror. Then she panicked. She tried to run past them, but it was no use. Shaw's big arm encircled her waist and lifted her off her feet. His beefy hand over her mouth stifled her screams.

Chapter Seventeen

TUCK HAD TRIED to sleep, but managed only to lie down and rest. His mind was too full of plans and worries. Repeatedly and in endless detail he went over the plans for the morning. The wagons were only a few miles outside Holyoke. Hopkins, Waring, and Pemberton were in Springfield, prepared to ride to Holyoke with the payment in gold.

In his mind's eye Tuck visualized the scene: the sturdy wagons parking beside the inn, the crates, barrels, and the rest of the shipment being carried from the cave, up the steps, and loaded into the wagons, covered with hay and straw. Shaw, Clayton, and their men would do most of the work.

Shaw and Clayton would be suspicious, on guard against any monkey business. But there was nothing they could do. The deal was that payment would be made only when the wagons were loaded. What if Hopkins, Waring, and Pemberton refused to pay? No, that couldn't happen. They wouldn't live to tell about it. His plan was foolproof. Tuck was sure of it.

The biggest problem was Gretchen. Somehow he had to convince her to remain inside the inn, tending to her chores, paying no attention to what was going on outside. Up until now he had managed to distract her himself—with pleasure—but tomorrow his presence would be needed outside. He didn't want her even to step outside, and he counted on the presence of Hopkins and Waring to encourage that. She wanted nothing to do with either man.

Gretchen! Thank God this was about to be over. But then what? Could he expect her to understand and forgive him? And if she did, what kind of life could he offer her? She might not want it, and he could not blame her for that.

To avoid such black thoughts, Tuck got up earlier than he needed to, made himself some strong coffee, and proceeded to dress. Actually he put on two sets of clothes. The first had not been worn in some time, and it felt strange to see himself so attired. Once he had taken such pride in himself. Now, strangely, he wasn't so sure. Would Gretchen approve of him? He wished he could be certain of that. Over the first suit he donned his familiar attire. Somehow he felt more comfortable in it.

Before dawn he saddled up and rode several

miles. He knew the way and the darkness did not bother him, except to force him to ride more slowly. Light was just breaking when he approached a group of riders in a wooded area, reined in his horse, and touched the brim of his hat.

"Good morning, Loudon. Is everything ready at your end?"

"As ready as it's ever going to be. I anticipate no problems."

"Good. We're all set"—he chuckled—"for our grand entrance."

Tuck nodded, then counted heads. "Is this all your men?"

"Hardly. The others are behind us, breaking camp. There'll be fifteen of us, enough to handle anything that comes up."

"Good. Do you know the way?"

"We traversed it yesterday. We'll be johnny-on-the-spot."

"I hope so. Timing is everything. You must arrive just after the gold changes hands, not before."

"I understand perfectly, Loudon. We will not fail you."

"I'm sure not." He smiled. "Very well. I shall see you shortly." With that, Tuck spurred his horse and road away at greater speed than he had come.

Timothy Wolf, also on horseback, was awaiting him outside the inn. He dismounted when Tuck did, and both men tethered their horses to the rail. Then Tuck reached over and opened the collar of

Wolf's coat. "I see you're dressed for the occasion."

"I am, indeed. It feels good to put it on again, doesn't it?"

"Yes, it does." Tuck wished he really believed that.

"Everything's going just as we planned."

Tuck gave a small smile. "Not if you keep talking that way, Tim."

The burly barkeep grinned widely. "Whatcha mean? Is thar somethin' wrong 'bout the way I speak the king's English?" Now he laughed. "I've been talking that fool lingo so long, I'm starting to believe it's natural to me."

"Well, keep it up a while longer, hear? You know what you're supposed to do?"

"Yes, sir. I's to hep 'em blokes carry that stuff inta the wagons, keepin' my eye on 'em all the while."

"And one more thing. If Gretchen should come outside while I'm not around, be sure to get her back inside and out of the way."

"Gotcha. I won't let nothin' happen to yer lass, Tuck." Timothy Wolf teased. "Ya sure got it bad, donacha? Can't say I blames ya."

Gretchen had never been more uncomfortable in her life. She was bound hand and foot, with stout rope, her arms behind her back. And the bonds were too tight, making her extremities numb. Even worse was the gag. Something dirty had been shoved into her mouth, then another cloth tied around that. She was lucky to be able to breathe at all.

Shaw had thrown her into the hold of his ship, which Gretchen knew was moored at the wharf. She lay amid rope, canvas, and she didn't know what else. The door had been shut and barred, leaving her in total darkness—and misery. The space was too small for her even to sit up, leaving her to lie there in great discomfort.

But that was as nothing compared to her fear. What was going to happen to her? She had no idea, except that it would be horrible. Shaw had ripped open her blouse and chemise and fondled her breasts—uttering vile comments all the while—but he had not gone any further than that. Apparently the presence of Clayton, an even bigger man, inhibited him, for Clayton kept saying there wasn't time for that now. Shaw reluctantly agreed—for the moment, anyway—saying, "Yer gonna git yers, just as I promised. No person alive takes a stick to Buck Shaw."

She lay there in the dark, trying to control her terror. What good would it do? She was utterly helpless, almost unable to move, a prisoner of two men who could and would do whatever they wanted to her. She could not prevent it—even if death came. And surely it would. They would never dare let her escape.

And there was no one to help her. Tuck was their leader, one of them. Even if by some remote chance he did want to save her for himself, he couldn't. No one knew she had gone to the cave. No one knew where she was now. Bitter tears came to her eyes as she thought about Tuck. How could she have believed she loved him? What a mess she had made of everything. Who would want her now? Oh, what did it matter? She was never going to escape this.

She wept a little, then began to pray, asking God to forgive her and make her death painless. It was all she knew to do, and it did make her feel better.

Tuck had just gone down and opened the cave when Shaw and Clayton appeared. Both looked at him with hostility, but there was nothing novel in that. His relations with them had always been difficult. "The wagons will be here shortly. We might as well start carrying this stuff up the bluff. Are the other men coming?"

"They is, but I don' like it, not a'tall." Buck's voice was gruff. "If we load them wagons, whass to keep 'em from drivin' off before we gits paid?"

Tuck smiled. "I assume you are, Buck—Big John, too. I doubt if our so-called business partners are dumb enough to try not paying us."

"Still, it ain't right. They should pay us 'fore we load the wagons."

Now Tuck laughed. "Somehow I can't imagine that English fop, or even the others, carrying all this up that bluff."

"We'll do it affer we's paid."

"And you think they'll trust you any more than you do them? Look, I thought we had this settled. We load the wagon, then they pay. It's the way this sort of business is always done. They won't try any shenanigans, believe me."

Shaw hesitated, looking at Clayton for approval. "I guess it has to be, but them blokes better not try anythin' funny. I'll wring their necks."

"Which is precisely why they won't, my good man." Tuck laughed and pushed by them. "I'm going up and checking on the wagons."

"Say Tuck, when we's dun with all this, how's 'bout comin' down to my boat for a bit."

Tuck saw Buck reveal his yellow and brown teeth in what passed for a smile. "Be glad to, but why?"

"Oh, just a visit. Wanna show ya somethin'."

"Like what?"

"Ya'll see. Be real in t'ressin'."

Tuck knew exactly what Shaw had in mind—a bullet or a drowning, maybe both. "I can hardly wait, Buck."

When Tuck climbed back up the bluff, he saw the wagons circling the green, led by Wolf on horseback, preparing to pull up in front of the North Inn. There were four heavy wagons pulled by oxen and mules. He wondered what the drivers knew about all this and what they were being paid. Well, that information would come out later.

Now he entered the North Inn. Ruth Brown was industriously cleaning the tavern. "Is Gretchen up and about yet?"

The dark-skinned girl looked at him shyly. "She must be, for she's not here."

"Not here? Do you mean she's still in bed?"

"No, sir. She's not in her room, nor any of the rooms."

"The kitchen, then?"

"No, sir. I haven't seen her this morning. She must have gone out."

"Out where?" Tuck demanded.

"Don't know that, sir. Maybe the store—or for a walk. She does that sometimes."

Tuck was puzzled but there was nothing he could do about it. "Well, when she comes back, tell her this business out front will be over shortly. She might be wise to stay inside."

"I'll tell her," Ruth promised.

"And stay inside yourself," he added.

"Yes, sir."

Outside Tuck saw that a good bit of the material had been lugged up the bluff from the cave, but none had been placed in the wagons. Buck Shaw said, "I ain't movin' nuttin' more till I see the color o' gold."

There could be no disputing that. Where were Hopkins and the others? They could foul up everything. In a moment he saw them approaching on horseback, obviously taking their time. Tuck smiled with relief. "It looks like you're about to get your gold, Buck."

"I don' trust 'em. I wanna see it."

It seemed to take forever, but ultimately Hopkins, Waring, and Pemberton reined to a stop in front of them. "I thought you would have the wagons loaded by now."

Tuck looked up at Hopkins and smiled, masking his true feelings of intense dislike for the man. "We have a small problem, Sir Clive. It seems my compatriots would like to see the color of your gold."

"Not you, Loudon?"

"Oh, I thoroughly trust you gentlemen. I fear my companions don't share my view, however."

A small smile spread the peer's lips. "Very well. Show them your money, Waring."

The gaunt, hook-nosed Bostonian slowly slid a hand inside his coat and extracted a heavy purse, dangling it in front of them.

Buck Shaw's eyes lit with greed, but he said, "Fine-lookin' purse, Warin', but it ain't the right color."

Hopkins laughed. "I believe our esteemed friend here has in mind something with more glint to it. Show him, Waring." In a moment bright gold coins filled one of Waring's hands. "Is that the right color, gentlemen?" Hopkins asked.

Shaw gaped at it a moment. "Sure 'tis." He turned. "Load up them wagons, men."

"Hold it just one moment," Hopkins interjected. "What is good for the goose is good for the gander. Waring, be good enough to dismount and check the merchandise. We wouldn't want any errors in our purchases, would we?"

Now it was Tuck's turn to laugh. "I can't believe you really think we'd cheat you. Such distrust! What is the world coming to?"

As Waring dismounted and headed for the stack of smuggled goods, Hopkins remarked, "I'd hoped to encounter the lovely Miss North this morning."

"I'm afraid that won't be possible, Sir Clive."

"And why not?" Hopkins wanted to know.

"She's gone off somewhere this morning. An urgent errand, I understand."

"Too bad. A most comely lass, don't you agree?"

"Oh, quite." Behind him he heard Waring and Shaw raise their voices in argument. Tuck went over and asked what the problem was.

"This barrel of sugar has been opened. Some of the bolts of fabric, too. The goods are damaged," Waring asserted.

"Naw, they ain't. Ya kin see they ain't," Shaw disagreed.

Tuck inspected the merchandise. He was as surprised as Waring to see the tampering, but he also recognized Waring's ploy to drive the price down. "I agree with Mr. Shaw. Nothing is damaged, as you can see for yourself."

"Then why were these things opened?"

Tuck was ready with a quick answer, if not a truthful one. "As you can imagine, Mr. Waring, we wanted to inspect the goods ourselves. Wouldn't want to cheat you gentlemen. We were satisfied, as I'm sure you must be." He turned to Clayton. "Seal up that barrel and those bolts, then put them on the wagons. Enough of this folderol." Drawing Shaw aside, Tuck murmured, "Who opened that stuff?"

"Dunno."

It seemed to Tuck that Shaw was rather hesitant and evasive. "Well, somebody surely did."

"One o' the men musta checked to see what was there, like ya said."

Tuck accepted this explanation because he had no other choice, but it struck him that Shaw knew more than he was saying.

The loading of the wagons proceeded with a lot of grunts and swearing. Timothy Wolf supervised, seeing that the weight was approximately equal on each wagon and balanced for proper transport. But it seemed to Tuck to take a long time, and that made him nervous. He glanced frequently across the green to the woods beyond the village. The men should be there by now, but he could catch no sight of them. Just as well. If he saw them, others might also. Surely they were there and well hidden. They'd better be.

Hopkins, who had dismounted, wanted to go into the tavern for a rum. Tuck knew he had to keep him very much in sight. "They're cleaning up the place, Sir Clive. I'll fetch you a rum—join you myself." He hurried away before Hopkins could protest. Inside he learned that Gretchen still had not returned. How very strange. Where could she have gone?

He emerged from the inn carrying two rums, a stiff one for Hopkins, a small one for himself. Even that he didn't intend to drink. He wanted a clear head.

"It's been a pleasure doing business with you, Loudon."

"And profitable," Tuck rejoined. He glanced at Hopkins, although his mind was elsewhere. His stomach roiled with nervous anticipation and worry—that something might yet go wrong, that

Gretchen might show up at the worst moment and ruin everything.

"Profitable, indeed. We should do this again soon."

Tuck forced a smile. "You off-load the goods from your ships. We'll bring it upriver anytime you want."

"As long as I bring the gold," Hopkins chortled. "Let's see how this business turns out first."

Now Tuck's smile was more genuine. "What could possibly go wrong?"

He turned away and went to inspect the wagons. The last of the contraband had been carried up the steps and was being put aboard. Now hay and straw was spread over the top.

"That does it, gents. Pay up." Shaw was nothing if not eager.

"All in good time, my man." Hopkins ambled over, joined by Waring and Pemberton, to inspect the wagons. They seemed to have all the time in the world. "This hay and straw should be tied down with ropes. It's a long journey. Can't have it sliding off en route."

Shaw swore his indignation, but Tuck said, "Good thinking, Sir Clive. Shaw, you and your men get at it. It will only take a minute."

It took longer than that, but soon the loads were secure. Shaw's voice was highly belligerent as he pronounced, "'Nuff lalligaggin'. Pay us whatcha owe—now!"

Hopkins casually mounted his horse, then looked down, an insipid smile on his face. "My, but you're impatient, Mr. Shaw." He turned to his companion. "Very well, Waring, give them their money."

Tuck was aware of Shaw's hand thrust out toward Waring, but his attention was focused on the woods in the distance. *Now! Come now!*

"The deal was with Loudon. He accepts the money. What he does with it is his affair."

Waring's words intruded on Tuck's thoughts, but he recovered in time. "Right you are, Waring." He extended his hand and felt the heavy pouch fall into it.

Hopkins raised his voice. "All right, wagons, let's move."

Tuck glanced toward the woods in desperation. "Hold it a minute, Hopkins. We count the money first, don't we, men?" Shaw quickly agreed and grabbed hold of the bridle of Hopkins's horse. Clayton did the same to Waring's.

"I assure you the tally is correct, Loudon."

Tuck bowed politely. "I've no doubt, Sir Clive. But one cannot be too careful, can one?"

Desperate to gain time, Tuck began to open the drawstring of the purse. He reached inside and pulled out a gold coin. *Where were they?* He slipped the coin between his teeth and bit down. "It's gold, all right, men. His Majesty's finest gold sovereign."

Shaw's eyes were bright, but he was consumed with impatience. "Count 'em, blast ya."

"I am, I am." Stalling for as much time as he could, Tuck began to count, calling Timothy over to hold some of the coins. "I count twenty gold sovereigns, men, each containing one hundred

thirteen grains of His Majesty's gold." He grinned.
"I think you could say we're all rich, men."

Shaw was beside himself. He let go of Hopkins's
horse and reached out greedily for the coins. Tuck
pulled away. "They're not all yours, Shaw."

"Then divide it up now," Shaw demanded.

"Good idea." Moving as slowly as he could,
Tuck counted. "I get a quarter share." He stuck
five coins in his pocket, then dumped the remain-
ing fifteen back into the purse and closed it. "You
pay off your men as you see fit, Shaw." He tossed
the purse toward him.

Hopkins said, his voice dry, "Now may we
leave?"

Tuck knew he'd lost. All his work had been in
vain. But what had gone wrong? His mind raced
for some excuse to delay them, but he could think
of nothing. What was the use? He had failed.
Dejected, he glanced again toward the woods. To
his relief he saw horsemen burst from the trees at
full gallop. He smiled up at Hopkins. "I doubt if
you're going anywhere, Sir Clive."

"What do you mean?"

The sound of the horses was his answer. They
all turned. It a thrilling sight—a dozen soldiers at
full gallop, sabers glistening in the sun.

"Redcoats!" someone shouted.

"Let's get outta here," said another.

As the men scattered Tuck tried to stop Shaw,
but the big man shoved him aside, knocking him
to the ground like a rag doll as he dashed for the
steps. Despite his greater girth, Timothy had no
better luck with Clayton. From the ground, Tuck

shouted, "Stop! In the King's name, stop!" It did no good. First Clayton, then Shaw bolted down the steps. Tuck got to his feet, ran to the top of the steps, and extracted his pistol. It took a moment to insert the cartridge and powder. He took careful aim, for he had only one shot. Shaw and Clayton were more than halfway down the steps when he pulled the trigger. Shaw seemed to stagger a little, but both men kept running. Damn!

"Captain Loudon!"

He turned to see Major Henry Dalton, his superior. "I've got to go for those two," Tuck said.

"Let them be. We'll get them later."

Chapter Eighteen

GRETCHEN THOUGHT SHE heard a commotion, then a shot, but it was so far away she wasn't sure. Now she heard heavy footsteps, men running, a sudden sway of the boat, then the raised, angry voices of Shaw and Clayton. After a moment she felt the boat move. They were floating downriver. Oh God, where were they taking her?

She lay quiet—what else could she do?—listening to the voices from on deck. Shaw was cursing heartily and he seemed to groan in pain a lot. She heard the words *blood* and *ball*. Was he wounded? She had heard a shot. Then came Clayton's voice, saying something about "digging it out," followed by huge bellows of pain, finally ending in quiet. This was most ominous of all to

Gretchen. Where were they going? What would happen to her?

Waring and Pemberton, not very good horsemen, were easily caught and captured. Clive Hopkins made a spirited run for it, but even he was no match for the king's cavalry. He was brought back in bonds to stand with his associates, glowering at Tuck, who had removed his outer garb and now stood resplendent in full uniform.

"I knew there was something fishy about you, Loudon," Hopkins spat. "I didn't know you were dealing in fish, Sir Clive," Tuck replied. "I don't believe you'd be in quite so much trouble if you were."

"You won't get away with this, you bloody bastard. I've friends in high places."

"Which we trust you will tell us all about. It may make things go easier for you." He turned to Waring. "The same goes for you, my romantic friend."

Waring was cowed, nearly quivering with fear. "I'm innocent. I-I just followed John North's orders."

Tuck raised an eyebrow doubtfully. "Tell us all about it, Waring. I'm sure it's fascinating."

Waring got no chance to reply, for Major Dalton joined them, saying, "All in good time, Captain. Right now the important thing is to get these men to Springfield, where there is a proper jail." Now he chuckled. "It was very good of you to have this contraband loaded on wagons, Sir Clive. It makes it much easier for us to move it."

"You can't seize it," Hopkins protested hotly.

"I already have, Sir Clive—in the king's name, of course."

"I planned to pay customs on it."

"A little late, my friend," Tuck said. "I am very much a witness to what you planned to do."

"Enough." Dalton turned and barked orders for his men to get the wagons and the prisoners moving. Then he turned back to Tuck. "Good work, Captain. I'm sure there'll be a commendation for you, perhaps even a promotion."

"Thank you, sir, but it isn't finished. Most of the locals got away."

"I figure they're small fry."

"That's true for most, sir. They probably didn't know what was going on, just earning a few bob. But Buck Shaw and John Clayton are key to this whole smuggling operation. They'll try it again. I want to go after them." He saw doubt on his superior's face. "I've an idea where they might have gone, Major," he continued. "If Sergeant Wolf and I move quickly, I think we can catch up with them."

"I need you in Springfield, Tuck, when we go before the magistrate."

"It will take you most of the day to get these wagons to Springfield. They're heavy and you'll have to move slowly. Give Timothy and me a day. We'll meet you in Springfield tomorrow, regardless of what happens."

Dalton looked at him querulously. "Your dedication is admirable, Captain, but is that your only reason for staying behind?"

Tuck hesitated. "Not quite, sir," he admitted. "The proprietress of this inn seems to be missing. I want to make sure she's all right."

"And tell her you're a British officer working incognito—not a scalawag smuggler as you seemed."

He grinned bashfully. "Something like that."

"Very well, Captain. Do what you must, but I expect to see you in Springfield at midday tomorrow."

Tuck watched him ride off, quickly catching up with the slow-moving wagons.

"Do you really know where Shaw and Clayton went?" Wolf asked.

Tuck turned to Wolf, and clapped him on the back. "No, I don't, but if I wounded Shaw with my shot, they can't go far. They'll have to stop somewhere between here and the rapids. Maybe we can find their boat."

"Good thinking."

"Let's hope so. They may head inland, probably to the west. We'll need horses. Take ours down to the wharf and commandeer that ferry. It's the only craft at hand."

"The ferryman won't like that, Tuck."

"Tell him he'll be paid. Take the horses aboard and wait till I get there. Shouldn't be long."

Tuck left him and hurried back into the inn, worry gnawing at him steadily. "Gretchen back yet?"

The sloe-eyed cleaning girl answered, "Not yet, sir."

"Where in blazes can she have gone? Have you checked her room?"

"Yes, sir, more than once. She's not there." Ruth Brown hesitated. "I'm worried, Mr. Loudon. It doesn't look as though she slept there all night."

"Good God!" Tuck grabbed the keys and raced up to Gretchen's room. It was neat and tidy, the bed made, the chamber pot unused. She hadn't been there all night. Panic rose in him, but he forced himself to look around carefully, hoping she might have left a note or some clue to where she was going. But there was nothing.

He bolted downstairs and questioned Ruth Brown again. "She said nothing to you about where she was going?"

"No, sir. I haven't seen her since yesterday noon."

He burst into the kitchen and confronted Molly Dugan. "Have you seen Gretchen this morning?"

"I ain't seen nobody. Too busy," Molly snapped.

"Any idea where she might have gone?"

"Nope. Got my own problems. Somebody stole my best knife. How'm I gonna cut meat wit'out it?"

Tuck swore under his breath. "Well, somebody must know where she is." He ran through the tavern and outside, looking across the green and around the village for some sign of her. Then he saw Miles Burnett, stumbling out of the stable, holding his head. Apparently, he had been so drunk he slept through all the commotion. "Have you seen Gretchen North?"

"Wha'?" he mumbled.

Tuck grabbed the small man's shoulders, shook him hard. "Gretchen. Do you know where she went?"

Miles's answer was a loud groan of pain. "Lemme be. I don't know nuttin'."

Tuck shoved him aside and ran to Follen's store. All he encountered was surprise at the sight of him in his red uniform. They knew nothing of Gretchen. Desperate now, he even ran to his own home, hoping she might have gone there for some reasons. She hadn't.

He stormed outside, looking frantically up and down the street. His first thought was to have Timothy return with the horses and begin a search of the area. But search where? Gretchen simply would not have wandered off somewhere. She knew the wagons were coming. She had been very interested. Suddenly he realized he was thinking more calmly. Yes, she had to be somewhere, and he ought to be able to figure it out. Racing around like a madman was not helping a bit.

Walking back toward the inn, he remembered the last time he'd seen her. She'd told him she'd found the cave. She had suspected what was in it, and even accused him of being a smuggler. He thought he'd convinced her he wasn't. But what if he hadn't? Could she have gone back to the cave? He shook his head. No. He'd been to the cave himself this morning. She hadn't been there. but could she have gone last night? Maybe her body was lying behind the cartons. Maybe she'd fallen down the cliff!

Running now, he reached the top of the steps and bolted downward, unmindful of his peril. He searched the cliff below for the body but found nothing. Now he turned into the path and entered the cave. The canvas had been removed and he could see the interior clearly. Gretchen was not there.

But he did see something else. He bent to pick it up. It was a large knife—probably the one that was missing from the kitchen of the inn. Suddenly he remembered—the opened keg, the slit bolts of fabric. Gretchen must have come here last night and used the knife to see for herself what was hidden here. Damn!

Then a new, more agonizing memory came to him—Shaw's inviting him to his boat, grinning like a cheshire cat.

Frantic now, Tuck raced down to the wharf and jumped on the ferry. "Let's go!" he called to Wolf. "Shaw's got Gretchen with him!"

The noise of the door to the hold opening jolted Gretchen from her half-conscious state. In an instant she was blinded by a sudden shaft of light. In horror she realized Clayton was climbing down to her. Oh, God, it was going to happen now.

"Ya gotta hep Buck," Clayton grunted.

Gretchen managed to open her eyes enough to see a knife in Clayton's hand. She tried to scream, but made only a squealing noise as she tried to move away from him.

"I ain't gonna hurtcha—not now, anyways."

Then she realized the knife was to cut her bonds. The tug at her ankles brought blessed relief, and when the knife cut through the ropes at her wrists, a sharp tingling came to her hands. But she had little chance for her circulation to return, as Clayton roughly took her arm and pulled her after him up the steps to the deck.

The sunlight was blinding. Gretchen sucked in the fresh air. It was heavenly after her confinement. At length she could open her eyes. They were floating downriver.

"Buck's hurt. Take care o' him, hear?"

She saw him then. He was lying on the deck on his back, shirtless. Blood oozed from a nasty black hole in his right shoulder. He was groaning. The sight made Gretchen squeamish, and she backed away.

"G'wan, do it, 'fore I beltcha good," Clayton threatened.

She raised her hands to remove the gag.

"Let it be. Ya don't need to talk."

But she persisted, removing the binding, then taking the horrid rag from her mouth.

"If ya scream, ya'll join the fishes," the big man warned.

She shook her head hard, for her mouth was so dry she couldn't speak. Seeing the open water barrel, she pointed, pleading with her eyes. Clayton let her go and she stumbled to the barrel on wooden legs and stuck her face into the water. It tasted dreadful, but Gretchen was too parched to care. Greedily she drank great gulps of water.

"'Nuff. Take care o' Buck," Clayton growled.

She drank a little more, then stood up, wiping the water from her face with her fingers. Again she looked around. The shore looked familiar. Yes, she had seen those rocks from the canoe, that day she'd spent with Tuck.

"Ya better not try to jump o'erboard."

She had indeed been thinking of it. "I won't. I can't swim."

Shaw emitted another loud groan, prompting Clayton to say, "Tend to Buck."

He shoved Gretchen toward the wounded man, but she went only a couple of steps. "I don't know what to do."

"Sure ya does. All women do."

He jerked her by the arm until she stood over the prone figure. "What happened to him?" she asked.

"That bloody Loudon shot him."

"Tuck?" She was incredulous. "But how?"

"He's a damned turncoat, that's what he is. But it don't matter none, as long as we keeps movin'. Fix him up."

Clayton twisted her arm, forcing her to her knees beside Shaw. He opened his eyes, looked at her, and made a growling sound. His eyes were still full of hate, but they were also glazed with pain now. Gretchen felt a kind of pity. Timorously she reached a hand toward the wound.

"What do you want me to do? Is the bullet still in him?"

"I dug it out. Bandage him. Stop the bleedin'."

She swallowed hard and looked up at Clayton. "I'll need some cloths of some kind."

That seemed to stymie him for a moment, then he kicked Buck's bloody shirt toward her. "Use that."

She picked it up gingerly, for it was incredibly filthy. But it was all she had. She began to tear it in strips, while her mind raced with possibilities, trying to understand what had happened. Tuck had wounded him. That must have been the shot she'd heard. But why? Why was Tuck shooting at Shaw if they were working together?

It came almost as a physical blow. Buck's big hand, his good left one, clamped to her jaw, squeezing her cheeks hard. There was pure malice in his eyes. "Yer gonna get it, wench."

"Leave her be, Buck. We gotta think what to do."

Buck held her a moment longer, intensifying the pressure, then shook her quite viciously. "Yer gonna wish ya was dead."

Clayton reached down and gripped his wrist. "Let go, Buck, so she kin fix yer wound."

Slowly, reluctantly, giving a deep, evil growl, Buck released her. "Gimme some rum."

Clayton brought a dipperful. Buck swallowed some, then poured the rest over his open wound, bellowing from the pain. She thought he had fainted again, but apparently not, for he barked, "Now tie iddup."

She began the task, folding the cleanest part of the shirt over the wound, then winding strips of the cloth around his shoulder and arm as tightly as she could.

"We's gotta get off this river, Buck. Them redcoats'll find us, sure as hell."

Gretchen blinked. Redcoats? What was he talking about?

"I knows," Shaw agreed.

"Kin ya walk?"

"Not fer 'nuff." He grunted under Gretchen's ministrations. "We needs horses."

"'At ain't easy, Buck."

"I knows." Again he groaned. "Dammit, wench, ya's hurtin' me."

She wasn't making any particular effort to be gentle. "You want the bleeding to stop, don't you?"

"Hey, what 'bout ol' Pinkie? He got horses, don't he?"

"Mules, anyway. But he wouldn't give 'em up."

"We's got gold. We kin buy 'em."

Gretchen rose and moved away. "That's the best I can do, Mr. Shaw." But she didn't move far enough or quick enough, for Shaw's good hand shot out again, this time gripping her ankle tightly. His face spread into a yellow leer.

"Maybe we won't haf to buy 'em. We's got somethin' to trade."

Clayton laughed wickedly. "If I know ol' Pinkie, he'll love her. Ya hold on ta her. I'll work the tiller."

* * *

The ferry was little more than a log raft with a small shed on top. It was slung to a heavy rope and guided back and forth across the river by a huge paddle. Once Tuck unhooked from the rope, it careened wildly downriver, leaving Timothy with the devil's own time trying to steer it even a little. Tuck had hoped to persuade the ferryman to come along to help. But he would have no part of it, and Tuck couldn't blame him.

Expending great energy, Timothy somehow managed to guide the raft close to the far bank, while Tuck quieted the skittery horses—they didn't like the ride at all—and kept a sharp eye on both shores. He was looking for Shaw's boat. They'd probably tie it up to shore, maybe hiding it under some trees. His guess was that it would be on the far shore so Clayton and Shaw could head west, but he couldn't be certain of that.

His hope for an early discovery soon faded. Minutes dragged agonizingly by, and he was consumed with worry about what they might do to Gretchen. If he didn't catch up to them soon, he would be too late. He watched the riverbanks constantly, concentrating as hard as he could, but saw nothing. He must have missed them. They couldn't have gone this far. The rapids weren't far away. They'd best go ashore with the horses and try to pick up a trail.

"There it is!"

Tuck turned to where Timothy pointed. The boat was hidden coming downriver, but clearly visible when seen from below. "Let's go. Mount up, Tim!"

"What about the raft?"

"The king will buy him a new one. Come."

He waited only a moment for Wolf to jump on his horse, then both leaped into the water. The horses were glad to be off the spinning raft. The water was deeper than Tuck expected, and the horses had to swim some distance before finding footing. But both made it ashore safely. At once Tuck went back to where Shaw's boat was.

Wolf dismounted and examined the ground, finally declaring, "Three sets of footprints, Tuck, two big and heavy, one smaller and lighter."

"That has to be Gretchen. Which way did they head?"

Timothy bent to his task, scanning the ground closely for a few yards. "One of the men and the woman—Gretchen I guess—went on ahead. The other man's following behind, but slower. Seems to stop often. He's dragging his feet or lurching."

"That has to be Shaw. I did wing the bastard. Mount up! Let's go after them."

Gretchen had hoped to jump overboard and run through the woods as soon as the boat touched shore. It was her only chance. But it was not to be. Shaw held tightly to her wrists while Clayton piloted the craft to shore and tied it to a tree. Then Clayton came to her, a wide, malicious grin on his bearded face. "Thinkin' o' makin' a run fer it, are ya? Fat chance o' that. Big John's too smart fer ya."

He tied her hands behind her back, leaving a long tether which he tied around his waist. Then he looked at her and laughed. "Where I goes, you goes, dearie."

There was no path; they simply set out through the woods. Branches whipped Gretchen's face and body, and painful briars and thorns tore her clothing and bloodied her skin. The area was infested with mosquitoes and gnats. With her hands tied she could only endure the bites.

Gretchen felt like a slave being led to auction—and painfully so. Clayton was in a hurry, and he set off through the woods at a vigorous pace, leaving Shaw to lumber after them as best he could. Gretchen had to run just to keep up with him, which was difficult with her arms tied behind her back. She stumbled and fell often, scraping her knees and shins, and each time she fell it brought a painful jerking on the tether, until she felt her arms would be pulled from their sockets.

She had no idea how long the trek went on. She knew only that she had never been more tired, winded, and miserable in her life. Her thoughts were heavy with despair. There was no hope for her.

Finally they burst into a small clearing. Gretchen saw a ramshackle log cabin with smoke puffing from the stone chimney, a corral with two scrawny horses and a mule, and lots of hides drying on wooden racks. Gretchen knew it must be a trapper's home.

"Hey, Pinkie, is ya here?" Clayton bellowed. When there was no answer, he added, "It's Big

John and ol' Buck come to visit ya. Gotta s'prise fer ya."

Finally the door opened and a figure of a man appeared in the doorway. He was carrying a hunting rifle. Gretchen gasped in revulsion, for the person was more apparition than man. She could see why they called him Pinkie, for he had a huge, misshapen head, devoid of hair, that was a rosy pink color. Dressed in hides, his body was heavy, with a burly chest and shoulders and the longest, meatiest arms she had ever seen. She almost couldn't bear to look at the man's face, for one bulging eye was lower than the other, and his thick lips drooped to one side. He had no nose, just two holes in the center of his face.

"That you, Big John?" His voice was guttural, coming from deep inside him, and almost unintelligible. Drool began to form in his mouth almost at once.

"Sure 'tis, Pinkie. Ol' Buck, too." Gretchen turned to look. Shaw had just broken into the clearing behind them.

"Whatcha want?" Pinkie made a step outside his door, but still clutched his rifle. Clearly he was suspicious of people.

"Buck's been shot, Pinkie, as ya kin see. He's hurt bad, can't make it far on foot. We needs a coupla horses."

The grotesque figure glanced at his animals protectively and clutched his rifle tighter. "Nope. Need's my horses."

"Make ya a real good deal, Pinkie." Grinning,

Clayton came to Gretchen and gripped her shoulder. "Trade ya this here woman fer yer horses."

Gretchen gasped in horror. He couldn't be serious!

"Ya always said how offen ya wished ya had a woman, Pinkie. Gotta real good'un fer ya." He twisted her neck around. "Betcha ne'er saw such hair. Like gold, 'tis." He shoved her toward the gnomelike man. "Real purty, ain't she? Take a good look, Pinkie."

Gretchen said a silent prayer as the man fixed his bulging blue eyes on her. He seemed to take the longest time to look her over. Finally she found her voice. "No, please, I—"

"Too skinny," Pinkie declared.

"Whatcha talkin' 'bout?" Shaw had come up beside her. "Take a good look." In one quick motion, using his left hand, he ripped open her torn dress and chemise, exposing her breasts. He gripped one tightly. "E'er see the like o' them thar?"

Gretchen could only stand there, shaking all over in revulsion, as the grotesque eyes leered at her in what she knew was lust.

"Make ya a real good woman, Pinkie," Clayton continued. "Ya ain't ne'er gonna get a woman like this here one."

Pinkie seemed to appraise her for a long time, drool spinning a long thread from his lip. Finally, he made up his mind. "No horses. Just the mule."

"Aw, c'mon, Pinkie," Buck protested. "She's worth more'n a mule."

Clayton shoved her toward him again. "Take a good look. Feel how soft she is."

To Gretchen's horror, Pinkie reached out a hand toward her, his eyes fixed on her breasts. Then slowly, he withdrew it. "Nope. Just a mule."

Shaw and Clayton argued with him, but he remained adamant. They had no choice but to agree. "Ya drives a hard bargain, Pinkie, but we's no choice." Shaw turned to her and spat. "I knewed ya warn't much. Only worth a mule."

Clayton shoved her toward the woodsman, pushing her hard, and she fell to the ground. "She's all yers, Pinkie. Take good care o' her, hear?" Laughing, Clayton untied the tether and headed for the corral with Buck.

Gretchen lay facedown on the ground, as if embracing it for protection. Then all her accumulated pain, dread, and confusion overwhelmed her and she began to sob, wailing out her desperation with the last of her energy.

So loud were her cries she did not hear the horses' hooves, but rather felt their vibrations from the ground. Then came shots and shouts. She half raised herself and through blurry eyes saw two men on horseback, wearing red coats, charging the corral. Buck fell where he stood, but Clayton ran into the woods, one red-coated horsemen after him. What was going on? Then in a moment she heard another gunshot, then a terrible bellow of pain. What did it matter? All was lost for her. New sobs tore at her throat, and she collapsed against the ground.

In a moment she heard, "God, Gretchen! Am I

in time?" Suddenly her hands were free and she was pulled to a sitting position, held within strong arms.

A face swam in her vision. "Tuck?"

"Yes, my darling. You're safe now."

His hands stroked her hair and wiped the tears and dirt from her face. She looked up and saw Timothy Wolf, also in a red uniform, holding the woodsman, whose hands were raised above his head as he blubbered his terror. She looked back at Tuck, shaking her head. "I don't . . . understand."

He held her close. "Let's go home. I'll explain everything, my darling."

Chapter Nineteen

WITH THE RESILIENCY of youth, Gretchen's cuts and bruises healed quickly—her spirits, too, although she still trembled occasionally at the thought of what almost happened to her. To her mind, the grotesque Pinkie had become more pathetic than menacing. He had not harmed her, and she was glad Tuck had let him go in peace. Buck Shaw and John Clayton did not share in her compassion. Both were dead, and she did not mourn them.

Tuck and Timothy had taken her back to the inn in Shaw's boat, explaining to her all that had happened. She had been correct about the smuggling ring—but how very wrong she'd been about Tuck. Imagine, a captain in the army sent here to infiltrate and break up the smuggling ring. She should have seen it, but he'd been so clever in his lies to her. Perhaps a greater surprise was the discovery that Timothy Wolf was a sergeant in the army. On the boat his accent and menacing manner disappeared, replaced by laughter and friendliness. She'd found herself liking him at once.

Tuck had returned her to the inn, told Meg Gwynne and the Browns to look after her, then ridden off, saying he had to finish with this business. Gretchen had not seen or heard from him since.

Gretchen rested a good bit of the first day after her rescue, then rose and tried to operate the inn. It was difficult, for she suddenly lacked a barkeep. How useful Timothy had been, and she hadn't appreciated it. She and Meg took turns running the taps and serving and somehow managed.

It soon became apparent to Gretchen that a change had occurred. At first she thought it was just the absence of Shaw, Clayton, and their friends, but it was more than that, for most of the regulars remained. Much of the loudness and lewdness were gone, although there were still plenty of laughter and fun. The patrons, she finally realized, were treating her with new respect and courtesy. She overheard people talking about her, recounting her adventure in rather exaggerated terms. It hadn't been that dangerous, after all, she told herself now. She had a sense of people bragging that they knew her and speaking to her with affection. Best of all, Bill Follen came in for an ale with some of the men from the village. Ezra

Brown even put in an appearance. Was she being accepted at last?

Her answer was not long in coming. The next day Esther Follen greeted her warmly in the store, and the other women approached her and said how much they appreciated what she'd done— cleaning out that nest of thieves. She was even asked to join the quilting bee. And at church that Sunday the sermon was on courage in the face of adversity. Best of all, lodgers—proper lodgers— began to stop for dinner and the night.

It was midafternoon of the fifty day when Tuck returned. Gretchen had missed him, but she had accepted the fact that he wasn't coming back this day, when there he was, just inside the door, looking at her as she stood behind the counter at the cash drawer.

"You're back—obviously." She smiled, then laughed at her stupid observation.

"Sorry I was gone so long. Had to go to Boston." He stepped toward her. "How are you feeling?"

"Better. Good as new, in fact." She studied him. How handsome he was in his red tunic. "I like you in your uniform." She felt suddenly shy.

He had hesitated about wearing it, but it was a fact between them. He was a British officer. "Sorry I had to deceive you about who I am."

"You said that before. I understand—now. What happened?"

He was at the counter opposite her. She wore only a simple blouse and skirt, but she was beautiful to him, all golden hair and blue eyes. Her scent was almost hypnotizing. "Hopkins is on his way to London. He faces charges of privateering and smuggling. The Crown will make him pay." Tuck hesitated. "I'm sorry I could not . . . protect you from him."

"You did the best you could. The others?"

"Waring and Pemberton face trial in Boston." He hesitated. "I'm sorry, but your uncle has been arrested and charged also. Waring couldn't stop talking, it seems."

His seriousness affected her. He really was sorry about her Uncle John. But strangely, she felt nothing. "I'm sure he will get only what he deserves."

"You don't care?"

"I should, I know," she said quietly. "But I do not." She paused. "Was my father a party to all this?"

"No." At her questioning look, he assured her, "I speak the truth. Your father had fallen into drunkenness. I wish I could spare you that, but I cannot. Yet he remained an honorable man. He had tried to control his drink, because—or so I believe—he thought you were coming. He truly loved you, Gretchen."

Her eyes misted. "Thank you."

"I believe he learned what was happening here—the smuggling. He was killed because of it."

"His own brother killed him!"

"In a round about way, I'm afraid so." He looked down at his hands. "I wish there was some way to spare you this, Gretchen, but I don't know how to. Winthrop North was rather late in learning of the smuggling—because of his condition. I'm sure Shaw, Clayton, and the others contributed to how much he drank, and deliberately so. They didn't want him to catch on to how he was being used."

"But he did learn?"

"Yes, and he tried to stop it. He was killed for it—taken downriver and drowned." He reached across the counter and gripped her trembling hand. "I'm sorry."

Her eyes filled with tears. "It's all right. It is enough to know that my father was not one of them."

"He was not. You may take pride in him, Gretchen." Tuck fished a handkerchief from inside his tunic and handed it to her. "Now you know why I tried to drive you away. If you discovered the smuggling—" He paused. "I was so afraid what happened to your father would also happen to you—and that I wouldn't be able to save you . . . any more than I was able to save your father."

She dabbed at her eyes, blew her nose, then came around the counter. Clasping her hands in back of his neck, she gazed at him a long moment. "Oh, Tuck, I misjudged you so."

"I wanted you to. I treated you shabbily."

"You were only doing your duty."

Her lips, so smooth and soft, were maddening to him. "I simply couldn't resist you. You are all I've ever wanted in a woman." He kissed her softly, but the sensation was wholly electric. "I love you, Gretchen." His voice was husky, barely audible. "I did not lie to you about that."

"I-I wanted . . . to believe you." She kissed

him then with far more passion, felt herself being immersed in it. "Oh, Tuck!"

"Can you love me now, after all the lies, knowing who I really am?"

Gretchen squeezed him tightly. "Yes."

"Can you love a British officer?"

She pulled her head back and smiled. "I can't imagine why not."

"I can. I've thought of nothing else." He pulled her hands away from his neck and strode away from her. "How can I ask for your hand, Gretchen? What have I to offer you but absence and poverty?"

"Yourself." But she realized how very serious he was. "Absence?"

"Yes. I serve at the command of others. Hopefully I will be posted somewhere here in America, but I cannot be sure of that. I could be returned to England—even sent to India, God knows where. Serving the king is sometimes hard."

"And you could be wounded—even killed." She looked at him most somberly. "I don't believe I'd like that."

"Nor I, certainly." He tried to smile, but not very successfully. "Oh, Gretchen, I cannot bear to be away from you."

Gretchen paused for a moment, then said, "Then I will accompany you wherever I can."

"You will give up all this?" He made a gesture. "The inn, all you're building here?"

"It is beginning to come along. I have hopes of its becoming profitable, but, yes, I will give it up for you."

"You would do that for me?"

Gretchen nodded. "For the man I love, yes."

Now his smile was broader and far more genuine. "I won't hear of it."

She was surprised. "And why not?" Relaxed now, he ambled behind the counter and began to pour himself an ale. "Who's going to be your bartender now that Timothy is gone? He sends his regards, by the way. I'm to tell you how much he enjoyed working with you."

"Where is he now?" Gretchen asked.

Gone to join His Majesty's troops at Fort Niagara. Oh, yes—he also said you are an excellent innkeeper, sure to make a success of this place." His mug full, he took a large draught. "He went so far as to add that I ought to remain here as your barkeep. You do need one, don't you?"

Gretchen was startled. "Yes, very much so."

"Well, then, I apply for the job."

"But you're in the army. You can't—"

"I'm thinking of resigning my commission. I like it out here. This is a new country, Gretchen. There's land to be had, good land. I was thinking of building a house, raising a family. A man has to settle down sometime, you know."

She saw a serious glint in his irresistible brown eyes, but still couldn't believe it. "Are you sure?"

"Never more. You aren't the only one willing to give up everything for love." His tone softened. "Actually, I'm not giving up much. I'm gaining everything I want."

She saw his arms stretched toward her, and she came around the counter to fill them.

**Don't miss the next sizzling novel in the THIR-
TEEN COLONIES series, FRONTIER ROGUE,
available from Dell in August.**

Fort Niagara
New York
1765

Thorn Durham strode through the woods with
markedly less caution than usual. What the hell
had ever possessed Victor to bring his daughter
with him? Damn the lack of communication between here and civilization!

Despite the worry crowding his mind, Thorn
became aware of an unusual sound among the
birds in the trees. He shook his head slightly. It
sounded like a woman singing by the pond where
the beavers had dammed the creek. But it couldn't
be. Careful not to make any noise, Thorn crept
toward the creek and parted the bushes lining it.
Good lord! Even *she* couldn't be that stupid! He
stared in amazement.

Chastity stood knee-deep in the clear water.
Granted, she still wore her chemise and panta-
loons, but they clung to her soaking-wet body,

outlining every chill bump, and other more sub-stantial curves, too. Surely she couldn't be naive enough to come out here alone—not with the situation between the British soldiers and the Iroquois the way it was.

If Pontiac and his men were to hear her voice, however lovely and melodious, the sound would soon change to screams of terror at their hands. Still, she had spirit, he had to admit. Thorn watched as Chastity vigorously worked the soap into her hair, suds running down her shapely body. Though partially hidden by the water, she was tall enough, he guessed, with long, shapely legs and a well-rounded bottom. She dipped slightly into the water, and a tremor ran through Thorn's lower body as the soap washed away and he saw her more clearly.

Thorn caught sight of a small stick swirling in the current a few feet from Chastity, and a wicked gleam came into his eyes. The stick floated closer to her, but Thorn bided his time until it bumped her, and then called out.

"Chastity! Snake!"

Chastity's scream split the air. Her eyes flew open, only to be engulfed by the soap suds run-ning down her face. Frantically, she scrubbed at her eyes and ducked her face under the water.

"The bath sheet! Jeremiah, the sheet!"

Jeremiah? The fool woman thought he was her servant! Well, he wasn't about to tell her otherwise—yet.

Chastity stumbled onto the bank and Thorn nonchalantly picked up the linen cloth she had left hanging on a bush and held it within reach of her groping hand.

Grabbing it, Chastity scrubbed at her face. When the burning in her eyes subsided somewhat, she blinked until she was able to focus. "You weren't supposed to be watching me, Jere . . ." She stopped short as she realized who he was. Then she glanced down at her figure, easily visible through the translucent went cotton that clung to her. Chastity could feel the heat rising to her cheeks as she sputtered, "What are *you* doing here!?"

Thorn leaned back against the tree and re-crossed his arms. "I guess I was saving you from a snake."

The nerve of the infuriating rogue! He wasn't going to get away with it. "The only snake I see is standing upright under that tree!" She wrapped the bath sheet around her and whirled away to where her clothes hung on another branch. Thorn's arm jerked her back.

"Let go of me!" Chastity tried to break free of his grasp, but it was too powerful.

Thorn grabbed her other arm and pushed her back against the tree. He dodged the kick she threw at him with her bare foot and held her firmly against the rough tree bark. Chastity struggled, but the cloth provided little protection against the bark and its rough edges bit into her skin. With a smirk, Thorn stepped closer and pressed his body against hers to still her. His raw strength made it impossible for her to move, despite her efforts.

"You're going to listen to me if I have to hold

you here all night!" Thorn spoke through gritted teeth now, both in an effort to get her attention and to ignore the tightening in his buckskin breeches that the scent of her soap and the feel of her body had stirred. He had to make a conscious effort to keep his fingers from stroking the silky skin under his hands.

"Get your bloody hands off me!" Again she tried to release herself.

"If the Indians had found you rather than me, you'd have a damned sight more to worry about than a man's *hands* on you! What the hell do you think you're doing out here?"

"What do *you* think I was doing? Obviously, I was bathing." Chastity spoke defiantly, focusing her blue eyes beyond his shoulder.

"I can see that much." Thorn's hands loosened somewhat and he moved an inch or so away from her. His dark gaze raked over her body. "Just tell me why you decided to come *here* and do it. Didn't your father explain the danger you'd be in?"

"You bastard!" Chastity took advantage of the small space between them. Her knee came up viciously, missing the aimed-for mark by just a hair—and then only because of Thorn's quick reaction. He jumped back, swearing, and his fury allowed her time to scrabble to where the rifles leaned against the tree. But he caught up to Chastity before she reached them and pulled her to the ground, close against him.

"You bastard!"

Thorn chuckled. "You've already used that word. Seems to me a *lady* of your breeding would have a larger vocabulary . . . and one not quite so unsavory!"

"My father will kill you!"

"What he *should* do is hold you over his lap and take a cane to you. If I *ever* catch you pulling a stupid stunt like this again, you can be sure I'll gladly perform that duty for him!" Thorn rolled away from her and rose to his feet. "Now, get your clothes back on so we can get out of here. God knows how many Iroquois you've drawn to this place with all that caterwauling you were making."

Chastity's anger rendered her voice useless. She leaped to her feet and grabbed her buckskin skirt from the bushes, then threw it back over the branch and waded into the water.

"What the hell are you doing?"

"Washing the soap out of my hair!"

Thorn let out an exasperated groan. He watched the surrounding woods for any signs of movement or threat, waiting until she emerged from the water again and wrapped the bath sheet around her.

Chastity saw him staring at her. "Turn around!" she commanded imperiously.

"Why?" he asked. There was a taunting look in his dark eyes. "I've already seen everything you've got to offer. And, might I add, most of it's fairly adequate."

She was not amused. "I said, turn around!"

Now it was Thorn's turn to get annoyed. "Let's get one more thing straight right here: You don't give the orders around here. I work for your father."

Chastity glowered at him, furious at the arrogant superiority in his voice. But even her anger couldn't quell the tingling awareness spreading through her body while his eyes scanned over her. Suddenly, a desperate desire to get into her clothing overcame her. Thorn's attitude made it plain he would stand there and watch her every move. Muttering an oath, she turned her back to him and threw off the bath sheet to begin pulling on her blouse. She would not look at him, but spoke to him over her shoulder, using a voice of cool authority. "And as I am his heir, you'll be working for me some day."

"I wouldn't count on that if I were you . . ."

FREE FROM DELL

with purchase plus postage and handling

Congratulations! You have just purchased one or more titles featured in Dell's Romance 1990 Promotion. Our goal is to provide you with quality reading and entertainment, so we are pleased to extend to you a limited offer to receive a selected Dell romance title(s) *free* (plus $1.00 postage and handling per title) for each romance title purchased. Please read and follow all instructions carefully to avoid delays in your order.

1) Fill in your name and address on the coupon printed below. No facsimiles or copies of the coupon allowed.

2) The Dell Romance books are the only books featured in Dell's Romance 1990 Promotion. Any other Dell titles are not eligible for this offer.

3) Enclose your original cash register receipt with the price of the book(s) circled plus $1.00 **per book** for postage and handling, payable in check or money order to: Dell Romance 1990 Offer. Please do not send cash in the mail.
Canadian customers: Enclose your original cash register receipt with the price of the book(s) circled plus $1.00 **per book** for postage and handling in U.S. funds.

4) This offer is only in effect until March 29, 1991. Free Dell Romance requests postmarked after March 22, 1991 will not be honored, but your check for postage and handling will be returned.

5) Please allow 6-8 weeks for processing. Void where taxed or prohibited.

Mail to: Dell Romance 1990 Offer
       P.O. Box 2088
       Young America, MN 55399-2088

NAME_____

ADDRESS_____

CITY_____STATE_____ZIP_____

BOOKS PURCHASED AT_____

AGE_____

(Continued)

Book(s) purchased: _____

_____

_____

I understand I may choose one free book for each Dell Romance book purchased (plus applicable postage and handling). Please send me the following:

(Write the number of copies of each title selected next to that title.)

MY ENEMY, MY LOVE
Elaine Coffman
From an award-winning author comes this compelling historical novel that pits a spirited beauty against a hard-nosed gunslinger hired to forcibly bring her home to her father. But the gunslinger finds himself unable to resist his captive.

AVENGING ANGEL
Lori Copeland
Jilted by her thieving fiancé, a woman rides west seeking revenge, only to wind up in the arms of her enemy's brother.

A WOMAN'S ESTATE
Roberta Gellis
An American woman in the early 1800s finds herself ensnared in a web of family intrigue and dangerous passions when her English nobleman husband passes away.

THE RAVEN AND THE ROSE
Virginia Henley
A fast-paced, sexy novel of the 15th century that tells a tale of royal intrigue, spirited love, and reckless abandon.

THE WINDFLOWER
Laura London
She longed for a pirate's kisses. . . even though she was kidnapped in error and forced to sail the seas on his pirate ship, forever a prisoner of her own reckless desire.

TO LOVE AN EAGLE
Joanne Redd
Winner of the 1987 *Romantic Times* Reviewer's Choice Award for Best Western Romance by a New Author.

SAVAGE HEAT
Nan Ryan
The spoiled young daughter of a U.S. Army General is kidnapped by a Sioux chieftain out of revenge and is at first infuriated, and finally hopelessly aroused by him.

BLIND CHANCE
Meryl Sawyer
Every woman wants to be a star, but what happens when the one nude scene she'd performed in front of the cameras haunts her, turning her into an underground sex symbol?

DIAMOND FIRE
Helen Mittermeyer
A gorgeous and stubborn young woman must choose between protecting the dangerous secrets of her past or trusting and loving a mysterious millionaire who has secrets of his own.

LOVERS AND LIARS
Brenda Joyce
She loved him for love's sake, he seduced her for the sake of sweet revenge. This is a story set in Hollywood, where there are two types of people—lovers and liars.

MY WICKED ENCHANTRESS
Meagan McKinney
Set in 18th-century Louisiana, this is the tempestuous and sensuous story of an impoverished Scottish heiress and the handsome American plantation owner who saves her life, then uses her in a dangerous game of revenge.

EVERY TIME I LOVE YOU
Heather Graham
A bestselling romance of a rebel Colonist and a beautiful Tory loyalist who reincarnate their fiery affair 200 years later through the lives of two lovers.

TOTAL NUMBER OF FREE BOOKS SELECTED _____ X $1.00
= $_____ (Amount Enclosed)

Dell has other great books in print by these authors. If you enjoy them, check your local book outlets for other titles.